T0253097

PUCK&
Prejudice

Also by Lia Riley

Regals Hockey Romances
Puck and Prejudice

Hellions Hockey Romances
Mister Hockey
Head Coach
Virgin Territory

Brightwater Series
Last First Kiss
Right Wrong Guy
Best Worst Mistake

Everland, Georgia Series
It Happened on Love Street
The Corner of Forever and Always

Off the Map Series
Upside Down
Sideswiped
Inside Out

Anthologies
Snowbound at Christmas

PUCK&
Prejudice

A
NOVEL

LIA RILEY

AVON

An Imprint of HarperCollins Publishers

PUCK AND PREJUDICE. Copyright © 2024 by Lia Riley. All rights reserved. Printed in the United States of America. No part of this book may be used or reproduced in any manner whatsoever without written permission except in the case of brief quotations embodied in critical articles and reviews. For information, address HarperCollins Publishers, 195 Broadway, New York, NY 10007.

HarperCollins books may be purchased for educational, business, or sales promotional use. For information, please email the Special Markets Department at SPsales@harpercollins.com.

FIRST EDITION

Interior text design by Diahann Sturge-Campbell
Hockey puck illustration © Vector Tradition/Stock.Adobe.com
Open book illustration © ~Bitter~/Stock.Adobe.com

Library of Congress Cataloging-in-Publication Data has been applied for.

ISBN 978-0-06-341232-3

24 25 26 27 28 LBC 5 4 3 2 1

To MYG: 👍 Future's Going to Be Okay

*And Lexi: For befriending a stranger on the internet
and liking so many important things*

PUCK &
Prejudice

CHAPTER ONE

Tucker Taylor walked across the sticky floor carrying a second round of drinks for the table. The pub's best days were probably a few centuries ago, but that fact didn't seem to faze his companions, their voices rising from the dimly lit booth.

His younger sister, Nora, gave a cursory nod as she reached for a pint and continued her argument. "Clearly, Jane Austen's impact is the most far-reaching. Her insights into social issues were way ahead of her time, and her exploration of class and society remains as relevant today as in the nineteenth century."

"Oh, come off it!" Her friend Pip slumped back, her freckled features contorted. "The Brontë sisters were literary rebels. They gave us Mr. Rochester, the ultimate bad boy, and Heathcliff, who originated the idea of a situationship."

These two had been going in circles about dead writers for forty minutes. Tuck slid into his seat and absentmindedly checked his phone for the umpteenth time. Maybe something cool would pop up, like underwater hockey trick shots, kitten rescue shorts, or the mating habits of Peruvian giant yellow-leg centipedes. At this point, he'd honestly settle for a weather update.

"You'd prefer gloom-and-doomery over wit, charm, and financial stability?" Nora scoffed. "Who needs unhinged passion when you can have a comfortable marriage with a side of banter? Bro . . ." She gestured to him with a *weigh in here* motion. "Who'd you choose: the boss who harasses you and totally doesn't have a wife locked away in his attic—"

"Or," Pip interjected, "the snobby wanker who is embarrassed to be infatuated with you?"

"Uh?" Tuck froze, hoping he didn't look like a deer in headlights. "Neither?"

Both women groaned, exchanging eye rolls before resuming their debate.

Nora, studying British literature at the University of Bath, had already booked a short friend trip to the village of Hallow's Gate when Tucker had sprung his surprise visit on her. She'd insisted that he tag along. Tonight, they had all gone to celebrate Yule at Ye Olde King's Head in the town square.

"What happened to the new king's head?" Tucker had mumbled when they parked out front. Pip, another student from Nora's department, offered a lukewarm grin, her facial muscles barely going through the motions. So, he'd decided to zone out, only half listening to which literary icon was the GOAT . . . Jane Austen or the Brontë sisters.

Who'd he pick for best goalie? Brodeur? Nah, probably Hasek. Weirdest? Hard to say. Maybe Bryzgalov—that dude was a bag of feral cats draped in a jersey, just as likely to start talking about bears as he was to ponder time travel.

He took a sip of beer, the amber liquid disappearing down his throat as he swiped at the foam clinging to his upper lip. It didn't take long for his mind to go back on airplane mode.

An hour later, Nora and her friend still hadn't come up for air. He'd passed the time packing down battered fish with thick-cut, golden-brown fries—*sorry, chips*—mushy peas, and a giant bowl of sticky toffee pudding while sending furtive texts to teammates.

Thousands of miles away, it was game day—the Austin Regals versus the Denver Hellions—and he wasn't playing. Again. He should be eating his lucky pregame meal—buttered bowtie pasta and a Coke—while wearing his superstitious boxers, the ones with cartoon axolotls. His teammates teased him for his habits while secretly revering them. After all, being a goalie came with tacit permission to be odd. But no rituals had ever prepared him for the team doc finding a lump in his armpit last spring or the diagnosis of stage 1A Hodgkin lymphoma. The good news? It had been easily cured. But treatment had been hell, and he'd be sidelined for much—if not all—of the season.

"Hey." Nora reached over and poked him. "We're boring you, huh?"

"No, it's all good." He swallowed back a jaw-cracking yawn. "But I don't have a lot to contribute."

Pip's lips quirked to the side. "You'd rather tell us about how you hit a puck super hard?"

He couldn't tell if she was joking or being a pain in the ass. Maybe both. "Actually, my job is to stop them."

"Come on, guys," Nora pleaded, flashing a peace sign. "I'm positive there's some conversational sweet spot on the Venn diagram here."

Tuck shared a brief glance with Pip, and they both silently agreed to let their differences be like the one sock that always disappears in the laundry—mysterious and unresolved.

"Why don't you two stay put and bookworm to your heart's

content. I'll walk back to the B and B and catch some z's. We'll reconvene in the morning for crumpets or whatever counts as breakfast around here."

"Really?" Nora furrowed her brow. "Pip and I can leave too. You do look tired."

"Nah. I'm fine." The lie rolled off easily. He'd been saying it enough.

"I know you'd choose hockey over South Hampshire any day of the week." Nora squeezed his shoulders in a half hug. "But I *am* excited to play tourist together. You haven't gotten much of a chance to see the world beyond the arena. It's good out here. I promise."

"Sounds like a plan." He playfully yanked one of her braids.

She slid her hand over. It took him a second to realize she was passing him her car keys.

"No." His answer was firm. "I'll walk."

"You'd be doing me a favor," Nora wheedled. "We need to drink a lot more before we start on the Romantic poets, and you've only had a beer and a half."

"At least we agree Percy Bysshe Shelley is the worst," Pip muttered into her glass.

"He took his second wife, Mary's, virginity on her mother's grave," Nora explained, like that cleared up everything. "Then that same Mary went and wrote *Frankenstein.*"

"Huh." Not going to lie—it was kinda cool being related to a walking Wikipedia.

"Anyway, I digress. Take the car." Nora's tone was final. "Later, I'll text you and you can come back and get us."

"Deal." He fisted the keys. "Be good. Don't talk to strangers."

Nora gave him a double thumbs-up. "If anyone offers us a lolly, I'll kick 'em in the shins."

Tucker kept the smile plastered on his face until he walked through the door. Out in the square, he jammed his hands into the pockets of his jeans, the rhythmic strike of his footfalls echoing against the cobblestones. Night mist hung low, full of woodsmoke and the earthy scent of decaying leaves—a far cry from Zamboni fumes and chlorinated ice. The brick row houses flanking him on all four sides could be from a storybook, except he didn't believe in fairy tales. Only the hard truth scraping against the back of his mind.

Shouldn't be here.

Shouldn't be here.

He made his way over to Nora's Mini Cooper. It was as boxy as a toaster. He opened the door and frowned down at the passenger seat. Shit. Wrong side. Walking around, he made a mental note: *Drive on the left.*

Inside, his knees smashed against the steering wheel as he shoved the key in the ignition, and he had to drop his jaw down to his chest to fit. He snorted. This was a glorified go-cart. Reaching for the seat belt, he jumped as his elbow beeped the horn. Scratch that—this was a clown car.

Walking might have been easier. Even with the cold.

Downshifting and releasing the clutch, he eased into the empty laneway. Condensation veiled the windows, obscuring his view. With a reluctant grimace, he opened the window, bracing himself against the bitter gust of December air that rushed in like an uninvited guest. Crossing a stone bridge over a creek on the outskirts of town, he had just reached for the radio dial when a cry drowned out the trickle of water over rocks.

A sheepdog bolted from a farmhouse on the hill, heading straight for the road. Hot on its tail was a boy in flannel pajamas and too-big rubber boots. Tucker's stomach hollowed as he

stomped on the brakes. Shit. Black ice. The dog and kid, illumi-
nated by the headlights, froze in front of him, wide-eyed. Tires
screeched. This wasn't going to work. He'd strike them. Without a second thought, he violently jerked the wheel to the right,
throwing him off the road like a rodeo cowboy on a wild bull. He
bucked and bounced, out of control, through the snow toward a
frozen pond.

With a roll, the car hit on the driver's side, and there was a
heavy crack of breaking ice. Frigid water funneled through the
open window. As he clenched and unclenched his fists, he fought
to relax. He focused on the sensation of his nails digging into his
palms, the slight sting helping to ground him in the present moment. Calm down. No big deal. This was like the cold-water im-
mersion therapy the PT staff used to make him do to help muscle
recovery after tough games. He needed to breathe through it—
slow and steady. With a quick motion, he got the seat belt off, and
just in time. The car was sinking fast.

He pushed away the thought as he rattled the door. Stuck.
Damn. He'd have to squeeze through the window.

He was a pro athlete and used to be able to run through box
jumps, ladder drills, sprints, and cycling to keep his cardio fitness in top form. But last week, he'd gone jogging and had to dial
it down to a walk after a measly quarter mile.

Fuck cancer.

He still had his mental fortitude, though. He was paid to stay
cool under pressure. He needed to imagine himself by a roaring
fire, dry and warm, recounting the story to Nora. He rehearsed it,
visualized it, and, with a determined crawl, got halfway through
the open window before his belt caught on something.

He pushed, but his arms might as well have been made of wet
noodles. His strength leached out by the second.

Failure wasn't an option. He wouldn't go out like this. Not after everything he'd survived. He bit his cheek, wrangling his focus. He had to control and execute each movement efficiently—no room for error or wasted effort.

His heart jackhammered in his ears as he finally kicked free and started swimming for the surface. The top of his head cracked against a frozen ceiling. Unyielding. No way out. Everything was so cold, yet his lungs were a firestorm, burning with fierce intensity. He punched violently. His knuckles scraped a wall of ice. His nails tore, ripping and breaking. No exit. *Shit!* He felt his strength ebb as his cells screamed for oxygen. Black water pressed on all sides. He couldn't resist the urge. Had to breathe. As he reflexively gasped, the darkness rushed in. An intense emptiness took hold, coupled with a whirling chaos, a sense he was at the end of everything. And then . . . nothing.

CHAPTER TWO

My Most Neglectful Offspring,

I set pen to paper to address the conspicuous silence that followed my previous letter. I can only surmise that your leisurely diversions have left scant moments for correspondence.

This past Monday, I had the pleasure of taking an excursion through Kensington Gardens with Lavinia Throckmorton. Amidst this floral profusion, dear Lavinia unveiled a most astonishing revelation—her Augusta, at a mere eighteen years of age, has found herself betrothed. A marvel, considering you, my dear, have now completed seven and twenty orbits around the sun in solitary splendor.

In her usual delicate manner, Lavinia sought news of your well-being, and I conveyed that you were finding the rural air most invigorating. My dearest fugitive, you embarked upon your pastoral sojourn to visit your cousin with a promise to be gone for a fortnight. It's now been twice that time.

In your absence, your brother has undertaken the task (again) of identifying suitable gentlemen who, against all

odds, remain unattached. I don't have to remind you that op-
portunities for a union are diminishing with each passing day.
I eagerly await your prompt return.

With the deepest affection and a hint of maternal vexation,
Your Loving Mother

A hint? A hint! Lizzy dropped the letter to her lap with a snort.
Hell's teeth. Her self-proclaimed Loving Mother was ready to
paint the words "Please Marry My Daughter" on a bedsheet to
hang out the front window of the family's Mayfair home.

She knotted her hands into the blanket she perched on to keep
from shaking her fists at the ducks paddling in the pond down
the rise. The mallards were hunting watercress, minding their
own business. Her mother could take a lesson from them.

It was high time that woman developed a hobby. Archery, perhaps? Or the delicate art of watercolor? Possibly the solace of a
well-chosen book, preferably a scandalous one? Anything to draw
attention away from the subject of her daughter's matrimonial
prospects, or, rather, the lack thereof.

Her cousin Georgie was the lucky one. Though she'd buried her
husband, she'd grown her freedom. Here in Hallow's Gate, she
lived the independent life of a merry widow—a shining example
of all that was possible. The previous evening, during another of
Georgie's legendary dinner parties, a revelation had struck Lizzy
during the fish course. A fact so painfully obvious she had inclined her head toward her friend Jane and murmured, "It's a
quietly acknowledged truth that a single man in possession of
a good fortune would be welcome to make any sensible woman
a widow."

Jane had choked on a bite of capered trout, kicking her under the table with the pointed toe of her shoe: a silent order to behave.

But where was the lie? While mourning wear wouldn't be her first choice—black was most assuredly *not* her color—a quick review of the facts determined that the advantages of widowhood were many.

One: financial independence. Fortunate widows could inherit property and income and then control their own affairs. No more begging her brother or mother or—worse—a future husband for pin money.

Two: respectability. Widows might travel and socialize with less scrutiny and restrictions.

Three: freedom. Widows made decisions about their households, finances, and social lives. They were not subject to the authority of a husband or any tedious marital obligations and had the power to henceforth remain forever single.

Of course, if one allowed emotion to get tangled up in it, the experience of widowhood could be tainted by grief, or fear, like for her own mother after Father's sudden death ten years ago. But Mamma, uncertain how to manage without a husband, had remarried, to a wealthy if self-important businessman, Rufus Alby, thus squandering any opportunity for independence.

It must also be acknowledged that if one married a man of lesser means, a future widow would be put at a disadvantage. That's why the only real solution was to marry someone with a respectable fortune and then . . .

What? Wait for them to die?

Lizzy worried at her lower lip. Well, she certainly wasn't a murderess. Far from it—she couldn't even bring herself to kill spiders.

Could she ask her brother to confine his search to men who were known to be sickly? That would be *quite* the conversation.

Henry, please find me a wealthy husband, but could you be a dear and ensure he has advanced consumption?

She settled back on her elbows, ignoring the tendrils of hair coming loose from the artless knot at the nape of her neck, and took a bite out of the apple she'd pinched from the cellar.

Involving Henry would be a dreadful mistake. He'd undoubtedly run straight to Mamma with the information and she would persist in discussing it ad nauseam.

Lizzy took another bite, grimacing as she swallowed. The apple's flesh had a mealy texture, tasting more like a distant memory of the fruit, but chewing gave her something to do with the clenched feeling inside her—the one that wanted to break the rules that kept her as nothing more than a canary in an ornate cage.

It was unjust that she was compelled to return to London and feign interest in dull men who couldn't engage in conversation beyond the topics of weather, hunting, or the evening's dinner menu. And that was if she was lucky. If not, she'd be stuck listening to pontifications on horse breeding or, the worst of the worst, the gentleman's ailments, a gouty toe or watery bowels.

Talk about mental rot.

Georgie raised dogs and held female-only parties where women weren't encouraged to take dainty nibbles off their plates. No, they indulged with gusto. She had recently hosted a luncheon entirely composed of desserts! The table was piled high with trifles, jellies, macarons, cakes of all sizes, blancmange, syllabubs, and crème brûlée. They washed it all down with Irish whiskey, Madeira, and rum until one of the ladies retrieved a violin and played a lively tune that sent them into an unrestrained dance, devoid of any proper steps. They ended up collapsing against the walls or sprawling on the floor, laughter and panting echoing through the spinning room.

And in another South Hampshire village, their friend Jane not only wrote books, but had even published one: *Sense and Sensibility*. It might have been officially printed with the nom de plume "By A Lady" to protect her privacy, but she had done it. And because she was lovely, Jane had given her recent main character the same name as Lizzy.

Elizabeth Bennet.

Last Christmas, Jane had read one of Lizzy's little scribbles from one of her many vellum notebooks. In *The Enchanted Garden*, a certain Lady Genevieve Devereux, a young woman of remarkable intelligence, arrived at an estate to spend the summer. She carried with her the weight of societal expectations from her family, who pressured her to make an advantageous match. One fateful evening, as Lady Genevieve strolled through the moonlit gardens, she stumbled upon a hidden gate that led to an enchanted garden. There, she discovered a sparkling fountain said to grant wishes. As Lady Genevieve pondered the nature of her wish, she encountered a mysterious man who was no lord or gentleman of fortune, only a humble but strapping gardener . . .

Jane had said her scribblings "showed promise," and Lizzy concealed the compliment in a pocket of her heart.

Promise.

She would make good on that promise, if she didn't end up tucked away in some dusty house to warm a man's bed. Unfortunately, it appeared as if the very fabric of the universe was conspiring to make this outcome inevitable.

With a frustrated shriek, she threw her apple core into the

bulrushes and then froze, cocking her head. There had been a strange sound. What was that? A duck? A dying duck?

A very large, very dying duck?

Visions of a wretched, thrashing waterfowl flooded her mind, making her skin crawl.

How she loathed ducks.

She scrambled onto her feet and gathered her skirts, straining to peer into the bulrushes as they waved on their tall green stalks, velvety brown seed pods bobbing cheerfully.

Her shoulder blades uncinched a fraction. Never mind. Maybe it had been a trick of the wind. Or some echo from the village. Or . . .

There it was again.

Blood drained to the tips of her toes.

It didn't sound like a duck. Unless that duck happened to be a groaning man.

"Hello?" She took a tentative step forward, her throat drier than dust. "Is everything all right?" A perfectly ridiculous question. Whoever made the sound was in a murky pond. Of course they weren't all right. Far from it.

She suppressed a frown. Had a farmer drunk too many pints at the Ye Olde King's Head? Or perhaps earlier someone had slipped down the hill, rolling into the water.

No point dithering. She shoved the letter into her bodice and strode forward. If she was in for a penny, might as well make it a pound.

She crept to the shore, swatting back an overzealous dragonfly as her linen boots squelched in the mud, making it impossible to hide her approach. Gooseflesh prickled the backs of her arms, and she resisted the temptation to glance around as if someone might come and save her from this obligation. Never mind.

She'd handle this fine. If anything dangerous emerged, she'd . . . she'd . . . punch it in the nose. Georgie had been teaching her boxing. Or at least telling her she ought to learn.

Lizzy's breath caught in a sharp exhale as she pushed her arms into the bulrushes, shoving them apart. Her gaze fell, locking with the piercing eyes of a brutal-looking man. The blood smeared across his angular features added a raw, dangerous edge to his appearance that intensified the darkness of his stare as he glared up at her.

"W-what happened?" She got the words out, just, wary but clear.

He pushed himself to a sitting position with obvious effort and dabbed the end of his nose, wincing. "I got hit in the face with a fucking apple."

The accent. That guitar-plucked twang. She'd heard it before in town, but not often.

American.

And gads, he was big. She'd wager once standing he'd rise a head taller than herself, and she was by no means a delicate violet.

Dozens of questions piled up. Why did he crop his hair that short? His jacket was black, but why was the fabric peculiar—too shiny, and very puffy—with strange metal teeth holding it together along a central seam? And his long splayed-out legs were encased in a sturdy-looking cotton dyed a deep blue.

In turn, he gaped at her lavender walking dress, his expression shifting from coolly peeved to incredulous as he raked his intense gaze up, down, and back again. The depth of his focus sent an unexpected shiver through her body. She'd never been the object of such single-minded attention before. The sensation left her feeling strangely vulnerable yet exhilarated, as she resisted the urge to tame her wild hair, ignoring the fact her coif likely rivaled Medusa's. Instead, she held his stare, a silent challenge hanging between them as the palpable tension grew. She counted silently, *One . . . two . . . three . . . four . . .*

Beneath the swarthy shadow of stubble peppering his jaw, a muscle twitched, breaking the stillness.

Lizzy blinked first. Unsure why her face was suddenly afire.

"Sir." She paused, swallowing to steady her voice. "Are you sure that you're quite all ri—"

"What are you wearing?" he blurted.

CHAPTER THREE

"What am *I* wearing? Beg your pardon, but I believe that's the pot calling the kettle black." The woman looked him up and down as if *he* were the out-of-place one.

A faint buzzing hummed in Tuck's ears, reminiscent of standing beneath high-voltage power lines. What the hell had happened?

She was still talking, peppering him with questions, the words coming a mile a minute, but he couldn't concentrate, not when a wave of nausea knocked him forward on all fours, his stomach twisting as if it were being wrung out like a damp cloth. He heaved, vomiting water that tasted of silt and algae.

"Good heavens." The woman gave a muffled shriek. "None of that, please. Oh dear. I think I'm going to . . ." She spun away, hands bracing her hips, and gagged.

"Ma'am?" Tucker sat back on his heels and swiped his mouth as a few hard truths registered: it was daytime, warm instead of cold, he was soaking wet, and something was off about the surroundings. The old stone bridge had turned wooden, and while that farmhouse on the hill looked the same, the streetlights and road signs were gone. So was Nora's car.

She turned back around, her nose scrunching up. "Are you finished? I nearly cast up my lunch."

His pits were sweat soaked. The gentle breeze carried the scent of fresh grass. A bird swooped in and perched on the tip of a marsh weed. Gray-brown feathers? Orange chest? Some kind of Euro robin? His heart hammered behind his sternum. These were summer smells. Summer sights. The world was too hot, too bright.

Where was the snow? The ice? The cold night sky? Was he hallucinating? Or had he died in that fucking pond?

"Are you . . . ?" Shielding his gaze from the sun, he struggled to keep his hand steady. "Are you some sort of angel?" She had a striking presence with her fox-like eyes, long lashes, and round cheeks.

"If you aspire to be a poet, I recommend trying harder." Her low voice was tinged with amusement even as her expression remained unsettled. "That dreadful phrase never works."

Okay, at least he wasn't dead. He mentally crossed that option off the shortening list of possibilities.

"What's going on then?" His frustration hit critical mass. He needed to make sense of this. Of the seasonal shift. Of *her*. An idea flashed and he clung to it as though it might carry him back to sanity. "Wait." He snapped his fingers. "Is this one of those historical reenactments? You know, where you act like an old-timey cosplayer and run a blacksmith shop or whatever?"

"A blacksmith?" She flicked up her brows. "Precisely how hard did I hit you with that apple?"

A muscle twitched in his jaw. She had to be messing with him.

"I get it," he growled. "Nice work. You're good at your job. A ten-out-of-ten performance. But drop the act. Where's the car? I have to find my sister."

"Car?" She stared blankly. "You mean a cart, sir?"

"No, of course I don't." He released a frustrated sigh. "It can't be summer." The throbbing in the back of his head mirrored how he sometimes felt after colliding with a goalpost.

"It is Midsummer's Day."

The nausea returned. "What the hell happened to December?"

She clicked her tongue. "Perhaps if I fetch a doctor and—"

"No!" He threw up a hand, trying to think, trying to make this make sense. "Wait! Okay. Let's pretend for a second that you aren't an actor, and it's actually summer. This is still England, right?"

"Indeed. We're in Hallow's Gate, sir. Midway between Ropley and Bentworth."

Okay, okay. The place was the same. He was going to make a fool out of himself with the next question. But he had to. "W-what year is it?"

"Are you attempting to secure amusement at my expense?" she snapped.

"If I was, I could think of a dozen better ways that wouldn't involve getting my ass wet while asking stupid questions."

"Your point is well taken." She turned over his words before giving a small shrug. "It's 1812."

The strange electric buzzing ceased. The world went still—nothing but wind, birdsong, and water lapping the pond's shore. If this was a dream, he'd better wake up real damn soon.

"You don't appear happy with the news," she said.

"No, I—" He released a bark of laughter—no humor in it, but better than exploding. "Can't say that I am."

"I need a moment to collect my thoughts." She ripped out her bun, long waves of dark brown hair tumbling over her shoulders as she paced. "You've voided your stomach and are uncertain of the year. However, you don't appear mad or in your cups."

"My cups?"

"Pickled. Three sheets to the wind. Drunk as a lord." She paused, tapping her chin. "Something very strange appears to have happened."

"Understatement." He twisted his mouth into a humorless smile. "But yeah. You're not wrong. I'm from more recent times."

She digested that; he could practically hear her brain chewing through his words. "When? 1912?"

A hundred-year jump.

He snorted, scratching the back of his head. "Add another hundred years and then toss in some change."

"Oh." The color drained from her face before she stiffened her spine. "Prove it."

"How?" He snorted. "Want me to pull a newspaper out of my pocket?" He gestured to his outfit. "Do people dress like me around here?"

"No." On this point, at least, there was no hesitation.

He threw up his hands in exasperation. "So?"

"You are indeed dressed strangely. However, peculiar clothing does not mean you're a man from the future. You'll simply have to do better if you want to convince me."

"I'm not a magician." He shoved his hands in his jacket pockets as his eyes widened. "Wait. I know." He dug out his phone and tapped it, the screen lighting up. "Yes," he muttered, mostly to himself. "My phone case is damn near indestructible." He chuckled. "I still have eighty-nine percent battery. No Wi-Fi obviously." The cell connection was out too. No shit.

The woman took a step closer. "What *is* that?"

"A phone. You can call people on it. Hit numbers like this,

and see? That's my sister's, Nora's, number. If I press that green button it will call her phone and we can have a conversation. Or I can do this . . ." He pulled up the texts. "Type here and send her a message. We mostly do that. No one likes a cold call."

She glanced from the phone to his face, and back to the phone. "I—I'm afraid I don't understand."

"Hold on." He held up the phone and snapped a picture. "Look, it can do this too."

When he showed her the image of herself on-screen, she sank down with a weak sound, her arms wrapped around her knees. "You're truly from the future? How did you manage to come here?"

"Yes. And I don't know."

They remained like that for a long moment, each staring blankly at the other. Finally, she heaved a sigh and unfolded herself back to standing, smoothing a hand over her hair. "Well, you can't very well remain in Farmer Pennycook's cow pond, can you? Best I escort you straight to my cousin. Georgie will know what to do. She always has ideas."

The woman had a point. He couldn't stay here.

"Wait!" She lifted a finger in warning as he stirred. "Stop. I'll need to find you a disguise, won't I? And where will I locate that? Did you have to be quite so large?" Her tone was annoyed, like his height was a personal affront. "Never mind," she pushed on, and he wasn't sure if she spoke to him or herself. "But you can't be seen in those clothes."

He glanced at his down jacket, jeans, and sneakers. So yeah. He'd stick out. "They don't, uh, burn people for witchcraft in 1812 . . . do they?"

"Witch what?" She gaped with utter confusion. "Get ahold of yourself. This isn't the sixteen hundreds. Now if you don't mind,

I'm trying to come up with a plan. But if you keep interrupting me, I might be tempted to source an axe instead and become quite Henry the Eighth."

The look she shot him packed more spice than his favorite hot sauce. But it made him trust her—she was ready to find a solution.

A long silence dragged out before she glanced over again.

"There's nothing for it." Her words had a tone of finality. "You'll need to wait here until my return."

"Are you serious? I'm supposed to stand here in the muck and do what? Watch minnows and hope for the best? No way. I want to help."

"You can't be seen like this." She waved a hand, gesturing to his clothing. "The village would never speak of anything else again. No, you must wait and not make a sound, Mr. . . ." She trailed off. "Pardon. I didn't catch your name."

"Taylor. Tucker Taylor. But you can call me Tuck. Most people do."

"Tucker Taylor." She spoke his name with a slight frown, like tasting a strange new flavor. "How very . . . American."

It took all his will not to roll his eyes. "And you are?"

She straightened. "Miss Elizabeth Wooddash. My friends call me Lizzy, but Miss Wooddash will do fine for now, Mr. Taylor." She dusted her hands on her skirts and turned to leave. "I'll return within the hour. If anyone approaches, pretend you're a frog and croak."

CHAPTER FOUR

Lizzy pressed the backs of her hands to her cheeks as she rushed toward the village road, in truth scarcely more than a narrow lane lined by moss-covered stones. A tapestry of wildflowers blanketed the field as oak and birch stood sentinel in the nearby wood, and yet she barely registered their charms, so at odds with London's bedlam.

Her heart pounded fiercely, the rhythmic thud echoing in her ears. She half expected someone from the nearby cottages to emerge, curious about the thunderous noise, as if a regiment were marching through the vicinity. She tugged impatiently at her damp bodice. Honestly, her corset had a single duty—to lift and separate her bust—but presently it was more occupied with gathering perspiration. The humid air clung to her skin like a blanket, putting the efficacy of her soap to the test.

She slowed to a walk, panting, trying not to wriggle in discomfort. What if she ended up stinking like a stable while in the company of one of the most handsome gentlemen she had ever encountered?

Tuck's cropped hair might be an unusual style, but it suited the bold structure of his features, those narrow-set eyes, the slash of brows, and such straight, bright teeth. And then there was the matter of his size—the bulk of his shoulders, those massive hands with the thick scar banding one knuckle, the ridge of collarbone that revealed itself when he absently tugged at his shirt. A strange sensation coiled in her belly. Really, though, how were anyone's teeth so white, so perfect?

She pinched her lips together. Could she be more ridiculous? Just this morning, her biggest concern had been the dwindling state of her soap bar, wrapped in a scrap of silk, infused with lavender and thyme. She hadn't been sure if she should request more to be sent from town or if that would incite Mamma to pen a letter on the need for an unmarried woman to demonstrate frugality so as not to burden others. The idea of enduring that particular lecture felt as enjoyable as dozing off atop a wasp nest.

Slathered in honey.

Naked.

Who gave a fig about exorbitant soap prices when a man from the future had crawled from the old cow pond? Her life had rearranged itself in the span of minutes. And she couldn't put it back the way it had been before. A subtle shift filled the air, a crackling energy teeming with uncharted possibilities. It whispered of magic within reach, an unfolding adventure. The hair on her arms rose. For the first time in her life, she could truly say she didn't have the faintest idea what tomorrow would bring. And she wasn't sure if the notion was exhilarating or terrifying.

And what sort of name was Tucker Taylor? Perhaps one that was common enough in America. But here? A soft, nervous laugh escaped as she reached the road. He might as well call himself Beasley Weaselwood.

Wind feathered her face as she licked her parched lips, trying to concentrate on the gravel poking into her thin soles. She needed to feel the ground, let it steady the dizziness threatening to spin her heart into her stomach.

Wait.

A new idea took hold. She hadn't gone stark raving mad and invented the whole thing, right? *Impossible.* She slid her hand beneath the thick coil of hair and kneaded her tight neck muscles. For starters, mad people don't worry about being mad. They'd simply accept a time traveler with a shrug and go off making daisy chains.

No need to risk a bruise by pinching herself. She seldom dreamed, and on the rare occasion when she succumbed to reverie while asleep, her dreams involved her teeth falling out or flying around Westminster. Never hitting a time traveler in the face with an apple.

The only viable choice was to entertain the truth of his wild claim and provide assistance in resolving the matter. Georgie's estate lay just shy of a mile away. Successfully leading Tuck there without incident depended on her ability to conjure appropriate male garb. How was that supposed to happen? A snap of the fingers? Luck?

Movement caught her eye, and she instinctively turned, silently thanking whichever guardian spirit watched over her. Beyond the yellow gate sat a farm—a humble brick abode half covered in ivy and bordered by vibrant flower and vegetable gardens. On a hedgerow near the barn hung linen smocks, a few pairs of darned wool stockings, a neatly patched brown coat, a few plain shirts, and two pairs of breeches. How fortunate it was that the farmer had chosen today as his washing day—these were precisely what she needed.

Except she couldn't approach the front door and say, "Greetings, sir, delightful summer weather we're presently enjoying, don't you think? Now, if you would be so kind, I have an urgent need for your breeches."

But if she dared to snatch any clothes in broad daylight and was apprehended in the act, she'd end up in front of the local authorities before she could hum "Greensleeves." Then Mother would lock her in their Mayfair attic out of sheer embarrassment, and Tuck would remain stuck in that stinking swamp until he did turn into a frog.

What to do, what to do?

She thoughtfully nibbled at her inner cheek. She needed a diversion—nothing grand, merely sufficient enough to draw attention away from the hedgerow. Then she'd grab enough clothing to get Tuck dressed for the walk to Georgie's, where a wardrobe was waiting full of her cousin's late husband's clothes. In a few days, she'd return the pilfered items by pretending she'd found them scattered along the roadside.

Was this a good plan? That was open to debate. However, seeing as it was her only plan, it would have to suffice.

She scanned the surroundings, unleashing a too-tight breath. In the chicken coop, a dozen hens pecked and scratched under the watchful eye of a squat rooster, his prolific blue-green tail feathers catching the breeze. She resisted the urge to roll her eyes at his typical male self-importance. To the left, an old sheepdog snoozed in the barn's shadow.

No time to hesitate. Any moment someone could appear and her plan would be ruined. Quickly, she ran over, unlatched the coop, seized the nearest hen, and tossed her plump form into the yard. The dog, half-awake, raised a head as a few more hens followed, happily exploring the barnyard and clucking over the long grass.

"Go on," she hissed to the dog. "Chase them."

One second passed. And then five more. His tail thumped once. Twice. His mouth opened in a wide yawn.

"Do it, blast you!"

The animal sprang to its paws, erupting into a cacophony of barks. The chickens, startled and in disarray, cackled their panic while the rooster attempted to marshal his harem. After unsuccessfully corralling them, he turned toward the dog with a defiant crow. Lunging forward, Lizzy secured a smock and a pair of breeches as muffled curses erupted from behind the barn. With panic thrumming through her veins, she hurried to the open gate, skillfully rolling the clothes into a tight bundle tucked securely under her arm.

Only a few feet to freedom. But her relief was short-lived.

"Hello there? Miss?" the farmer called, appearing around the side of the barn. "Can I be of service?"

Double blast! Her breakfast nearly emerged as she turned, doing her best to appear composed and only a little curious. "Oh, yes. I was passing by, heard the commotion, and . . ." And what? Her mind froze.

"No need to be alarmed, it's just me senile dog making a mess of things as usual." The farmer had an openhearted grin. No trace of suspicion lurked in his ruddy features.

"Goodness." She fought the urge to cringe at her overly enthusiastic tone, a feeble attempt to hide the fact that she was currently pilfering from him.

As his eyes assumed a familiar gleam, a wave of relief washed over her. It was the same look she often received from gentlemen who inspected her appearance with a critical eye, scrutinizing every detail from her hair to the size of her nostrils. Within moments, they would come to the conclusion that she was not so remarkable as to evoke insecurity but rather pleasantly agreeable enough for them to relax their guard.

These unimaginative men assumed her life's goals centered around tending to her family, delighting in a well-kept household, and contemplating the joys of future parenthood. The notion that she might desire to engage in conversations beyond these domestic realms—such as her aspirations to travel the Continent, her writing, or even preferring cats over dogs—appeared to entirely evade their notice. They didn't see *her*; they merely perceived the shell, her outward appearance, oblivious to the wealth of her inner world, vibrant with hopes, dreams, and yearnings. Very well. Let this fellow look too—and see nothing.

She'd misdirect.

Lizzy tossed her head, thankful for the effort she'd put into wrapping her hair into curling papers the previous night, ensuring the aid of a few bouncing ringlets. She fluttered her lashes and allowed her front teeth to latch onto the corner of her bottom lip just so before releasing it with an audible pop. And with that simple act, the farmer's focus shifted entirely. He ceased to concern himself with the roaming hens, completely ignoring the bundled clothing tucked under her arm.

"I must also confess a little secret." She changed her voice, elevating its pitch and infusing the words with a breathy, conspiratorial tone. "I couldn't resist coming closer to steal a glance at your flowers. They're lovely. You possess quite a talent in the garden."

She secretly swore at her use of the word "steal." But the farmer's mouth opened and closed like a fresh-caught trout on a riverbank.

Thank goodness for dimples.

She hoped that her flushed complexion would contribute to a

demure impression. She tucked a loose strand of hair behind her ear with her free hand, praying it added to the effect. "But I am shy with strangers. I think it best that I now depart." She allowed a slight quaver to enter her voice. With a small bob, she turned and resumed walking, fighting the overwhelming urge to bolt.

But the ruse worked. He didn't give chase.

Tonight, curled under her bedclothes, she could ponder the frequency with which men underestimated women. So much so that one could slip away with stolen goods under their very nose, evading notice, all the while adorned with an inscrutable smile and employing a soft-spoken manner. However, in the present, there was no room for moral qualms. Descending the hill, retracing her steps toward the pond, she narrowed her eyes, scrutinizing the surroundings. The tranquility appeared almost too flawless—two blackbirds flitting about, a frog croaking from the shadows. Was he still present? Her pace hastened, and she pursed her lips, emitting a low whistle.

It took effort to maintain her composure when Tuck emerged at the sound. The firm hold of his jaw eased a fraction, subtle relief relaxing his features before he intentionally masked the expression. The familiarity of his gesture caught her off guard, feeling oddly relatable. Concealing her genuine sentiments was a practice she engaged in so frequently that it had become habitual. It was discomfiting to see the gesture mimicked on another.

"You came back." His deep voice, carrying the faint twang, resonated with a mix of gratitude and irritation.

Her throat grew tight, words sticking like honey. "Of course. I promised, didn't I?"

"Good." Gold ringed his pupils like a sunburst. "Good." Before she could breathe, he was turning away. "What's the game plan?"

"First"—she frowned—"this isn't a game. Second, here." She advanced, grimacing when her boot heel squelched into the mud. "You can change into these."

He unrolled the clothing and went still, unreadable. "No."

"No?" Confusion swiftly transformed into ire. "*No* what, exactly?" Her already thin patience had reached its limit in the past hour. Was he about to act ungracious, even after she had freed chickens from a coop and dealt with the flirtatious farmer? Tucker Taylor, from his mud wallow, was going to tell her no?

Indeed not.

"Those aren't even real pants," he said. "They're capris. I'll look like a joke."

She didn't understand all his words, but red flashed behind her narrowed eyes.

"Allow me to be straightforward." Her gaze flickered disapprovingly over his attire. "We can't justify your current dress if we encounter anyone. I understand that these clothing choices lack style or sophistication, but the only joke here will be you if you're caught in your current dress. We need to cross two fields and an entire stretch of woods to reach my cousin's residence, all the while hoping that no one comes too close as it is. I don't even have stockings for you."

The wind picked up, carrying the scent of rain. She glanced over a shoulder and pinched the bridge of her nose. Dark clouds loomed. Just their luck.

Except . . .

Her gloomy thoughts vanished instantly—yes, rain clouds!

It *was* luck.

With the weather taking a turn for the worse, they'd be less likely to run into anyone else on a pleasure stroll or social call.

"Sir." She turned around to face him, not as if he were a handsome stranger or a time traveler but rather a poorly behaved child. "If you want my continued support, I'm going to insist that you don't waste my time or your air by telling me all the reasons you cannot wear the clothing, and in fact just get on with it. From the look of those clouds, it won't take long until the rain starts in earnest. We can't remain."

"I am not sure how to put these things on," he grumbled.

Her hands flew to her hips. He might be acting like a baby, but she was not his mother. "If you require coddling, Mr. Taylor, you'd better look elsewhere. I'm not setting a single foot into that swamp to dress you."

"Tuck. Tucker." He glanced up as if he'd surprised himself by the force of his words. "Please. Call me by my name."

"I'll call you by whatever name that you so desire if you are sorted within the next two minutes." But she wouldn't. Not really. She couldn't imagine calling a stranger by their given name.

He blinked before narrowing his eyes slightly. "You don't take any crap, do you?"

Crap? Her brows furrowed as she tried to recall the meaning of the word. "Like castoffs?" She nodded in dawning comprehension; the term wasn't commonly used. "No, I won't tolerate being treated as inconsequential or having my ideas casually dismissed. I do not wish to take such *crap* from anyone if I can help it. You are not a child." She refused to let her gaze travel the span of his shoulders. Heavens, they seemed wider than the English Channel.

"No, I'm not." He scrutinized her in a manner that was so unlike the farmer's. No focusing on the bounce of her curls, or the turn of her nose, but trying to push deeper, see further.

She fought the urge to take a step back.

"How old are you?" he asked in that low lilt of his, drawing out the *o* sound, almost kneading the word.

She never saw the point in women hiding their years. "Seven and twenty. You?"

"Thirty."

"All the more reason to act your age." It was impossible to keep the snap from her voice. Probably because she wasn't sure if she should swoon or strangle him. Possibly both.

"I'm more of a grow-old-disgracefully kind of guy."

He disappeared into the weeds, and she resisted the temptation to sneak even a single secret glance. Well, maybe one, but certainly not more than two.

In no time, his distinctive puffed jacket came flying out, landing in a heap beside her. She quickly grabbed it before it could get wet. Following suit, a navy-and-white shirt appeared, its long sleeves featuring a peculiar shiny texture. A crown and the word "Austin" were on the front, while the back declared "13" and "Taylor." Yet she couldn't dwell on the specifics because he emerged from between the reeds . . . almost naked.

CHAPTER FIVE

Lizzy's clear blue eyes zeroed in on his torso, her gaze inscribing a secret message across his skin. Tuck ran his tongue behind his top teeth, making a conscious effort not to cover his chest. Why the sudden self-consciousness? He wasn't a stranger to female attention—everyone from infatuated fans to chemo nurses slid into his DMs. Maybe it was because he wasn't accustomed to feeling this out of control. Here, he had no idea how to play it cool or figure out his next play.

He was in 1812? What the fuck.

He hiked up the micro pants and rolled his shoulders to release some tension, flexing and relaxing the muscles in his chest.

Lizzy let out a sound that was a cross between stepping on a dog's toy and letting the air out of a balloon.

Tuck glanced down to see if he'd grown a third nipple in the day's chaos, but everything appeared as usual—dark hair whorling across his chest. "What?"

"You're in a . . . a . . . a . . ." She craned her face skyward, her pulse fluttering in her throat as she flapped her arms like a hyperactive hummingbird.

He cocked a brow. He wasn't imagining things. Lizzy might

seem as prim as a nun, but she'd just checked him out. So what if he wasn't as shredded as when he was in peak NHL shape? His muscles had been responding to his recovery workouts.

"You're in a state of nature," she blurted.

That was a new one, but he could guess what she was getting at. And it was sort of cute, seeing her perform this little thrashing dance.

He didn't have a specific type of woman he was attracted to—no particular look or interest. The moments of chemistry happened when and where there was some kind of alchemy in the blend of personality and atmosphere.

This sure as shit wasn't a good time for any of that. And yet . . . here it was, that warm curiosity tapping him on the shoulder.

"What's the nature I'm stating?" he asked, more to calm down a notch than win any comedic points.

"Do you truly require me to articulate the word? Naked." Thunder clapped through the gathering clouds with a dramatic punctuation. "You. Are. Naked!"

Why was she acting like she'd never seen a shirtless guy? Did people here go around fully covered at all times? That couldn't be true. What about at the beach? Or exercise?

But if she kept hyperventilating, she was going to pass out— hard to feel flattered if a woman went unconscious.

"Shhhh. Look. I'm wearing your tiny pants, okay?" He'd gotten into them—just. But breathing was going to be a challenge.

She slid him a sideways look, her gaze traveling down from his navel to his happy trail before she slapped her hands over her eyes.

The warm feeling ebbed as exasperation took hold. Christ. It wasn't like he was out here swinging his dick in the wind. "Hang on. Can we stick to the real issue?" He fisted the flowy white linen shirt she'd given him. "Like the fact you got me a *dress* to be inconspicuous? Kinda defeats the purpose."

She went from peeking through her fingers to planting her hands on her hips—her protests ceased. The stony silence lasted a beat, broken only by a cow lowing nearby. He smothered a grin at the return of her queen-bee attitude. She might be a handful. But there was no denying she was cute as hell.

"Please be so kind as to remind me what you did while I went through considerable risk and no small embarrassment procuring that disguise?" She tapped the center of her chin with a pointer finger. "Oh, yes, I recall. You remained right there, sinking ever deeper into the mud."

He drew himself to his full height. "That was not my—"

She cut him off with a derisive huff, holding up her hand to silence him. "I'm speaking now, and for starters, I didn't pilfer a dress." She pointed at the limp garment dangling from his fist. "That's a smock. Farmers wear them to cover the rest of their clothing from the elements. Plus, see how loose it is? You'll get much more ease of movement than ladies do, strapped into corsets with so much whalebone or cording that we can scarcely breathe."

"I'm not the fashion type," he mumbled. "More of a jeans and T-shirt guy, you know?"

Her blank face told him that she didn't. Of course not. She was dressed like she starred in one of those costume dramas that sent him snoring before the first waltz.

Here it was the norm for guys to wear micro pants, and God forbid showing any bare chest. If she saw the inside of the Regals locker room, she'd have a stroke. This time period was too different. Too uptight. Too two hundred fucking years ago. What was he going to do? A dozen questions crept to the tip of his tongue, but he swallowed them back.

He needed to get out of here, stat. If a pathway to the past opened, then it was only logical that it could unlock in the other direction. He'd tried diving back in when she was off looking for clothes, but nothing lurked under the water but mud and weeds. No one was coming to the rescue—it was on him to figure out how to escape.

He poked his tongue into the side of his cheek, a headache brewing. Somewhere, apparently in another dimension, a bottle of ibuprofen sat in the top drawer of his dresser at the B and B. Regrets were useless, but if he'd only stuck it in his jacket pocket before heading to the pub. He had a feeling he'd need some pain-killers in the coming . . . Damn it, how long would he be trapped here? Regular folks lived by a clock or a calendar. He was a pro athlete. He lived by a schedule. Practice days. Game days. Team meals. Off days. Since being out on medical leave, he'd gotten disoriented. Lost track of days and sometimes his purpose. And now this . . .

"Oh, do make haste," she snapped, glancing over her shoulder. "Should anyone chance upon us in your current state, we'd be marched straight to the nearest altar. And I can assure you that matrimony does not feature on my list of intentions."

"For real?" He paused. The last thing he wanted was to put her in a compromising situation. "Sorry. I'm serious. You didn't ask for this, and I don't want to cause any problems."

She met his gaze and then looked away. "Apology accepted as long as you understand that from this point on, I insist that you notify me whenever you remove even a stitch of clothing. Afford me the courtesy to remove myself."

"That's absolutely fair." Who cared about clothes? He had bigger things to worry about and she'd made a genuine effort to source this smock from God knows where, so time to put up or shut up. There wasn't a chance he'd fit in here, but he could do his best to look the part.

He slipped the garment over his head. It stretched tight across his chest and the sleeves weren't going to cover his wrists. "It doesn't fit."

"It will have to suffice," Lizzy ordered, cutting off any more complaints in a preemptive strike. "And if you remain like that, a bird will relieve itself on your lip."

He jerked back. "What are you talking about?"

"It's an expression my mother used whenever I was petulant as a child. And the way you hold your mouth like so." She mimicked a sulky expression, lower lip pushed out. "I don't care where you come from. That's a pout in any time."

He snorted. "Whatever you say."

"Yes. And I say pout," she muttered, as she turned to start walking. "Gather your things."

He shoved his Regals shirt and jeans into his down jacket, compressing the entire thing under one arm before giving chase. If fate existed, then why in the hell had it forced him to travel two hundred–plus years, not to save the world or do anything heroic . . . just to bicker with this woman? But to give proper credit, she was taking this all in stride in a way that was remarkable.

She was scrappy.

He liked scrappy.

"We'll go through the rocky field. Wait. That won't do. There's that farm with the seven children. No. It must be the forest. The path will be muddier in this weather, but it's direct." She glanced over, brows furrowed. "I'm choosing the best way to move unobserved." She gestured as he slid on his sneakers. "Because those shoes don't belong here."

"None of me does."

A few hours ago, his top concern was being benched for the season. Now he was dressed as if for a Renaissance festival, caught up in a Tom-and-Jerry routine with a woman who seemed genetically engineered to push all his buttons. He had no idea where he was going or what was going to happen next. Lightning forked in the sky, and thunder cracked again, closer this time.

Heading toward the forest's edge, he couldn't help but notice the absence of streetlights, stop signs, cars, and phones. The back of his neck tingled. It was as though this place was both familiar and alien, sort of like landing on Mars and discovering it resembled the park near his house. The notion hurt his brain. Maybe he should have gotten drunk last night.

It didn't help that Lizzy was giving him another one of her assessing looks. "Is everyone . . ." She slammed her mouth shut. "Never mind."

"If we're going to be a team, we need to trust each other."

Lizzy scrunched up her nose, making it look like a tiny accordion, a hint that she wanted to start yet another argument, but raindrops began falling in thick plops.

She startled, hugging herself. "Pardon me. I don't care much for storms."

He glanced at her eyes and his chest tightened as he noticed fear clouding her formerly vibrant expression. The only way he could think to calm her down was to keep the conversation going, leaving no room for silence, or a chance for her thoughts to spiral out of control. "Hey, remind me how far we are going again? I got a bit distracted with all the clothing excitement."

"A-about a m-mile," she stammered.

He flicked moisture from his hair. "Then we might as well accept that we are going to get wet. You've already seen me half-naked. No secrets, all right?" His attempt at humor was a bit clumsy, but his intentions were good. "What were you going to say a minute ago?"

Normally, he had a knack for reading a room, a rink, or a person. His approach involved sharp observation, analyzing possible plays, and anticipating the next move, especially when it came to the puck's trajectory. He knew what others expected from him: fans wanted wins, teammates needed him to be unbeatable, the press hoped for another oddball goalie with good sound bites, lovers desired him to be superhuman. But this woman was different. She wasn't trying to get anything from him. And she hadn't signed up to be a cosmic chaos cleaner today.

"It wasn't anything intelligent or captivating. Just a fleeting thought." A dimple appeared with her shy smile. "You are notably tall, you see, surpassing most gentlemen I've encountered. And more— How do I express this delicately . . . ?" She gestured at the breadth of his chest. "Are men from your place of origin generally as imposing as yourself?"

He processed her question, still adjusting to how she spoke.

A soft patter of raindrops whispered through the air.

It took a beat to figure out she was asking if guys in his time were as ripped as he was. Standing at six-two, he was average by NHL standards. "I'm taller than most," he said, keeping his face neutral so as to avoid showing his satisfaction and closing her off. "And to answer your other question, no, not everyone is as, uh, muscular." Despite the rain, despite the disorienting strangeness of the day, the corner of his mouth twitched, a smile emerging. When all was said and done, he kinda liked this weirdo.

So would Nora. Lizzy was her type of person.

Shit.

Lizzy read his face, her hair clinging to her cheeks in wet tendrils. "What's the matter?"

He meant to say his usual "Nothing," but the truth snuck out before he could catch himself. "My sister . . . She won't know what happened to me. She's going to be frantic and there's nothing I can do. And I'm all she's got, since our parents, well, they don't really . . ." He swallowed back the words. He wouldn't bring any of their nonsense here.

She turned her head, surveying him with surprise. "You hold your sister in high regard?"

"Yeah, but I don't always show it," he admitted. "I'm cold, standoffish, even, and—"

"Always believe you know best?" she broke in.

"Oh no, she's the brains." Tuck wiped a wide hand over his face. "I got the brawn, as you pointed out. She's studying here, actually. Well, England. The University of Bath."

"She's permitted to do advanced study?" Lizzy repeated the fact under her breath as if it were unusual. "But there is no University of Bath."

"Dunno." Tuck shrugged. "Must have been built later. But it definitely exists in my time and she's there getting a master's degree in British literature."

"British literature? What does that mean?"

"She's always talking about this one writer . . . something Austen."

The rain intensified, fat droplets pelting their skin as they stood facing each other.

"Austen," she parroted blankly, loosening a breath. "I'm sorry— what was the rest of the author's name?"

He frowned slightly, trying to remember. "It was like . . . Janette or something. Pretty sure it started with a *J.*"

"Jane." The color leached from her cheeks.

"Bingo." He snapped his fingers before silently swearing at her frown. He needed to quit saying words she wouldn't understand.

"Jane Austen. Are you certain?" There was energy behind the question, an urgency that he didn't understand.

"Yeah. Why? Is Jane Austen a big deal now too?" He shook his head. "What's with the hype?"

CHAPTER SIX

"*You* know Jane Austen?" Lizzy asked.

What made her head swim more, the sudden knowledge of her friend's fame or Tuck's intent eyes? How had she overlooked those lashes? Or the fact that his irises were less brown and more copper, a near shade match to a three-pence coin?

"I guess even the frogs back in that pond know her. Let me guess, you're a fan too?"

Too? "I—I—I." She veiled her stammer with a delicate cough. "I'm beyond familiar with Jane; we're close friends. Very close. She's completed one book, under a nom de plume, titled *Sense and Sensibility*. A London publishing house distributed it in three volumes last autumn, though she bore the printing costs and— Oh!"

Lizzy slipped on a mushroom patch, half concealed by the sodden undergrowth on the forest floor. Arms windmilling, she twisted to steady herself on a nearby oak trunk, but Tuck moved faster, wrapping one hand around her upper arm while sliding the other beneath her lower back, ensuring she regained her balance.

"Whoa now, Pocket Rocket." His unexpected touch vanished as quickly as it had come, but the shock of it, combined with his knowledge of Jane, kept her unstable. Fortunately, he opted not to make a fuss about the physical contact. In her present state of confusion, his lack of acknowledgment regarding the breach of propriety suited her perfectly. She needed a moment to steady her jangled nerves, not be forced to soothe him.

However, as she peered over, he didn't seem remotely flustered by the contact; rather, he appeared to be pondering something.

"What is it?" She wasn't miffed that he wasn't affected by their unexpected embrace. Not at all. In fact, she was feeling much better herself. It must have been a momentary bout of vertigo brought on by the day's excitement.

"Sorry." He clicked his tongue, snapping back to attention. "I know I keep using words that you won't understand. Describing a rocket is tricky. I meant—"

"I know what rockets are." She bristled. He might come from the future, but that hardly meant she was an unsophisticated rustic. "My stepfather took us to Hyde Park three years ago to watch the fireworks display commemorating King George the Third's jubilee. Red, gold, green, and blue rockets shot through the sky as the band played, their colors reflecting off Serpentine Lake."

"Really? Huh. Fireworks," he muttered almost to himself. "You have those, good to know." For a moment he looked exactly like what he was . . . a man lost, far from home or friends.

Lizzy drew a full breath, the scents of rain and wet earth steadying her. The weather had ushered in mist; the forest was ghostly with fog.

"What are all those bumps in the ground over there?" He pointed at low humps of earth set amid gnarled trees, their twisted branches forming a dense green canopy of dappled light.

She crossed her arms, a conscious effort to resist the impulse to reach out for one of his big-boned hands. There was no rational explanation for her sudden desire.

"Those? I've heard them referred to as barrows. I'm uncertain of their origins or purpose, but they are quite ancient," she murmured, her attention divided between his scarred knuckle and a strange inclination to run her tongue over the jagged line.

The mad impulse coursed through her, a cold river of shame containing a trickle of something thick and warm with rose-colored tendrils. She rubbed her forehead as if that could erase the idea. Better to forget he had hands and focus on a subject change. "How are you feeling?" she asked after clearing her throat. "If I were to emerge from a pond into an entirely different era, I'd be quite beside myself."

"It's not like I have much of a choice. Plus . . ." He trailed off with a half shrug. "I gotta be honest. I'm half expecting to wake up any minute. Maybe I knocked myself out on the car wheel. You could be a symptom from one hell of a concussion."

He'd used that word before. She cocked her head. "What's a car?"

"Uh." He opened his mouth and then slammed it closed, lips tight. "Never mind. As wild as it seems, you don't appear to be a random electrical zap in my brain. And if you're real, and this situation is actually happening, then it's probably not a good idea to say much."

"I beg your pardon?" That pullback demanded a response. "And what exactly do you mean by that?"

"It's dangerous to tell you too much about the future." Two deep creases appeared between his brows. "I've seen enough movies and they always—"

"Moo-vies?" There he went with yet another unfamiliar word.

"Shit. I don't know how to do this." He snapped a twig underfoot. Somewhere high above, a squirrel scolded them for destroying the peace. "I don't want to mess up time or say something I shouldn't and kick off a chain of events that could unmake the universe or whatever. Can we start walking again? And no talking. I need time to think."

In spite of her intense temptation to resist, challenge, and extract the future from him—glean whatever insights he might possess—there lingered a chill of unease. He genuinely knew what was to come, not like a fortune teller seeking coins on a city corner.

"Very well." As they strode along, Lizzy breathed in the earthy smell of the rain and pondered his peculiar words. *Car. Movie.* However, his unique insights posed their own peril. If others knew about his knowledge, to what extremes might they resort in their attempts to extract it from him? A protective instinct surged within her. She was determined to shield this man, even if he happened to be one of the most imposing individuals she had ever encountered. She'd find a way to keep him safe here in her world.

Everything about Mr. Taylor was a surprise. And she'd had precious few of those in her life. Most days blended into the next like a watercolor scene gone muddy, overmixing until it was impossible to discern individual elements. This morning had given no hint that today would be an exception. She wore her usual purple walking dress and ate her breakfast the same way she always did—with a honey cake, boiled egg, and souchong tea.

Afterward, she would retreat to her room and her lap desk, confronting the blank pages of her notebook. Paradoxically, the surplus of time in the countryside had left her immobilized. Despite the boundless tranquility and quiet that should have provided her with ample time to devote to what felt like her calling, she found herself stumbling in the execution. How could she persuade her family that she deserved a life free to pursue her craft if she couldn't muster the necessary motivation to fulfill the task at hand?

No, that wasn't accurate either.

It wasn't the lack of words or motivation that was daunting. It was the idea of completing something and discovering it wasn't very good.

And now, to discover that her dear friend was crafting stories that would be remembered far into the future? The notion ignited a spark of envy deep in Lizzy's heart. She despised it too. If there was anything worse than jealousy, it was feeling that vile emotion toward a dear friend who deserved every ounce of good fortune and success.

"What's wrong?"

Tuck's deep voice tugged her back to the here and now, where she was saturated from the rain and her predictable little life had just been upended.

"Have you ever measured your own merit against some elusive standard only to be left with a feeling that you are forever falling short of the mark?"

He made a noncommittal sound, a sort of thoughtful hum that encouraged her to keep going.

"Because I have. Constantly. It's a stroll through a portrait gallery of perceived shortcomings. Each flaw is framed in gold, reinforcing the notion that no matter my effort, I will never be enough."

He shot her a glance that bespoke incredulity and amusement, but not with any mean-spiritedness. "That's all sitting in your head waiting to come out?"

"Oh, you have no idea." She cast him a grim smile. "What do your thoughts tell you?"

"Well, I don't think in words. Certainly not like you just shared."

"How?" She frowned. "You must have an occasional thought rattle through that big square head."

"Square, huh?" He laughed, his eyes never straying from her face. "I think in pictures, and, if I were to try to describe it, in feelings too. I mean, if I had to force myself, I could do it, but it would get annoying."

"I've never pondered how I think before."

"It's not a typical conversation people go around having. But that doesn't explain what upset you."

Her head emptied out. No excuses or wit. Just the ugly little truth. "It's embarrassing."

"I promise I won't tell anyone. Given you're the only person I know in 1812, the odds are high that I can keep my word."

Fate had put them together. They were going to have to trust each other. At least enough to share some honesty.

"Very well." She squared her shoulders. "You recognized my friend's name. The writer. Jane."

"Jane Austen." He made a noise in the back of his throat. "I mean, look. Full disclosure. I haven't read a single word she's written. But my sister . . . It's sort of her thing. Jane Austen is one of her favorite authors."

"Your sister will read our Jane over two hundred years from now." Imagine having made that sort of impact.

"I do know there are movies—which are like plays, I guess you could say—made of her books. People take trips to see where she lived, at least according to Nora."

"And that's wonderful. Truly. I mean it, even though I am going to sound like one of the worst people possible. It's . . ." She squeezed her eyes shut and said as quickly as she could, "I am trying to write a book too. But I haven't even managed a satisfactory first chapter. No one's discussing Lizzy Wooddash in your time, are they?" She opened one eye, checking.

He contemplated for a moment. "Can't say I've heard of the name, but don't let that worry you. I'm not much of a reader either—at least of old books. But look, you write? That means you're a player too. Maybe you aren't signing the eight-year, eighty-million-dollar contract, but that doesn't mean you aren't in the game. That's what matters."

"I'm sorry. Who is signing what for when?"

He winced. "I tried to make a hockey analogy, sorry."

"Hockey?"

"That's a whole conversation." He gave a small sigh. "Hockey's my work. And life too, honestly."

"Ah, I see." She let the falsehood fall effortlessly. In truth, it might as well be midnight for how little she saw. However, she loathed to appear uninformed. "Hockey is a sort of trade?"

"A sport."

She blinked twice, reviewing the sports she knew: hunting, fishing, racing, shooting. But no gentleman did such things for money. Maybe boxing—she'd heard vague stories about pugilists who did illegal matches for payment in town. She crossed her arms, both from annoyance and an attempt to keep warm in this rain. "I don't understand."

"I don't know—does it matter if I talk about it?" He rubbed the top of his head, his big hand flattening the short locks. "I can't see how learning about hockey will have too big of an impact. Okay, let's do this. In my time, there are plenty of sports. If you excel at playing one—and I mean truly excel, not just being good—then yeah, you can make a living off it."

"How is this hockey played?"

"On ice. To make it sound simple, the players try to hit a puck into a net. Whatever team does that the most wins."

"Puck." She smoothed her damp skirt. "There's a Puck in *A Midsummer Night's Dream*. Shakespeare. But I presume you're not referring to a fairy?"

He barked out a surprised laugh. "That would be a no. A puck is round, black, and made of rub— Wait, I don't know if that material's been invented yet. It's designed to glide on ice."

"And you hit it."

"My job is to keep it out of the net."

She kept her chin high, unwilling to admit she was utterly baffled. "Like . . . bandy?"

He shook his head. "I don't know what that is."

"When it's cold enough in winter, sometimes men hit balls on the ice for fun. They call the game bandy."

"I mean, maybe that's somewhat close," he replied, rubbing the back of his neck. "I don't know."

Her curiosity was piqued. "And you can make a living doing this hockey?"

A small smile played on his lips. "I do all right."

"Because you stop a disc from going in a net. Fascinating."

"Hey now." His ears tinged pink. "There's a lot more to it, all right? The plays, the arenas, the crowd, the lights. It's physical. It's aggressive. It's a highly structured competition."

"How positively gladiatorial." It wasn't difficult to picture Mr. Taylor in the midst of the Colosseum. Those big corded muscles slick with sweat. His chest heaving. A wild sort of primitive bloodlust in his eyes. She swallowed nervously.

"Sure. Whatever you say." A beat passed.

She stared.

He stared back.

She held her breath, wondering if he could hear her wildly pounding heart. Here she was, Elizabeth H. Wooddash, poised to have an adventure. The very notion sent a frisson of excitement through her. She trembled with barely suppressed anticipation. For the first time in her life, she didn't have the faintest idea what was going to happen next.

A muscle feathered in his jaw, and he abruptly turned away. "There's something ahead."

Fortunately, the trees thinned, revealing the outline of a well-appointed two-story home with all the necessary outbuildings and gardens needed to run a small estate. Five chimneys punctuated the pitched tile roof, and four gabled windows faced the forest view that bestowed the property with its name.

"There it is! That's the Woodlands," she said with a sigh of relief, her legs going weak with a sudden bone-deep weariness. Uncertainty was equal parts exciting and exhausting. "We made it."

He gave a low whistle. "Heck of a house."

"My cousin married a gentleman, Mr. Edward Gardiner, who died of typhoid fever the better part of a decade ago. Before his demise, he settled a generous jointure on her. He had no debts, so she's been allowed to enjoy a life of considerable independence and—"

A long, resounding howl reverberated through the yard, shattering the silence as the echoes bounced off tree trunks.

"Oh, Goliath." She rolled her eyes. "Do give it a rest."

"What the hell was that?" Tuck halted. "Your cousin doesn't raise wolves, does she?"

"Ah." Lizzy raised a finger. "I forgot to mention. You don't have an issue with large dogs, do you?" She leaned in, catching his scent—a subtle woody undertone, despite having marinated in the pond. Suppressing the urge to take a second, longer sniff, she added, "'Large' doesn't quite capture his size."

"I'm fine." He turned back toward the deep baying. "Your cousin's a dog person, I take it?"

"That's a modest description. Georgie is engrossed in the world of breeding mastiffs; it defines her entire persona. If you happen to mention anything related to the breed, prepare to devote hours to the conversation. And I'm not overstating—I mean hours."

"Noted."

A few servants bustled by in gray dresses and white caps; one used a stick to herd a large pig into its sty while the other was stooped, carrying two buckets of water.

"Are you sure your cousin is going to be okay having me here?" Mr. Taylor glanced at his clothing. "I must not look like your usual visitors."

Lizzy mashed her lips at his understatement. "She'll be fine. But she won't act like it. Her bark is far worse than her bite. Just don't talk too much. She detests overbearing men."

Turning the corner around the home to access the inconspicuous back door, they nearly collided with Georgie, who was setting down a bowl filled with what appeared to be a robust meat stew for two enormous whining dogs. Her frizzy blond waves were pulled back with a brown ribbon, resembling a horse's tail.

"Oh, all right," she crooned. "That's enough of all that fuss. Here's your supper, my loves. Keep your petticoats on." Stepping back, she affectionately stroked Goliath's apricot-colored fur. He maintained a single-minded focus on the bowl's contents, while his mate, Daisy, gulped some down beside him, ensuring she got her due.

While Mr. Taylor had a gladiator somewhere in his family

tree, Georgie clearly descended from the Viking invaders who had once plundered these shores. Everything about her, from her loud laugh to her broad bosom to her iron-forged sense of self, branded her as a local hoyden. The best part was that Georgie never seemed to notice how she bent the world to her will; she accepted it as her due.

Her money gave her independence and a begrudging respect—even from Lizzy's snobbish mother.

"Elizabeth, my dear, you bear a striking resemblance to a drowned rat," observed Georgie in her characteristic bluntness, never one to tiptoe around pleasantries. She cast a swift, assessing glance at Tuck, her good-humored eyes contrasting with her resolute jaw. "And who's this big buck? You weren't found poaching, were you?"

"Cousin." Lizzy conjured her most charming smile even as her spine wobbled like jelly. They needed to get out of the yard before the servants got a long look at him and his odd attire. "Best to go indoors for this particular conversation. I suggest the drawing room. And do you have any more Irish whiskey? We'll need it."

"I don't like that expression one bit, girl," Georgie said with a grunt. "It hints that peace and quiet aren't in my future."

Five minutes later, Georgie was pouring her second glass of amber liquid into a crystal tumbler, a servant dispatched to locate Jane, who was also visiting the Woodlands from Chawton Cottage, some twenty miles due west.

"Fancy that," Georgie muttered for the third time, dabbing her handkerchief at the sweat pebbling her temple. "I've heard the old stories, of course, from servants back when I was getting settled into these parts as a young bride. I must confess that I didn't pay them much heed, but there are things that can't be explained, like Hamlet was always going on about."

"'There are more things in heaven and earth, Horatio, than are dreamt of in your philosophy,'" Lizzy rejoined. "That's the verbatim quote."

"Oooh, look at the clever one. A pity I don't have a sweet in my pocket." Her cousin patted at her dun-colored skirts in mock bemusement. "I'd give you one as a reward."

Tuck's chuckle turned into a hoarse cough when Lizzy shot him a furious glare.

"I'm not showing off," she said testily. "I simply think if one is going to quote a famous play, one should do it properly."

"And as you can see, 'proper' is my middle name." Georgie gave Tuck a wink.

"But why *not* aim for accuracy?" There were moments when Georgie—and even Jane—could irk her. Perhaps they teased her because she was younger or they were closer friends. Yet, when it occurred, she couldn't shake the unpleasant feeling of being on the outside of the circle. And she detested it. "I'm sure Shakespeare put effort into those words."

"Too bad I can't apologize to old Will. But since his plays are mostly dirty jokes stuck between moments of plot, I suppose he's got a good sense of humor about life." Georgie turned to Tuck, her thin eyebrows raised. "Serious Lizzy here is my second uncle's daughter. There are people worse than Uncle Leopold was, but few as boring. How he and my foolish aunt managed to have a child as dear as Lizzy is one of life's mysteries." She put her empty glass on a carved table and gestured to the piano. "Play something for us."

Lizzy recoiled. "You can't be serious. Now is not the time for music."

"Isn't it, though?" Georgie gestured at the drawing room door with a knowing look. "The servants will either hear you abusing the ivory or us regaling Jane with how you discovered a man from another time in a cow pond. What's your choice?"

"A waltz it is." Lizzy marched to the pianoforte. "Please make allowances, everyone. This will not be pleasant. I'm not falsely modest. I am not an accomplished player."

"I'm sure you're fine," Tuck said, reaching out to pick up a bronze candle snuffer. He regarded it in bewilderment and inexplicably sniffed the end.

"You use it to put out candles, Mr. Taylor," Lizzy snapped, arranging her skirts on the bench. What did he mean with his *fine*? Did he mean he was indifferent? Dismissive? And why was he so fidgety? She'd already observed him poking at snuffboxes, sconces, and even an inkwell, before frowning at the fireplace screen and then the chandelier.

"Ah." He set it back down. "But why don't you blow them out?"

"You'd bend the wick if you did that," she said.

"Dear Lizzy is a cross between a child and a little sister to me," Georgie continued, as if she'd been the only one speaking. "I never had children of my own. Indeed, I have no real inclination to be maternal, but I do enjoy companionship."

"She seems good company," Mr. Taylor said.

"I've been fond of her ever since I met her bald and croupy. A proper banshee, this one was. And scrawny too. Imagine a skinny baby. No, don't, you shouldn't like to think of such a thing."

"Cousin, thank you," Lizzy uttered through gritted teeth, hitting a wrong note that made everyone jump. "I am certain Mr. Taylor wishes to occupy his thoughts with far more urgent matters than tales of my infancy." She wasn't oversensitive. It was merely that those she held dear seldom took the time to regard her as anything beyond an extension of their own narratives—a supporting character offering occasional amusement or, at worst, an obligation, a burden, a weight.

"Ma'am?" A servant appeared at the door. "Miss Austen will join you momentarily."

CHAPTER SEVEN

The woman hustled into the drawing room, her white dress swishing with each step. While her hair was mostly covered by a lace cap, a few curls peeked out. "I hope this is important," she said, her voice equal parts annoyance and curiosity. "I've had an aching head, barely managed to write a page, walked to the village to purchase more paper, got caught out in the rain, and was about to take a nap. We indulged in far too much wine last night, Georgie. Look at my hands; they're trembling. I wonder if—" She halted upon noticing Tuck. "Oh."

Tuck fought the urge to squirm. Her bright eyes bore into him like he was a fish in a bowl being observed by a curious cat. Time to do what he did best: give nothing away.

"I was not aware we were to have callers." She beelined toward the velvet couch where Georgie was perched and parked herself. "I confess, my curiosity is piqued."

"Jane." Lizzy spoke from her bench at the piano as she plonked out what sounded vaguely like Beethoven's Moonlight Sonata. "Allow me the pleasure of introducing you to Mr. Tucker Taylor."

"Mr. Tucker. Taylor." Jane enunciated each word slowly, as if the name was as weird as someone shouting "hippopotamus" in a crowded bar.

"Pleased to make your acquaintance." Tuck offered his most charming drawl and added a small bow for good measure. He wasn't a born-and-raised Texan, but this Michigan kid had lived in the Lone Star State long enough to have absorbed a few southern manners.

Jane's eyes widened ever so slightly.

"Yes. You heard him correctly. Mr. Taylor's American." Lizzy's tone could mean anything from "What did I do to deserve this?" to "We must all suffer together." She hit another discordant note on the keys, the jarring sound making everyone flinch.

Tuck was suddenly tired. Tired of the headache that lingered behind his eyes. Tired of the fact that he felt half starved and sick from swallowing so much swamp water. Tired of standing in these fun-sized pants and too-tight shirt, hoping his next deep breath didn't split a seam and send all these proper women into fainting fits. Tired of Lizzy butchering Beethoven to mask their whispers.

"I'm sensing quite a tale," Jane remarked, stating the obvious.

Georgie exhaled a windstorm through her nose.

Lizzy told the story, while her cousin interrupted most sentences with an exclamation or a curse. Jane listened in absolute silence, almost quivering with concentration.

When Lizzy was done talking, her words seemed to hang in the air, each one hitting Tuck like a gut punch. His mind reeled as he tried to process everything that had occurred in the past few hours. The tension coiled up inside him until he could barely draw a breath.

"Absolutely preposterous," Jane whispered. "Completely impossible." As Lizzy stood from the piano bench, ready to argue, Jane raised a hand to stop her. "But," she continued, "there have been local legends." She glanced at Georgie with an unreadable expression. "You know them too."

Georgie nodded as Jane continued. "Folks arriving from other times or vanishing for good during the full moon. This land has ancient roots, what with all the barrows, and then the stones."

"Barrows?" Tuck asked. "You mean—"

"Yes, the mounds back in the forest," Lizzy finished.

"Druids, and those who came before them—the Old Ones," Georgie interjected. "They understood the land's magic, the ancient knowledge that's been long forgotten. When Christianity arrived with its priests, they forbade everything interesting and wild."

"That's heresy," Jane murmured. Although, she didn't sound as shocked as Tuck had expected.

"I know you're a curate's daughter." Georgie spoke calmly, soothingly, even. "But I'm not wrong. It's only a day's ride out to the Salisbury Plain to see the rock ring at Stonehenge. The Old Ones understood the world in ways we don't. Magic is likely all around, and they knew how to read the signs. We've lost the ability in this modern world."

Tuck's mind swirled as he rocked back on his heels, but Georgie was right. This was the modern world. To them at least.

"But without proof . . ." Jane rose and walked to one of the large windows, idly flicking the fringe on the curtain.

"His clothing," Lizzy hissed so loudly it might as well have been a shout. "Look at the shoes he is wearing. I've never seen anything like them. None of us have."

He glanced at his Nike Dunks. Would he have to burn them? Bury them? Hide them away? The idea of someone a few hundred years from now opening up a trunk and finding the mystery of his shoes was a little funny.

"Show them the talking device that took that portrait of me," Lizzy ordered.

"A talking device?" Georgie leaned in, intrigued. "What do you mean by that?"

"Yeah. I have something. I don't want to show you much because—" He glanced at Lizzy, mentally willing her to help him explain.

"He fears we'll disrupt the future should we possess too much knowledge," she clarified.

"My goodness. He's quite right. That does require an adjustment," Jane said to no one in particular as Tucker went to his jacket and unzipped the inner pocket, taking out his phone.

Georgie, Jane, and Lizzy drew in close, attracted to what he was holding, making small noises of wonder. Lizzy reached out and poked the glass.

"Wait until you see what it can do," she breathed.

He pulled up the photo he'd taken of Lizzy by the pond. Before they finished gasping, he swiped to a picture that Nora had snapped last night, a selfie with Tucker from inside the pub.

"This is me and my younger sister."

"I know this place," Georgie breathed. "That's Ye Olde King's Head. You can tell from the fireplace."

"I've never seen such a painting." Jane covered her mouth with her hands. "How is it like looking in a mirror?"

Tuck couldn't explain how phones worked even if he wanted to; he'd always used them without thinking about the technology involved. "We take a lot of these kind of pictures in my time."

"You use such a strange little thing to record the world?" Georgie spoke in a tone of reverence, as if they discussed the lost Ark of the Covenant and not a device that people used to record themselves doing funny dances to trending music.

"You can use it for all sorts of things. Imagine Lizzy is out, and you want to reach her, ask her a question or whatever. You can enter some numbers in a special order, and a connection is formed to her phone. Then she can go ahead and talk to you, even if she's miles away. Hundreds or thousands of miles. There's way more to it, but that's probably saying enough. Plus, it's better to save the battery. I don't know how long it'll last." He turned it off and shoved it back in his pocket.

"So, we need your creative mind, Jane," Lizzy said, "to figure out how we can get Mr. Taylor home and craft a believable story for him while he's here. We can't very well just have him go back to the pond and try to dive under."

"I already tried that anyway," Tuck interjected. "When you went to find the clothing, I swam down to the bottom, but nothing happened."

Lizzy's expression registered shock, but it vanished so quickly that he must have imagined it.

"First things first," Jane said. "We must incorporate clever details and hints grounded in half-truths and plausible explanations. However, it should be mundane enough to deter anyone from delving into further inquiries."

"Then please don't ask him how he makes a living," Lizzy muttered, letting out a snort.

"Hey now." He turned toward her. "Play nice."

"Let me guess," Jane said. "Given your size and bearing, I'm going to guess you're a soldier."

"In a roundabout way." Lizzy shrugged. "He guards a net with a stick and people try to hit discs at him."

"It's a game," Tucker broke in, exasperation tinging his words. "I play a sport for a living. It's all skill and speed."

"Like gladiators," Lizzy blurted. "Engaging in a battle, except no one is dying."

"No, no," Tuck protested.

"You are employed to play to crowds who are invested in your wins or losses."

Jane mulled it over. "I must say, it does sound fascinating."

"But it's not a story we can tell others," Lizzy said.

"To be sure, to be sure," Jane agreed. "Why not say that he is a merchant from Baltimore. I encountered such a man once, dreadfully dull. I daresay, if you mention trade and Baltimore, very few people will press for additional details. Why don't you claim to specialize in dry goods? As soon as you utter those words, people will be eager to discuss anything else."

"I don't have a Baltimore accent." Tuck frowned.

"You are an American. That's enough for around here."

Tuck went to the whiskey decanter. A drink sounded better and better. He wasn't much of a hard-alcohol guy as a rule. A beer or two usually sufficed. But nothing made sense now. He was no longer a goalie for the Austin Regals; he wasn't even a player on medical leave. He was going to masquerade as a dry goods merchant from Baltimore visiting England, but for what purpose? "What should I be doing here again, professionally speaking?"

"Expanding trade contacts in teas and ceramics," Jane stated matter-of-factly. "Your duty is to be believably boring while we figure out what is to be done about you."

"And there is that nasty business with the growing tensions," Georgie broke in. "I haven't heard it so bad since the war. According to the papers, the Americans are seething over the press gangs."

"What gangs are pressing who?" Tuck poured a double and drained the contents in a searing swallow.

He caught Lizzy staring at his throat. Her cheeks flushed as their eyes locked.

He arched a brow, just a fraction, and the pink crept even higher on her cheeks. But she didn't look away shyly this time. Rather, she held his gaze, her lashes not so much as fluttering in a blink. It was as if she silently challenged him. *Yeah, I was looking. What are you going to do about it?*

She was seriously attractive, in a way that made him want to crack the code. Her nose was a bit on the larger side and her mouth was pretty wide, but somehow her face just came together perfectly. It had been a while since he'd been with anyone, even before he got sick. That must be why she hit him like a one-timer, catching him completely off guard. His drive was coming back, stirring up reactions he'd nearly forgotten he could feel.

But not here.

Not now.

"My brother recently wrote, mentioning that British sailors have boarded American ships in the Atlantic, forcing them into service," Jane said.

"Is that allowed?" A stupid question, Tuck understood, as the weight of the era's injustices crashed down on him. People were enslaved. Women couldn't vote.

"Some in the navy appear to believe that once a British subject, always a British subject, and use that as justification for impressment, or forcible recruitment," Jane said. "Of course, your country disagrees. It's an awful fuss, and a topic that could be raised in company."

"I think we all agree that Tuck should avoid conversations that attempt to draw him in about the tense relationship between our two countries. But what else shall we do? Hide him at the Woodlands until we figure out how to return him home?" Lizzy asked.

"He can't stay here!" Georgie was adamant. "Not for a prolonged time with just you and me. Out of the question. Not unless you want to see your reputation gone forever and whatever is left of mine go up in smoke on a pyre of scandal."

"But"—Lizzy gaped—"I thought you don't mind what people say."

"That's true. But I do care if we are never invited to any home to dine or dance again. I do like to go out from time to time to have a chat or a laugh."

"What, then?"

"Just a moment." Jane rose to her feet. "My goodness. He is perfect." She circled Tuck like an angular shark. "Do you remember, Lizzy darling, how you shared a desire to be a widow, to have the independence of our Georgie?"

"Yes, but I don't see—"

"Marry Tuck."

"And murder him?" Lizzy yelped.

"Uh, ladies?" Tuck took three steps away from the iron poker next to the fireplace.

"Of course not. What on earth do you take me for?" Jane seemed aghast. "You marry and that will give credence to him remaining in your company as we work to find a solution. I'm not suggesting it's a real marriage of body and mind, simply legal protection for you both."

"But you told me once that anything is to be endured rather than marrying without affection." Lizzy swayed on her feet, her face drained of color.

"In regular circumstances, yes. But do not overlook the opportunity such an unusual moment affords. Mr. Taylor made his way here. And he will find a way home. When that happens, you tell the world he went swimming at sea and never returned to shore. Afterwards, you can move permanently to the Woodlands and work on your writing. I'll visit when I can and do the same. Someday Georgie can bequeath her estate to you, and you will not have to rely on support from your brother. Trust me when I say, from firsthand knowledge, it is not comfortable to be in a brother's debt."

"What a terrible, marvelous idea!" Georgie threw herself back against the sofa and kicked her feet. "You are an evil genius."

"Cousin!" Lizzy hissed. "You can't be condoning this."

"With all my heart I am."

Tuck wasn't a piece of meat, so why was Georgie eyeing him like he was a tasty snack? In another moment, she might pinch his biceps or poke his abs.

"You two are both mad." Lizzy spun to face him. "How can I marry you?"

Marry? Tuck's brain short-circuited. It felt like a joke, but the eager, earnest faces of the two older women told him it was all too real.

"If he wants to get back to his time, then he needs assistance," Georgie continued matter-of-factly. "Between us, we know scholars, but also villagers and even some mystics. But there is no possibility he can keep respectable company with us unless it's sanctioned."

"By a minister?" Tuck croaked.

"A Scottish blacksmith," Georgie said firmly, as Jane added, "In Gretna Green."

CHAPTER EIGHT

"Honestly, you two. This isn't some idle amusement for your afternoon's entertainment." Lizzy sank into a chair. The sunlight streaming through the window did little to warm the chill that seeped through her damp dress and into her bones. "I came to you seeking genuine guidance, not jokes."

"No one is questioning your sincerity here." Jane's words conveyed conviction, her tone and posture reflecting such. "And that's precisely why my plan holds merit."

"I've already had to explain to Mr. Taylor that if anyone caught a glimpse of us while he was in a state of undress, we'd be dragged to the altar." Lizzy stood abruptly, rubbing her arms as she resumed her agitated pacing. The need to keep moving, to outrun the absurdity of the situation, drove her on. "And now you want me to parade him across all of England, leaving a trail of scandal in our wake?"

"Earlier, you said that simply changing my shirt in your presence could ruin your reputation. Think about it." Mr. Taylor spoke slowly. "This world . . . I can't navigate it alone. It's too foreign. And I can't stay here, trapped. I need to find a way back—back to my family, my life. I have too much to lose. This arrangement could help us both."

"As fortune would have it, I'm dealing with the subject of elopement in my current book," Jane said. "I have two characters—one a reckless younger sister, who is the definition of silly, and the other a cad who gives her a false promise of marriage. She sends a note to her family announcing she will be going to Gretna Green. When the gentleman's true nature as a scoundrel is exposed, and they are discovered in London, the family is thrown into turmoil. However, a hasty marriage is arranged to salvage some semblance of honor from the wreckage of her disgrace."

Lizzy dug her teeth into the soft flesh inside her cheek, struggling to hold in the sudden sharp sting of tears.

How was she on the verge of crying?

It all felt so absurd.

Marriage was crafted to ensnare a woman. Once she said "I do," nothing in her life was hers anymore. The institution was a relinquishment of power in exchange for an illusion of safety, a trade-off where freedom was sacrificed for the semblance of a home and the illusion of authority in running it, while the husband remained the ultimate decision-maker. And to make the bitter pill more palatable, it was wrapped in the sweet, pretty lie of love.

She *knew* this. So why was the idea of a false marriage jarring? Did she harbor some undercurrent of romantic sensibilities?

"I don't mean to be indelicate, but it cannot have escaped anyone's notice that Mr. Taylor does not have means. And being a poor widow is not—"

"Forget the need for a rich man." Georgie waved her hand dismissively. "I have the resources to provide you a substantial dowry. This keeps you captain of your own ship."

To have financial security and the means to pursue her own

interests was tempting indeed. And yet, entering into a false union, even for practical convenience, left her unsettled.

"Enough plotting." Georgie seemed to sense Lizzy reaching a breaking point and stood up briskly. "Before we can think of elopement, we need to get our guest changed and have an early dinner."

"That would be advisable." Jane gave a delicate cough. "In his current attire, Mr. Taylor looks as though he resides under a mushroom."

Tuck glanced down. "I feel like an overgrown leprechaun."

"Very well, then," Georgie declared, striding purposefully toward the hall. "Let us investigate the contents of Edward's wardrobe."

The trio flanked Mr. Taylor as they went up the stairs and entered Georgie's late husband's bedchamber.

The walls exhibited soft hues of light blue and cream, providing a serene backdrop to the robust furniture. The central focus was a majestic four-poster bed. The room remained free of dust, suggesting the occupant had only momentarily stepped away rather than embarked on a permanent journey. Delicate porcelain figurines on a writing desk and a dressing table adorned with a toiletry set, cologne, and hair tonics contributed to the room's ambiance. Oriental rugs covered the hardwood floor, infusing warmth into the space.

"It's as if he could enter at any moment," Jane remarked, trailing a finger over the damask bedspread. "Poor Neddy. He was a good man."

"Indeed," Georgie said as she approached the wardrobe. "Mr. Taylor, I daresay if the ghost of my ex-husband still haunts these walls, he will be most delighted to see you in his bed."

Jane let out a choked noise as Tuck cleared his throat.

"That's him, Edward, or cousin Neddy," Lizzy announced, stepping forward to touch Tuck's arm lightly, her gaze drawn to the gilded portrait of a kindly faced man with thinning hair and a sharp chin, his expression tinged with amusement. She felt the hard muscles beneath her palm as she cleared her throat, hoping he hadn't noticed her reaction, and gestured toward another portrait of Goliath. "He adored his dogs. Do you have any back at home?" Incredible to think somewhere he had a life, a home, a family.

"Nah, not me." Tuck passed a hand over his jaw, the hair there faintly visible against his bronze skin. "Someday, maybe. But my life is too busy now. I travel a lot. Or I did."

"I see," she murmured, though she didn't really, but even while Jane and Georgie were occupied, ferrying armloads of Edward's clothes to arrange on the bed, they both strained to catch every word exchanged between them, and it made her self-conscious. "I prefer cats. They make me sneeze, but I adore them."

He gave a stiff nod while averting his gaze. On the surface, it seemed as if he wasn't paying much attention, but his inward expression hinted at a deeper focus, as if he were meticulously cataloging every word she uttered, placing "adores cats" on a mental shelf that he'd consider at length in some later private time. It might have been foolish, but a small thrill surged through her chest at the notion.

"I'll call in my best manservant," Georgie was saying. "He's discreet, loyal to the house, and will see you dressed for dinner. You're welcome to anything in this room that feels useful. Lizzy? Jane? Let's go downstairs. Dinner will be served within the hour."

"Will you manage all right?" Lizzy whispered as he stared at the pile of clothing with open puzzlement, as if seeing some articles for the first time.

"I don't think I have much of a choice, do I?" he muttered.

She wasn't sure if he meant the clothing or everything. Despite her hollow stomach, she wished she could skip dinner and retreat to bed. Either today would turn out to be a dream, despite all evidence to the contrary, or she would at least gather the strength to face tomorrow and all the strange questions it would bring.

She inclined her head in what hopefully passed for sympathetic agreement and turned to follow the two older women.

She noticed Jane's sideways looks as they advanced along the corridor.

"Oh, what is it?" She didn't mean to sound quite so sharp.

"You like him." Jane's answer was perfectly bland, but an ocean of subtext lingered beneath the polite tone.

"I don't even *know* him." And that was the truth.

"Is that a requirement?" Jane's forthrightness, though it might seem bordering on blunt, served her well. Perhaps it was because she spoke without judgment, relying solely on her wry observations. "Nevertheless, his presence proves beneficial."

Jane was someone who spoke the truth, with insight that could pierce through obstructions or deflections. It was why having her here was so vital. Her cousin and her friend were honest with her in a way that made her trust herself as she never did in London.

As they waited in the dining room, Lizzy accepted the offer of a drink, swirling the Madeira in the crystal glass like she could read her fortune inside.

And then, as if summoned by her thoughts, Mr. Taylor appeared, filling the doorway—and her mind. The clothing hugged his large frame, the navy wool jacket with its fitted silhouette emphasizing his stature. Beneath it, a gray herringbone waistcoat adorned a crisp white shirt topped with a loosely tied cravat. His trousers clung to his muscular thighs, further emphasized by a pair of polished Hessian boots.

The sight left her pulse pounding in her ears.

"Darling, close your mouth before you catch a fly." Georgie beckoned to Mr. Taylor. "Right here, we've prepared a place setting for you. Don't be timid."

Seizing the opportunity provided by Georgie's assertiveness, Lizzy surreptitiously dabbed at her chin with a deft flick of her wrist, checking for any sign of drool. To her relief, there was no mortifying moisture leaking from her mouth.

It wasn't as though Mr. Taylor had been entirely without appeal in his previous appearance, be it squelching in the swamp or navigating the woods. On the contrary, he possessed a certain charm. However, seeing him now, attired like a country gentleman, odd haircut notwithstanding, sent a shot through her, as precise as an arrow. It was as if he were suddenly more within reach.

He sat in the chair beside her. "A man dressed me upstairs," he murmured, leaning close. "Like I was a little child."

Overhearing his comment, Jane responded, "It was merely a bit of guidance to ensure you get it all right."

"I say, you look marvelous," Georgie chimed in. "Don't you agree, Jane?"

"The effect is tidy and refined, and no one could cast a shadow of impropriety on you." Jane poked at the slice of beef. She never ate enough. Georgie insisted she take some berries, bread, and butter. While they good-naturedly squabbled, Lizzy noticed that Mr. Taylor kept fidgeting.

"Is everything all right?" she murmured, helping herself to a pasty and a little salad.

"Where's the bathroom?"

"You wish to take a bath?" she whispered. "At this precise moment?"

"No. The guy upstairs told me to go in a porcelain bucket in the corner of the room."

"I see. You mean to relieve yourself," Lizzy remarked, edging slightly closer. She caught his scent. Despite her writerly ambitions, she found herself unable to conjure an adjective better than "good." He smelled good. Such a feeble word for a scent that was so much more than that.

She froze.

Here he was discussing chamber pots, and she was tempted to bury her nose in his neck and inhale. This was a fine form of madness.

What she should have said was that this wasn't a suitable conversation for a lady and a man to have anywhere, let alone at a dining table. But she didn't know what they had in the future—apparently not chamber pots.

"Yes, and I used it, but it's weird. I don't want to leave it sitting there."

"A servant will come. It's probably already dealt with."

He grunted. "That doesn't make me feel better."

"You could use the privy. It's located outside, near the stables. As much as I wish to claim curiosity about such private matters, I'd rather not be a liar."

The fact that she could draw laughter from him, coupled with the way his shoulders shook, as if the noise traveled through his whole body, pleased her more than she liked to admit. She took a small, deliberate sip of wine, recognizing the need for caution. There was something about being in this man's space that lit her up like a candelabra. She'd barely had more than a few mouthfuls of Madeira, so the giddiness couldn't be attributed to that.

Blotting the side of her mouth with the cloth napkin, she caught him in a stare, his focus lingering on her lips. "Oh dear." She brushed her fingers over them. "I don't have food on my face, do I?" He shifted his gaze to his own plate, suddenly engrossed in chasing peas around in a shallow pool of gravy.

"These are excellent boiled potatoes. Compliments to whoever among you is the chef."

"We didn't cook this meal." Jane turned toward him sharply. "Georgie can afford staff."

She didn't tack on the phrase "you idiot," but it hung in the air. Something seemed to amuse her because she repeated, "Excellent boiled potatoes" under her breath to no one in particular.

"Is the clothing to your liking, Mr. Taylor?" Georgie held court across the table. "I must say, you clean up nicely. Doesn't he, Jane?"

"He has a pleasant countenance," Jane said, covering her glass when Georgie attempted to pour in more wine. "And I will not let you coax me into another night of drinking, as we have more than enough diversions to occupy our minds. For example, if Mr. Taylor is going to be successful, he shall require proper education. For starters, when is it acceptable for a gentleman to rest his elbows on the dining room table?"

Tucker glanced down at his relaxed posture. "Between courses?"

"Never." Jane's reply hit the mark, and he jolted back in his seat. "And in which direction do you pass a dish?" she continued.

"To whoever asks politely?"

"Left to right," she said simply.

Lizzy bristled. "You can't expect him to—"

"He must know enough to not cause offense. Of course, being American helps. You can explain away much ignorance on that point alone."

"At least he unfolded his napkin on his lap." It wasn't until the words left her lips, hanging there over the table, that she realized she was riding to his defense. Any hope she had of feigning indifference or of projecting an attitude of resigned obligation dimmed considerably.

The knowing glance between Jane and Georgie grated on her nerves.

"Let's review topics fit for discussion in social settings." Jane resumed a businesslike demeanor, all efficiency and seriousness. "The weather. Blue skies. Stormy skies. Dry spells. Fog. Discussing the weather is *always* safe." The corner of her lip curled. "You may die from boredom, but better to be too dull than daring."

"Makes sense." He gave a slow nod. "How's this? 'Hey, look out the window at this masterpiece we've got on display today. A perfect blend of gray and, uh, grayer. It's like Mother Nature took her palette and went, *Let's keep it simple, but make it fashionable.*'"

"There is a fine line between mockery and wit," Jane said dryly.

"And best not to discuss the American War at all," Georgie said. "If anyone asks, change the subject to—"

He turned to Lizzy. "What's the American War?"

"My mother's husband fought in it, and now he has a limp." Lizzy wrinkled her brow, bemused. "Certainly you know. It's when the colonies had their rebellion."

"Ah. The *Revolutionary* War." He nodded. "Got it."

"For the next few days, I propose that Tucker receive an education in being a gentleman of our time," Jane mused. "We'll all help, and I daresay we'll have our work cut out."

"You talk about me like I'm a barbarian."

"Not quite," Jane shot back. "You're more brawn than brute."

"Here, here," Georgie chimed in.

"And you're both incorrigible," Lizzy scolded. "Mr. Taylor . . . I'll help you."

The room went silent.

Her palms grew clammy, and she curled her fingers into her skirts, the fabric bunching beneath her grip. "I'll help you get home, even if it means we go to Gretna Green. This is for our mutual benefit. Your lessons will start tomorrow promptly after breakfast. We'll cover the broad strokes from history to current topics of interest to manners to literature."

"On one condition," he said.

"I don't believe you are in a position to negotiate."

"I'm serious. I can't tell you much about the future, okay? I don't want to be rude, but it's better that way. There's a theory known as the butterfly effect that says that even small actions, say, a butterfly flapping its wings, could lead to a big consequence, like causing a storm on the other side of the world. I don't know how history and time are connected, and I really don't want to be responsible for messing with the future or anyone's destiny in this room."

"How charming." Jane laughed. "Imagine any of us living lives that could be of lasting consequence."

Mr. Taylor nudged Lizzy's shoe with his boot. A signal. *Careful.*

"Yes." Lizzy gave a weak grin. "Imagine that."

CHAPTER NINE

The clinking and scraping of iron gradually penetrated Tuck's awareness, pulling him from his deep sleep. He blinked, fixing his gaze on a crack in the ceiling's plaster rosettes, his brain registering the pieces of his surroundings like a puzzle coming together. Nope. He wasn't in the hospital ready to tell Nora about his vivid dream. His ass was still firmly planted in 1812.

The room held an unfamiliar scent, a blend of cedar and beeswax underscored with a bit of old-home dampness. Tuck's gaze wandered over the four-poster bed, the high ceiling, and the walls painted in two tones, light blue and creamy white. Opposite the bed, the portrait of the room's former inhabitant, Edward, stared back from the canvas with an inscrutable expression.

"Thanks for lending me your room, old buddy," he murmured, wiping sleep from his eyes. Neddy may be gone, but that was just the tip of the iceberg. Everyone he'd met in the past twenty-four hours? They were all long dead and buried in his time. And now that included himself. They were a world of ghosts not knowing they were already history.

The great cosmic cycle could cave your head in.

Saluting Neddy, Tuck tossed off the blanket and swung his legs to the side, his bare feet sinking into the soft rug. First, he reached under the mattress and pulled out his phone, turning it on.

No signal.

No shit.

Still, it comforted him to see his screen saver, a Regals team shot from last season. He looked at the guys, the arena. Matty Vincenza, the backup goaltender, would step up. Coach would have called in an emergency backup too. Maybe a kid from UT Austin. Did they know he was missing yet over in England? He was out for most of the regular season, but they must have gotten word. What would they do? Give up his spot? No fucking way.

He powered off his phone and returned it to its hiding spot. Absentmindedly scratching his lower back, he wandered over to the window. He needed a distraction, so he decided to check what was making that noise outside.

A round-cheeked house servant yanked a chain, pulling a bucket up from the stone well in the middle of the yard. Hence the clatter of metal. He whistled under his breath. When he returned home, he'd never take indoor plumbing for granted again. He might even buy his toilet a top-of-the-line bowl brush.

The servant must have sensed his gaze because she turned to glance up. Suddenly aware that he had slept naked, Tuck leapt back into the safety of the shadows. The last thing he needed was to look like some pervert with a flashing fetish.

The door flew open behind him. "What the hell!" Tucker's snapped surprise earned him a frown from the gray-haired man who entered.

He grunted as Tuck clapped his hands over his dick. "Morning, sir." The male servant inclined his head in a stiff bow. "I'm here to see you dressed properly."

Not again.

"Why is this necessary?" Tuck asked. "I'm fine handling it on my own."

"Not from what I've seen," the servant drawled calmly, striding to a chair to inspect the clothing Tuck had tossed there the night before. He held up the jacket and clicked his tongue before moving to the wardrobe. "What I witnessed yesterday was a man in his underthings for all to see, even respectable ladies."

"I was in pants and a shirt." After a life of hockey, he was well accustomed to changing in front of others, even the media when they came through the locker room door hunting for a quote.

"That's right." The servant turned with a puzzled look. "No waistcoat. No jacket. No hat. And in front of Miss Wooddash, for shame. I don't know how you Americans behave across the pond, but here?" He made a disapproving sound that seemed to convey the words *You come to this house and try any funny business, I'll mess you up.*

And Tucker approved of that. Here was Lizzy, alone in the country, surrounded by nothing but deep dark woods. A territorial sensation clenched his gut as he forced logic into his head. The women in this house deserved physical protection, but from what he could see, they could take care of themselves just fine. Anyone attempting to break in would likely find themselves fleeing like the burglars in *Home Alone.*

While this servant was taking his sweet time selecting clothing, Tucker caught a glimpse of himself in the mirror. His skin had a natural olive tone, but he'd spent last summer indoors. The chemo port scar on his chest was a visible reminder of why. His abs were lean, lacking clear definition, sure, but his waist was trim.

Would Lizzy like it?

The thought rattled him like a shot off the crossbar. What did it matter? If she went along with whatever plot was being cooked up by her cousin and her friend, it was to serve her own purposes. Not because of his abs.

"Here we are, sir." The servant handed him a white linen shirt with a twinge of annoyance. "Don't stand there looking at it; put it on." Tuck took the shirt and pulled it on over his head; it hung to his mid-thighs.

"What's your name?"

"Robert, but most call me Robbie."

"Thank you, Robbie. And I think—"

"Please don't." Robbie cut him off. "Think, I mean. My job isn't to chat; it's to get you dressed so I can see to my other chores."

"Are you often sent to dress a guy?"

Robbie looked bewildered. "And why would I be doing that, seeing as we haven't had a man stay in here since the old master died? Not even Miss Wooddash's brother has visited, and him being a cousin of Miss Georgie too. But we can still do things properly."

"Fair enough." Tuck pulled on the proffered stockings, then underwear, essentially long white leggings. He fastened the top button and then stepped into the offered breeches.

Tuck had been close to Dixon, the Regals' equipment manager, who'd held the role for two decades. He anticipated Tuck's needs, often before Tuck did. A realization clicked into place. So Robbie here, now reaching for a waistcoat, was like the 1812 version. Instead of sharpening skates, breaking in sticks, and cleaning jerseys, he was ensuring all these items of clothing were ready to go.

This was another game, one that would take all his mental concentration and focus. And the stakes were higher. If he lost, he might not only be unable to ever return home, but something worse could happen. People could think he was crazy and lock him in some drafty asylum. Or he could get sick, spike a fever, and that would be it—game over. Worse, his cancer could come back. The thought sent ice water coursing through his veins.

Then what? There wasn't anything to put him back into remission here. As much as he hated chemo, despised the smell of hospitals, the thin scratchy fabric of hospital gowns, and the endless blood draws for labs—all of that allowed him to know he'd be okay. It assured him that he'd kick cancer's ass and have a setback that would turn into a comeback, not a decline.

"Sir?" Robbie's brows knit.

"What's wrong?"

"I asked if you wanted to see the result."

Tucker reached out and patted the man on the shoulder, realizing as Robbie flinched that casual touch maybe wasn't the norm here. While there were some correlations, 1812 was not—and would never be—home.

"When you put this much effort into turning me out? Of course I'll look. Tell you what, I probably won't recognize myself."

Robbie directed him to the mirror, and Tuck didn't know what to say. It couldn't be "I look like an asshole." But he kind of did. At least like a man who'd drink tea with his pinkie outstretched. A regular snob.

But this was the uniform. And he was in the game. He gave an approving nod. "Good."

"Anything else I can do for you before seeing myself out?"

Tuck ran the tip of his tongue over his teeth. "Actually, yeah. One more thing. Where do you keep extra toothbrushes in the house?"

Robbie blinked. "Sir?"

Tuck's heart sank as the steward gave a nervous smile. There were more than a few gaps where teeth had once lived. Four, by an initial count.

"Did a dentist pull yours?" Wasn't a puck or high stick.

"If you're talking about my teeth, I use my finger and soot every day, but if one gets to aching, I go to the barber, and he fixes me up all right. The one in Hallow's Gate is strong. One pull and *crack*!"

"Back it up. You go to a barber for teeth? I don't understand."

"Well, here in the country, we can't keep a full-time tooth puller employed. That's for the city. Of course, there could be the blacksmith."

The damn blacksmith again. It sounded like those guys could do everything from making a horseshoe to yanking out a rotten incisor to marrying you in a border town.

"A tooth what?"

Robbie leaned in with a grave face. "Scoundrels that wrench out your afflicted teeth from your very jaw, causing such a torment as to make a man lose his dignity."

As the conversation continued, Tuck grew increasingly less certain why he was asking these questions when he suddenly didn't want to know the answers. If he was reduced to rubbing ash on his teeth, he might resemble a poorly carved jack-o'-lantern when he finally returned to the twenty-first century.

At breakfast, he mentioned to Lizzy his conversation with Robbie. Georgie was out with her dogs, and Jane hadn't come down yet—Lizzy said Jane tended to sleep late.

"Do you use ash on your teeth too?" he asked.

"No, of course not." Lizzy wrinkled her nose before clapping a hand over her mouth. "I didn't mean it like that. You must think I'm a dreadful snob."

"I just want to clean my teeth."

"I use a method my mother taught me. It's salt with oven-dried sage crumbled through it."

"Salt?" He arched a brow, inwardly wincing when she flushed slightly, catching his reaction. "But no fingers?"

"I have a tooth scraper. How do you clean *your* teeth? They are quite brilliant."

He hesitated. His teeth looked good, but more than a few weren't the ones he was born with. Veneers felt like a lot to explain.

She rolled her eyes. "If I learn your mysterious secrets of brushing, will I cause some irreversible twist of fate for the whole of mankind?"

"When you put it like that? No." He took another sip of tea. The drink was okay, in a way anything that warm and wet was, but he'd kill for a protein shake. "We go see a dentist."

"Den-tist." She tasted the unfamiliar word.

"It's a doctor for teeth. And while sometimes people will get one pulled, for the most part, you go to keep them healthy and in place. There is a team of assistants who clean and polish each individual tooth and a dentist who fixes the harder problems."

"And so, as people get older, do they keep most of them?"

"Define *most*," he said.

"Half?"

"The majority of people where I'm from keep *all* their teeth, and if not, you can get a fake one put in."

Her brows knit. "I've seen people collecting teeth in the poorer areas, hoping to resell to the richer classes."

"That seems wrong," he said.

"It must feel very different here." She pursed her lips. "I'll have a tooth scraper located for you as well. But I also can't help but harbor the ongoing feeling that you must be laughing at us."

"Why?"

"For how simple we must seem. Your world is so different."

"That it is, yes."

"Here, now, a woman's legal identity is absorbed by her husband upon marriage. They cannot own property, enter into contracts, or control their earnings."

"Yeah, that's different in my time." He sat back in his chair. "Women can own their homes, work in any field, and do whatever they want with their money."

"A woman can get a job like a man?"

"Yes."

Her brows perked up. "And earn the same amount?"

"Well, no, not always." He swung his gaze to his plate. "Women often don't get paid the same."

"That is odd. In America, you have presidents. How many have been women?" she inquired.

"None."

Her smile dimmed. "Your country was formed in the eighteenth century and you've not had a woman rule even one time?"

"I mean, when you put it that way . . ." He trailed off sheepishly.

"What other way is there?" she challenged. "What about your sports job? Do ladies do it?"

He brightened. "Women play hockey, sure!"

"On your team?" she pressed.

"No, no. I'm with the NHL, the National Hockey League."

"Made up of men from your nation?"

"Yes. And no. Also, men from Canada. Norway. We have a Russian too."

"My head is starting to ache." She rubbed her temples. "Where do women play hockey for work?"

"Most don't." He frowned. "There have been some starts and

stops to get a female league. There is one now, but not that many cities are in it."

"So women don't do sports?"

"Many women play many different sports. But it's hard to get a lot of sports teams for women to earn a lot of money."

"Because men don't want to watch or value them," she concluded softly.

Shit.

She was right. Her reasoning got to the ugly truth.

And worse, he'd barely thought of it before. He'd known, of course. Everyone knew. But somehow the knowledge was so ingrained—the unfair dynamics of the two-tier reality of women in sports—that he'd come to accept it as the norm.

And fuck that.

Now he had to be here with this bright, beautiful woman who'd hoped that over time wrongs would be righted, and all he had to offer was . . . *It's pretty shitty. And I've done nothing to change it.*

Shame soured his stomach.

"Hundreds of years in the future and women still can't enjoy what a man can." Her laugh was forced, like someone replaced the real thing with a cheap plastic imitation. "I can't say I'm surprised."

And the hollowness in her voice—he hated it.

Right now, from what she'd shared, a woman was the property of her husband. And it didn't seem right that all he could offer her was that in the twenty-first century at least a woman could work a job that would usually pay her less than a man. Not much of a reason to take a victory lap. He wanted to say something honest, even if it wasn't much.

"I'm sorry. And worse, I could have done better. But I've been so focused on myself; my goals are big, it's a competitive world, there's a long line of guys waiting for me to mess up, so they can take my spot. But it shouldn't be *either-or*. It should be *both-and*."

"Be *both-and*?" Lizzy's smile pushed through like a tiny flower appearing in a sidewalk crack. "I like how you talk."

"Glad I amuse you," he said. "But if me showing up here can make a difference to you? Make it so you can work to become a writer? To live a life on your terms? To inherit this house? Then I'm going to say yes. Scotland. Gretna Green. Marriage. Let's do it."

"If you are willing to accept, then so am I."

He wasn't breathing. The hair on the backs of his forearms had gone extra sensitive.

"But I have a few rules. All are nonnegotiable." She held up three fingers.

The way she spoke, her voice quiet yet filled with intense focus—it was as if she had gained the power to redirect his blood straight to his brain, making him hyperaware of every single word.

Talk, idiot.

He cleared his throat, and the sound felt too loud. "Go for it."

"First, we respect each other's need for privacy and personal boundaries. We will be traveling together, but not as husband and wife. Eloping with you shall enrage my family. I prefer to mitigate that by behaving with decorum."

"Okay, deal. What else you got?"

"Second, social contracts. We will identify and agree on how to address each other in public. We can be unusual, but we must be convincing.

"Third, we support each of our goals. I assist you in returning home, and you will help me become a widow."

"Who grieves me terribly," he murmured wryly.

"Would you like that?" She cocked her head. "To be grieved?"

He frowned. "I'm afraid that's happening now. My sister—we aren't close in terms of interests or hobbies—but we get each other. And it kills me to think she's worrying. And then there are my parents. I was sick earlier this year. Nothing serious. Well, it was, but I'm fine now. I just prefer to do the worrying about the people who matter to me and not the other way around."

She held his gaze. "You are a good man."

"Sometimes." He cracked his knuckles. "Thank you."

"I am honored to pretend-marry you."

He raised his head. "Thought this was going to be legal."

"You know what I mean."

There was a knock on the dining room door. Robbie entered, hat in hand. "Sir? The mistress asked if you'd be available to come meet her at the stables."

"I think we are both finished with breakfast?" Lizzy gave Tuck a quick glance. "We can go out together."

"Sorry, miss." Robbie twisted his cap. "The mistress said only the gentleman was to come. You're to begin packing."

"Very bossy of her." Lizzy shrugged. "She probably wants to show you something with the dogs, as you mentioned an interest. I am quite sure she knows she has maximized all my goodwill on the topic."

Tuck nodded and gave her a convincing smile, even returning her wave as she exited the room.

As soon as her footsteps disappeared down the hall, he squared off with Robbie. "Okay. What's really going on?"

Robbie dropped the submissive pretense. "Mistress is in with the dogs, but she's not throwing Goliath a bone. She's polishing a pistol. Sorry, sir."

"That's all right. It's about what I was expecting."

Lizzy was clearly doted on as the younger relative. The gamble that Georgie and Jane were making was considerable. There was the potential this would all work out exactly the way they hoped. But he got it. They were protective. And it was time to face the music.

He walked out into the backyard and nearly into a goose, who honked at him like he was the rude one. "Excuse me," he muttered.

"In there." Robbie pointed down toward a small white-painted outbuilding. "And good luck, sir."

Tuck crossed his arms. "You reckon I'll need it?"

"Oh, very much." Robbie's rapid nods punctuated the sentence.

"Well, cover me," Tuck quipped. "I'm going in."

The stables were dark and shadowy compared to the bright morning light outside. Tucker looked around, waiting for his vision to correct; he heard Georgie rustling around somewhere.

"Thank you for taking the time to talk to us." She stepped from the back stall, a massive dog flanking her on either side. "Jane and I are grateful that you've agreed to this wild plot to take our Lizzy and travel to Gretna Green."

"Jane? Is she here?"

"Of course."

"Jesus!" Tuck jumped at the soft voice in his ear. He didn't startle easily, but this had gotten weird. Behind him was Jane in a dark dress, no cap, no smile. Was she holding a shovel? He glanced down. Yeah. That was a shovel. And a rusty one at that.

"You leave for Gretna Green tomorrow." Georgie didn't acknowledge she was holding a gun. The giant dogs weren't growling, but they didn't have a warm expression either. "We secured you a stagecoach from Salisbury. It's a long journey."

"Four nights," Jane murmured. "Four nights in inns without a chaperone."

"Easy." He held up his hands. "I know what you're thinking . . ."

"Do you, though?" Jane didn't move.

Tuck was boxed in between them.

"Is the gun necessary?" he asked Georgie. "If we could just have a reasonable conversation about this Scotland idea—that *you* both came up with, I might add."

"This is a dueling pistol." Georgie turned the weapon over in her hands; it had a smooth wood handle—walnut, maybe—a dark steel barrel, and intricate silver touches. "It belonged to my father."

"Used once. In a matter of honor," Jane said.

"You aren't from this time," Georgie said. "We wanted to impress upon you a few things."

"If you change your mind, and leave Lizzy without marriage, she will be ruined." Jane's tone was matter-of-fact. "It signifies a loss of respectability, social standing, and, for a young woman, the total collapse of other suitable marriage prospects. And it won't only affect her. It will affect her parents, her brother, his future wife, their future children."

"Who, to be sure, we don't give much care for," Georgie added. "But Lizzy does."

"And what Lizzy cares about, we care about."

"No cold feet," Tuck said. "I give you my word. I won't leave Lizzy."

"And if you do? I imagine you won't be hard to find. You will make any number of mistakes. People will talk," Jane said.

"I'll defend my family's honor." Georgie's fingers tightened on the gun.

"And I'll bury your body in a grave no one will ever find."

Jane's sweet, soft voice belied the threat. "Once my good opinion is lost, it is lost forevermore."

And Tuck had the impression they were absolutely serious.

But so was he.

"I'm not going to leave her. I promise. I swear it on my life. Is that good enough for you?"

"Not quite. Swear on the life of someone who matters to you," Jane said firmly. "We aren't more than acquaintances. I know you enjoy a good boiled potato. I'm rather less certain how much you value your own life."

His temper began to rise. He understood them wanting to make sure he wasn't going to be an asshole, but they shouldn't assume too much. "You don't know what I've done to stay alive. And I swear it on my sister Nora's life. I won't leave Lizzy. We made a deal. We need each other. I need to figure out how to get home. And, well, she needs me dead. But . . ." He pointed to the dueling pistol. "Not for real."

Georgie locked her gaze with his. "Very well. I trust you, Mr. Taylor."

"And I also place my faith in you," Jane declared. "But I must warn you, sir, if you prove false—"

"You shall find yourself in the Great Beyond," Georgie concluded with a serious tone. "And I dare say, you will find it quite impossible to return home from there."

Damn, these ladies were hardcore. But he kinda respected it.

"Once you've completed your task, make haste to London," Georgie instructed. "In the meantime, we'll research the history of the pond and other lore in the region. Perhaps we'll uncover some valuable insights."

"Very well." Jane set the shovel against the barn wall. "Since we aren't consigning you to the grave today, Mr. Taylor, I find myself quite eager to return to my book. My hero is about to make a mess out of everything by declaring his love for my heroine."

"And that's a bad thing?"

"It is when he is still obtuse about women. Are you obtuse about women, Mr. Taylor?"

"I think the women around me would be best equipped to answer that question."

Georgie barked out a laugh. "I don't often have a high opinion of your sex. But you might surprise us all."

CHAPTER TEN

The Two-Necked Goose was a stagecoach inn in Salisbury nestled beneath the shadow of the towering cathedral. The narrow cobblestone lanes resonated with the clip-clop of horse hooves, while gilded signboards swung in the breeze, enticing passersby with promises of fine silks, bespoke millinery, and rare curiosities. Lizzy hadn't missed London since departing for Hallow's Gate, although the display of ribbons and fabrics in the fashionable hues of the season at the mercer's emporium and the scent of linseed oil and pigment wafting from the open door of the printing press made it undeniably pleasant to be in the bustle of a town again.

The inn was a hive of activity, filled with a brisk utilitarian ambiance devoid of any debauchery. No dubious characters hunched around tables twirling whiskers or plotting nefarious schemes as Lizzy had fretted about before drifting off to sleep last night. Instead, travelers bustled about dragging trunks, anticipating the arriving stagecoaches. Lizzy reached into a concealed pocket in her dress and pulled out a golden watch, once Cousin Neddy's prized possession and now a treasured gift from Georgie.

"We are here in good time, are we not?" she remarked in Mr. Taylor's general direction. She couldn't think of him as *Tuck* in her head. It felt too personal. Too intimate. How incredible that she'd marry this man in a few days' time. Even though their motivations for this marriage were to achieve individual goals, the thought of standing before him and exchanging vows made her feel unsteady.

"Here you go." Tuck slid out a chair for her at a corner table and she almost stumbled while sitting. Wouldn't that take the biscuit, to fall into his arms? Heavens above, she knew somehow that he'd be gentle, but the notion sent a most peculiar sensation coursing through her, as if tiny butterflies waltzed across her skin.

She had to regain her senses. Immediately.

"I sometimes get ill when in a carriage too long," she blurted.

Lies.

That had never happened. She'd even ventured out on a boat with Papa before he died, near Portsmouth. Her legs had felt as steady as if she strode across dry land.

"Want something to drink?" Tuck glanced toward the kitchen door. "Get a bite to settle your stomach? The stagecoach is going to be enclosed, right? Being cooped up inside might make you feel worse."

"I'll endeavor to sleep." Here, Lizzy was finally truthful. Or at least partially. Her plan for the next few days was to feign sleep as much as possible. All the better to save herself the embarrassment of encountering strangers in a compromised position and to keep these confusing sentiments related to Tuck—Mr. Taylor—at bay. "But a pot of tea would be lovely as we wait—souchong, if they have it."

As he went to procure sustenance, she surveyed the interior. It was dim due to the ivy outside that grew over the windows. But far from invoking a sense of gloom, the subdued illumination cast the room in a sort of intimate coziness.

Mr. Taylor returned, and it didn't take long before a girl brought out the tea, along with a few cakes and the usual lemon, milk, and sugar.

"How do you take your tea?" she asked, pouring two porcelain cups.

"Not sure. Can't say I've drunk much before coming here. Why don't you give me the works?"

She was torn between the urge to laugh and the desire to scoff, compromising with a gasp. "Milk *and* lemon?"

"Sure. Sounds good. And sugar." His gaze trailed around the room's unpretentious interior as if he wasn't being infuriating.

"One can have milk and sugar. *Or* sugar and lemon. But not all three." On this point she was adamant.

He mulled her words for a moment. "Why not?"

"It's just not done," she explained. "The acid in the lemon will curdle the milk."

"Not if I drink it fast."

"This is serious. You are not a barbarian."

"You judge people based on how they take their tea?"

"If it's done incorrectly, yes," she snapped. "I'll not wed a savage, even if it is to gain my freedom."

Was this the moment when Tucker Taylor would reveal himself to be just another insufferable man? Was he the kind of person who would argue that black was white, who would resort to personal attacks against a woman making an argument instead of addressing the merits of the argument itself?

"What do you suggest?"

"A lemon slice," she answered.

"All right, then. I'll go with that. Sugar too. Hold the milk." He seemed wholly unfazed and willing to listen.

She blinked in surprise.

"How are you feeling about everything?" he asked after taking a cautious sip. "That's good, by the way. You were right."

She struggled to maintain a neutral expression, trying to hide her confusion. He'd listened to her without getting angry, frustrated, or closing his mind. "I'm . . . I'm fine."

"No. Don't do that." He placed the cup on the saucer and leaned forward on his elbows. "Not with me. I don't want the right answer. Give me the real one."

She hesitated a moment before admitting, "I'm a bit overwhelmed."

A hint of approval flickered in his eyes. "Good girl."

A thrill shot down her spine at the utterance of those two simple words. A curious thing, because she could sense within herself a strange and inexplicable urge to earn Tuck's favor. Not at the cost of her own sense of self, but from a desire to bask in his approval. In fact, the thought of hearing those words again gave her such pleasure that she feared she might ask for them, propriety be hanged.

Yet she was wary of giving him too much power, hesitant to lose the upper hand in whatever seesaw game they were playing, especially considering the audacious path upon which they were to embark.

At least Georgie and Jane had blessed this scheme.

"What are you thinking about now?" he asked.

She tucked her chin and widened her eyes, a flirtatious gesture she'd observed other women employ at balls or dinner parties when playing the coquette. It always worked too, because, in her experience, men were easily swayed by such tactics.

Mr. Taylor sat back, seeming unimpressed. "What are you doing?"

"Looking at you."

"Why the weird face?"

His blunt question caught her off guard. She tilted her head, adopting the picture of innocence, like a woman in a rococo painting. "I don't know what you mean. This is how I look."

"Yeah, sure." He passed a thick hand over his strong jaw with a snort. She noticed a small cut near his chin, likely from shaving.

She squared her shoulders, resisting the compulsion to lean in and gently blow on the wound.

"I think you wonder what I think of you," he stated, not a question.

"I'm curious about a great many things in this world, Mr. Taylor," she replied primly. "If you wish to share what you perceive as fact, I'll listen, although I may find it of little use."

His nostrils flared, gaze sharpening. Their verbal volleys felt like both a conversation and a game, leaving her dizzy despite having drunk only tea.

In a blink-and-miss-it moment, he ran a finger down her left hand. She glanced up, her coy smile slipping at his intense expression. She donned her most useful mask, the one that betrayed no thoughts.

He didn't break eye contact. "I think you have more courage in that little pinkie than most people have in their entire body."

She forced a brief laugh, pressing her knees together, but the tension persisted, and worse, intensified. The spot where he'd caressed her still felt warm. If one touch had this effect, what about more prolonged contact?

"That's quite a claim," she said. "And unfortunately incorrect, as I'm afraid of many things. You've yet to see me encounter a spider, or a duck."

"Duck?" His eyes crinkled with smile lines. "That sounds like a story."

"When I was a child, a mallard bit me. I was at a park in London, enjoying a particularly delicious muffin, when it gave chase. The sensation of its beak pinching the backs of my legs is something I'll never forget." She shuddered. "So, you see, I'm not exactly the type to lead the Spanish Armada into battle."

He cocked his head. "Everyone thinks I'm good at what I do because I have quick reflexes. But the reason I act fast is because I can predict. And I predict because I make it a point to study my opponents. I study them off and on the ice. I review games. I don't quit until I know the competition better than they know themselves. People sometimes want to believe my success is due to luck, talent, or genetics. Nah. It's due to observation."

"And I'm an opponent?"

His expression softened. "No, you're on my team."

She scuffed her boots against the floor in a nervous rhythm. "And what team is that?"

"Team Mutual Benefit. You win if I win. I win if you win. Our goal is that I return home and you get to pretend I'm dead."

"You're not too offended?" she murmured.

"I'd like to think you could enjoy me for the time we have. That I'm the kind of man you'll miss when I'm gone."

She wouldn't show how much his words touched her. "I'll tell you one secret," she replied breezily. "I don't look good in black. I probably won't be in mourning long."

His serious expression didn't alter. "I know how much you're risking by taking this trip, Pocket Rocket. And if things go wrong, what it could mean for your future, even for your family. I want to be straight before we climb into the stagecoach and go three feet from this place. I'm glad you're on my team."

The worst happened. Tears sheened her eyes before she could force them back. "I'm sorry," she blurted, fumbling for a handkerchief. "I don't know where those came from."

"My guess? You haven't had enough people in your life who root for your success. They're more about their own selfish goals. But look at yourself. You're a force of nature. When we met, you stayed cool, calm, and collected. You assessed the situation, figured out a plan, and executed. And now you're here ready to take on a trip to Scotland. And you know what? It's not because you trust me—although you absolutely should. No, it's because you trust yourself, and that takes a special kind of strength."

CHAPTER ELEVEN

Four hours into the journey, Lizzy found herself wedged between the stagecoach wall and Tucker Taylor. The limited space had become even more suffocating with the addition of five more passengers. A minister, who dozed off before they'd even left Salisbury's city limits, now filled the coach with thunderous snores, accompanied by the wet, snorting harmony of a naval officer. An elderly woman and her lady's maid, on their way to visit the woman's daughter, who had recently delivered her eighth child, occupied the seats opposite Lizzy. And across from Mr. Taylor sat a dark-haired naval officer who repeatedly attempted to discreetly insert a finger halfway up his hooked nose.

The stagecoach's incessant jostling on the uneven road only served to intensify Lizzy's discomfort. The rhythmic thumping emanating through the roof mirrored the throbbing ache in her head, each thud reverberating through her skull. Two youths, paying a reduced fare to perch on the top of the stagecoach, seemed blissfully unaware of the impact of their restless kicks and roughhousing. The elderly woman descended into fits of hysteria.

"Oh, Harriet! My poor nerves," she wailed to her maid, fumbling for a handkerchief to blot the sweat sheening her upper lip. Harriet, unmoved, clucked her tongue, adjusted her round wire spectacles, and buried herself once again in her book, the title of which had eluded Lizzy's attempts to discover it.

The stagecoach lurched as it struck a deep rut, the violent jolt threatening to catapult Lizzy across the interior. In a flash, Mr. Taylor shot out his arm, a silent protector keeping her firmly in place. His lightning reflexes prevented her from being tossed like a rag doll. She cast him a sidelong glance, a subtle nod of her head silently acknowledging his assistance.

"Careful, dear sister." A smirk played on his lips as a tacit understanding passed between them. Their fabricated narrative painted them as siblings who had recently returned from a prolonged stay in America, now journeying northward to visit an infirm uncle. The tale was riddled with more holes than a block of Swiss cheese, prompting them to steer clear of casual discourse, lest their deception be laid bare.

"Oh, Harriet, I've gone and had the most dreadful thought." The older woman's declaration sent a ripple of unease through the cramped confines.

"What if the coach goes off the road, plunges into a river, and we all drown in no more than a few feet of water? I heard about a man who drowned in an inch-deep puddle once."

"We're not passing a river, mum," the maid replied absentmindedly, engrossed in her book. "And there are no puddles on the road. So you'll be quite all right."

"What about if we are set upon by highwaymen?" Her frown made her look rather like a gorgon. "The villains could rob us and then do who knows what."

"She sounds a little too thrilled by the opportunity." Tuck's breath grazed Lizzy's ear, his words heating her already too-warm skin. She closed her eyes, breath hitching as she shifted in her seat. How did he manage to evoke so much with so little? Her corset felt constricting, as if her breasts were larger—an illusion, but they felt more sensitive, more tender.

The lady's maid turned the page. "That's why the coach driver has a guard."

Indeed, there was a guard. When they'd boarded, he stood sentinel at the door.

Lizzy crossed her arms and, with the hand closest to Mr. Taylor, delivered a sharp pinch to his side. He emitted a low grunt.

"A cup of cream."

It took Lizzy a moment to realize the older woman was addressing Mr. Taylor. He caught on a beat later. "Excuse me?"

"That's the best remedy for indigestion. I've heard that sound before, and mark my words, I know the cure. Take it the moment you begin to feel bilious."

He looked lost, confusion etched on his features.

Lizzy intervened. "What a good idea. We'll try that, won't we, brother?"

The older woman scoffed, and in that moment, Lizzy realized no one in the coach believed their pretense of being siblings. They likely imagined she was on a journey to ruin and damnation.

A sudden bang vibrated through the stagecoach, causing the entire carriage to shudder. Skinny legs appeared outside the window, kicking wildly. A cacophony of screams and curses filled the air, then silence settled in, an eerie calm after the storm.

"I say, what in God's name is this, man?" The naval officer, now shaken from his stupor, was at the door, yelling.

Outside the window, the boy with the kicking legs descended from the roof into the tall grass beside the road, pale but seemingly unharmed.

The older woman wept, and the maid's book lay on the floor, cover-side up. *Memoirs of a Woman of Pleasure*, by John Cleland.

Somewhere in the fog of Lizzy's mind, a small flicker of realization ignited. This book—she'd heard of it before, whispered about among friends who hinted of its shocking and provocative nature. Lizzy had never read a scandalous book and dearly wanted to try one. The lady's maid caught her staring, hastily grabbed it, and tucked it away in her carpetbag to shield it from prying eyes.

"The bloody wheel's lost a bearing," the coachman shouted from outside. "We're not far from the inn. Youse will all need to go the rest of the way on foot."

The stagecoach had broken down three miles from the inn on the outskirts of Bristol, where they were meant to rest overnight before continuing their journey. The Crown and Horns, as the coach driver had called it, was to be identified by its red-painted door.

Dinnertime approached, and Lizzy hadn't eaten since the tea and cakes at Salisbury, which now felt like a distant memory. This was the furthest she'd ever ventured from friends or family, and she realized that the only person who'd care if she made it to the inn unscathed was the man walking beside her.

"Are you quite sure you wouldn't like some help?" she asked Mr. Taylor again. He had both leather travel cases tucked under his arms.

"You concentrate on walking." He frowned at her linen boots. "Those shoes look like more trouble than they're worth."

The minister led the way, muttering what sounded more like complaints and curses than prayers for their safe arrival. The two boys from the roof darted about in the fields, playing tag and whooping it up. Meanwhile, the lady's maid and the elderly woman brought up the rear, convinced they were about to be hunted down like foxes by highwaymen.

"Would you say this is your worst day ever?" Lizzy asked him. "It seems to be the case for everyone else on this road at the moment."

"What? That wheel back there?" Mr. Taylor made a wry face. "Nah, a minor inconvenience at best. My legs were cramped. A walk feels good." He adjusted the portmanteaus for balance. "As a matter of fact, this is what I'd call a good day."

"A bold claim. Why would that be?"

"I don't like to sit and worry. Moving feels good. Feels like we're doing something, even though I don't know what that something is."

She nodded. "I'm like that too. Sitting and waiting and hoping for a change? I've done that long enough."

"And there's the matter of the company. It's not half bad."

"Oh." She pointed at herself. "Is that meant to mean me?"

"You? You're a pain. I meant the nose-picker and the snorer. They were great. Life of the party."

Her mouth turned up despite herself.

"I suppose I should work on getting to know you better, seeing as you are about to become my husband."

"That's up to you," he said. "I know plenty of married folks that don't know anything about the other. My parents, for example. I bet if you asked my dad what my mom's favorite color is, he wouldn't have a clue. Her middle name? Favorite food? They've been married thirty years, and I'd bet real money he couldn't tell you."

"That's horrible." Her heart ached at the thought.

"He likes getting taken care of, and she likes doing the caring. It's not how I ever want to be."

"Lavender," she said.

"What?"

"Lavender is my favorite color," she answered simply. "And to be specific, not the color they use for dresses or ribbons. It's close but it's never quite right. I mean the color of a lavender sprig plucked right from the bush. Someday—"

"When you're a widow," he said, finishing her thought.

"Yes, exactly. I want to have a field of lavender. I'll go out in it at sunset and sit and write and never have to talk to another person if I don't feel like doing so."

"What's your middle name?"

"Oh no, no, no." A nervous laugh escaped her. "I prefer not to say."

"Well, now you have to."

"I don't have to do anything of the sort. You may guess. But I'll not do it of my own free will."

"Mary?" he ventured, his eyes narrowed in thought.

She made a face. "Far too easy and common. No, of course not."

"Penelope, Mabel, Scarlet, Josephine," he rattled off.

"No, no, no, and no."

He shrugged, a hint of discomfort in the motion. "Favorite food?"

That was easy. "Pineapple," she shared, proudly. "Have you ever tried one?"

"Sure. Lots."

She tripped. "What do you mean by *lots*?"

He gave her a confused glance. "I mean that I've eaten pineapple a lot. Just like I said. What's the big deal?"

"Over five?"

"Five pineapples? Yeah?" His brows pulled tight. "I've been to Hawaii three times, plus it's at every hotel breakfast buffet."

"This is most shocking news." Lizzy tried to grasp what he was saying and failed. "You've traveled to the islands of Hawaii?"

"Yeah. Once with my parents on vacation, once in college, and once with a girlfriend."

Lizzy couldn't keep up. "How many pineapples have you eaten?"

He barked out a laugh. "This is the absolute last question I think I ever would have imagined answering."

"They are rare here, and very, very expensive. I had a taste of one at a Christmas dinner eight years ago." She sighed wistfully. "I've never forgotten the flavor."

"I didn't realize. Dang. If I'd known, I'd have stuffed one in my pocket to time travel with."

The inn came into view in the distance, the Crown and Horns.

She sighed. "We'll wash up and eat a very boring dinner without a single pineapple to be had."

At the inn, the keeper was flushed from the bustle of patrons. "I don't have as many rooms as I'd like," she said. "You'll have to be sharing. The lads can go into the barn. The two ladies in the room at the top of the stairs, the three gents can go to the one at the end of the hall, and my siblings here . . ." Her voice drew out, holding more than a trace of sarcasm. "You get the attic."

"Are you sure there's nothing else?" Lizzy breathed, her heart dropping into her stomach.

"Not unless you want to go with the two ladies in the room at the top of the stairs." The innkeeper arched a brow as if daring Lizzy to take the offer.

And listen to more prattle about highwaymen? Lizzy would prefer to do anything but. The attic it was.

When they entered their room, she gripped the doorframe for support. It was a tight space with one window, the glass coated with dirt and grime.

And pushed up under the sloping roof was a single sagging bed.

CHAPTER TWELVE

The room resembled a dust bunny orgy, but the sheets, at least, appeared clean. "I think we'll be fine for tonight, but I wouldn't recommend touching or licking anything," Tuck said, immediately regretting his choice of words.

Lizzy was rummaging through her trunk, focused like a squirrel searching for an acorn. For a moment, it seemed she had missed his comment entirely, but then she murmured, "And where shall *you* sleep?"

Her tone was a bit too casual.

She missed nothing.

"I'll rough it on the floor." Tuck gestured toward his own leather case with a half shrug. "There's a coat in there. I'll make do. I'm a pro at sleeping anywhere, anytime."

His teammates had envied that about him; they'd hop on a plane, and he'd be snoring before takeoff. His secret was simple: he'd close his eyes, take a few deep breaths, and imagine a scene from his childhood. Usually, he pictured rural Michigan, with rows of faded corn husks in a snow-covered field and a few flurries silently falling. He never shared this image with anyone; it sounded too bleak to be a believable happy place. But the sense of emptiness always relaxed him, even during treatment.

But right now, Lizzy's grimace as she surveyed the stain-splotched wood commanded his full focus. "That floor doesn't look as though it's been given a proper scrub since the reign of Queen Anne."

"Don't worry. I'd rather have you be comfortable."

She glanced his way. Her gaze felt like a language he'd once known, leaving him with an unsettling sensation. It was as though, if he concentrated hard enough, he might decipher the meaning behind her eyes.

"What's on your mind?" A curl tumbled over her forehead, teasing him, begging to be brushed aside.

"Do you really want to know?"

Her lips parted a fraction. "I think so."

"Don't believe everything you think, Pocket Rocket." The nickname rolled off his tongue. He liked calling her that. He liked way too much about her. They hadn't known each other long but already had this rhythm established, a back-and-forth that wasn't quite bickering but was closer to a dance. They kept making up the steps, changing the tune, forcing the other to react and adapt.

"Go on, then. Tell me." Her voice was tight, a guitar string on the verge of snapping.

"You've got pretty eyes." It wasn't everything he was thinking, not even close, but it felt like enough for now.

"Is that all?" She tilted her head, an undercurrent of bemusement in her tone.

His laugh took him by surprise, the sound filling the small room. "What more do you want?"

"It's customary for gentlemen to pay compliments to my eyes," she observed crisply. "It appears to be one of those pretty nothings your gender latches onto before admiring my gown, or inquiring about my accomplishments."

"Are you telling me that I'm basic?" He clutched his chest in mock offense.

"You had a rather interesting expression on your face a moment ago, and it made me curious to learn if there was an interesting thought to accompany it." She flicked a speck of dust off her sleeve. "But alas, you've dismissed that idea entirely." Despite her deadpan tone, those pretty eyes she'd shot him down for complimenting sparkled brightly with mischief.

The game was still on. She was poking and seeing if he'd poke back.

The problem was that if she kept this up, he'd want to do a hell of a lot more than poke. He'd never had a woman hand him his ass like this; she wasn't remotely intimidated or trying to impress.

"Okay, fine, give me another chance." He leaned in, dropping his voice to a low purr. "What about this . . . ? Your eyes look like moons when you smile, little crescent ones."

She pursed her lips, as if fighting an unwilling smile. "I still stand by my earlier assertion that you shouldn't trade hockey for poetry."

"Well, I might not be a poet, but I'm prepared to sleep on the ground for you. Although if I'm going to be honest, it's more for my own selfish reasons."

"Excuse me?" She bit, just like he knew she would. Two points for him.

"Well, I dunno if I should say it, but I should be honest, right?" He took his time with his shrug, enjoying the way she leaned in, curious despite herself. "You look like a bit of a blanket hog."

"A what!" Real outrage entered her voice.

"The kind of person who steals all the blankets."

"If you must know, I end up kicking most of them off in the

night. I get too hot, except for my . . ." She trailed off, blinking. "Never mind. Forget I said that."

Not a chance.

"Go on," he prompted.

"I should wash up. Long day on the road. And we have another one tomorrow." She fidgeted a moment before clasping her hands together. "I'm also starting to get peckish. They must have cheese and bread downstairs."

"Elizabeth Wooddash, don't you go changing the subject. Finish the thought—except for . . ."

"Oh, fine. It's just a bit of nonsense. I keep my feet covered for the monsters." Her words spilled out in a breathless rush. Noting his blank look, she hesitated. "You do know about the monsters, don't you?"

The corners of his mouth twitched. "I regret to say that I'm not on a first-name basis with any."

Her shoulders stiffened. "I am seven and twenty and well aware monsters do not truly exist and that such a notion is preposterous. Yet, when I sleep, I must ensure my feet remain covered, lest one of them should attempt to brush my foot with a clammy finger." A visible shudder rippled through her body.

"I see, so if there's a monster lurking around, that's how it's going to want to spend its time? Tickling your bare foot?"

"Unfortunately, yes." She wrinkled her nose. He was beginning to know that expression well, and the two little lines that appeared between her brows had become his good friends too.

"Well, you can rest easy. If I'm here, there won't be any monsters. Let those feet fly."

"I'm not so sure about that." Her eyes narrowed, a challenge lurking within their depths. "You look as though you're the type to snore. That could attract them."

"How do you figure?" Sparring with her was easy, comfortable. It made him feel more like himself than he had in a long time. Strange.

"You'll begin snoring, and I'm certain the creature will be drawn close, as though you're beckoning it."

"Singing the song of its people?"

She nodded sagely.

"Tell you what. You need water and food if you're going to fight monsters. I'll go down and get us some dinner." He pulled out a few coins Georgie had given him. "I don't like that I haven't earned this money."

"Don't worry about that." Lizzy was matter-of-fact. "Georgie is like any person born into money. She doesn't see its value the way others might."

"You weren't born wealthy?"

"Oh, I was. My family is respectable. But after Papa died, our situation became more precarious, before Mamma remarried. Those months of dire finances left an impression. And I've grown accustomed to hearing that every day I remain unwed is another day that I'm using up resources that could be directed to my brother."

"Your parents care about you, though, right?" He couldn't imagine any parent not being thrilled to have such a strange, feisty kid.

"It's not as if my parents had no regard for me. I'm quite sure Mamma does, in her own way. It's just that she's never truly *seen* me for who I am. I'm not sure she's capable of it." Lizzy's voice softened, a wistful note creeping in. "I've been me, the same me that is standing in front of you, my whole life. Yet, every time she glances my way, it's as if I'm reflecting something else back, a thing that's not measuring up, that's fundamentally lacking in some way.

"Please don't look at me like that; it's nothing to feel bad or sad about. It's my life. And now that won't matter, because soon what they'll see is the ring on my finger, and we'll be married." She blanched. "Oh no. The rings! I utterly forgot that we'll need some."

"Not to worry. Your cousin remembered. I have them stored away for safekeeping." In just a few days, he'd be sliding a gold band onto Lizzy's finger, binding them together in a way that he didn't want to dwell on. Better to push those thoughts aside and focus on current, less-complicated practicalities. "What do you want to eat? Something like stew?"

"Yes, but only if it's lamb."

"Okay. That's specific."

"Yes." Her chin lifted. "I know what I like."

Her words echoed in his mind as he made his way downstairs and into the inn's courtyard. The pump handle was cool beneath his palm, the damp metal unyielding as he worked it up and down. A week ago, he'd never have imagined himself here—pumping water in a world without cars and filled with carriages, dressed in breeches and boots. He'd give a lot for some gray sweats and a pair of slides.

But there wasn't room for stress or worry here; he had to focus on the task at hand, which was getting through each moment.

His thoughts drifted back to Lizzy and the certainty in her words: *I know what I like.* At least he could trust in her, trust the unexpected strength that radiated from her core.

What would that certainty be like in bed?

Images churned through his mind: Lizzy with her thick hair loose and wild, her skirts hiked up around her waist as she straddled him, sinking onto his hardness. Would she arch her back and roll her hips?

Or maybe she'd want to relinquish control, needing him to

grip her hair firmly and guide her down to her knees. Not out of weakness, but trust—toward the liberation that comes from surrendering to give and receive pleasure.

A sudden splash jolted him back to reality, and he realized two facts at once. First, he'd been pumping water into an already full bucket, creating a puddle at his feet, and second, he was hard.

Fuck. Come on. He wasn't some horny teenager. He needed to get a grip.

He grabbed the bucket and held it in front of himself, glancing around. Nobody was in sight, but that didn't mean they weren't watching. He ran through some old hockey stats, Bobby Orr's 1970–71 season—37 goals and 102 assists—or Wayne Gretzky's 39 goals in 50 games.

Gritting his teeth, and willing his erection to subside, he went into the inn. A quick conversation with the innkeeper yielded three points of information:

1. The stew was rabbit, not lamb.
2. The man had a hell of a time understanding an American accent.
3. A steak-and-kidney pie didn't sound all that great, so he went with the chicken option. Hopefully that would suit her.

While one of the keeper's children took the bucket to transfer the water into two glasses, he waited for the food.

"Pardon me." He turned to find a raven-haired woman behind him, her painted lips pursed in a knowing smile. "You owe me a drink, sir."

He glanced around to ensure she wasn't talking to someone else. "I think you've mistaken me."

"I was about to take a sip of wine when I noticed you. I'm afraid I immediately spilled my glass."

"Sorry." He shook his head. "What?"

With her height, her lips were almost at his ear when she whispered, "I'm trying to seduce you. Is that agreeable?"

"Ah." Her red dress. Her makeup. Her practiced aura of seduction. It all clicked into place. Jesus, he was distracted. "You're a working girl."

"Are you hard work?"

"I'm not your target market." He reached for the tray with the two chicken pies and waters he'd ordered. "And I have to go bring up dinner to someone, but good luck."

"Oh, I won't need it. That naval officer in the corner has been giving me cow's eyes for a few minutes, but you were more handsome." She glanced at the pies. "You have a woman waiting for you?"

"I do," he said simply. And it was true. He did. "We're to be married in a few days."

She tilted her head. "Isn't she lucky?"

"You'd have to ask her."

"You're a funny one, Yankee Doodle. I like that. Let me know if you both get bored tonight. I wouldn't mind joining your party. My guess is you have a pretty one." And after a mocking curtsy, she sauntered away.

It had been a minute since he'd been with a woman. At least a year. It wasn't that he strove for a monk's existence, but rather that he struggled to compartmentalize his life in the way his teammates seemed to manage so effectively. His dedication to studying opponents, rigorous workouts, and constant practice left little room for investing in a relationship. Despite occasional bouts of loneliness, he loved his work. Nothing was more fun.

But now he was here. Over two hundred years away from the Austin arena. From his teammates. From his routine. From the ice.

He stood outside the attic door, his arms laden with the dinner tray, unsure of how to alert Lizzy to his presence without startling her or dropping something. Kicking the door was too aggressive.

As if she'd read his thoughts, the door opened, revealing Lizzy standing on the other side.

"I heard you," she said simply. Her hair was fanned around her shoulders, and her face was pink. She'd changed out of her dress and was in a long white nightgown.

"Thank you for the water," she said, taking the glasses from him. "I'm so tired. And so hungry. I can't decide which I want to do more, eat or sleep."

"These chicken pies smell good." He set them on the table in the corner. "Eat one and then you can crash. You don't want to board the coach tomorrow on an empty stomach."

"Indeed not." She looked younger—no, that wasn't it, just more vulnerable. It was strange how something as simple as seeing her ready for sleep made it feel as if they were crossing a new threshold.

They ate quietly. Too tired for banter, but also, as the dusk turned to night outside the window and she lit the single lamp, it felt like the bed filled the room, growing at the same rate as the shadows. He washed up quickly, still not quite used to the fact that toothpaste here came as a powder. Although better not to complain, because at least he had clean teeth, thanks to the tooth scraper he got at the Woodlands.

He cleared the dishes and brought them downstairs. The officer and the lady in red were gone. When he got back to the room, Lizzy was sitting up in bed. There was a chill in the night air, and he could tell that her nipples were hard. It was difficult to think of anything else.

"Are you comfortable?" he asked, his hand hovering near the lamp, ready to extinguish the soft light.

She shifted, the bed creaking beneath her. "The mattress is not a cloud, but it will do."

"I'm going to turn the light out now, Lizzy." He twisted the knob at the base, the wick lowering into the oil. The room dimmed to darkness.

"Mr. Taylor." Her voice was soft, almost hesitant. "You don't have to sleep on the floor."

He had to keep his tone even. "It's okay."

"Mr. Taylor?" A moment of silence stretched between them. "What if I said you could sleep in the bed?"

His mouth went dry. "I'd say you are polite, but it's fine, really."

"What if I insisted?" she inquired.

He didn't know if it was a challenge, an invitation, or both. "Then I'd say you better call me Tuck or Tucker."

"Why does it matter so much?"

"Every time you call me Mr. Taylor it makes me feel like my dad," he said softly. "I'd rather be me."

"Very well, Tucker." The sheets rustled softly. "You may join me."

"I could sleep upside down to you."

"So, your face would be by my feet?"

A soft chuckle escaped him. "All the better to keep the monsters away, am I right?"

"But then your feet would be by *my* face."

"This is true," he conceded.

"Can't we sleep side by side like betrothed adults who have three more days of travel together?" A note of practicality entered her tone, weaving through the weariness.

"All right, then." He unfastened the buttons of his jacket one by one.

"What are you doing?"

"Taking my jacket off," he answered calmly, continuing the slow, purposeful movement of his hands.

"I trust you shall remain fully clothed?" Her words carried a hint of wariness.

"I already said I could sleep on the floor."

"I simply require assurance that you will be dressed."

"All right, all right. I'm keeping my clothing on. Just minus the jacket," he clarified before easing into the bed beside her. The narrow mattress forced him to hug the edge to avoid contact. The air separating their bodies was charged like static electricity.

"After enduring four days of travel, it is possible that we may still find ourselves needing to share a bed occasionally."

He could smell her soap. It was a flower he recognized but couldn't put his finger on, and something familiar yet spicy, like rosemary. "I hadn't thought about what comes next." He folded his hands over his stomach, clasping them tightly. It felt like he was playing the game Nora used to make him do in middle school: light as a feather, stiff as a board.

How was he going to sleep? Every single cell in his body was alert and at attention. His cornfield visualization seemed out of reach. He was too focused on wondering what she was doing. If the proximity affected her as well. He'd had women in his bed. But never like this. For some strange-ass reason, it was hotter to know she was there, so close, and so entirely off limits. If he so much as touched her cheek, it would have the same intent as pushing up her gown, sliding his hand beneath her parted thighs.

His cock jerked, flooding with heat. Shit. Why the fuck was he thinking about her nightgown? How it hid so much. Practically wrapped her up like a present. Imagining how slow it would be to open each button. The little reward each time he was successful, another flash of creamy skin. She was probably so soft, so warm, so fucking—

"Are you quite all right?" Her whisper made him start, as if he'd been caught out.

He cleared his throat, praying to whatever god wanted to listen that he didn't sound hoarse. "I'm falling asleep—why?"

She paused. "Never mind."

"Tell me."

"I don't want to make you feel bad."

Shit. Panic flooded him. She didn't sense his hard-on, did she?

"You're really stiff."

Oh God, she did.

"I'm sorry." What else could he say? Might as well admit it. Boners happen.

"I perceive your body's tension. You needn't worry. I shall refrain from any physical contact," she reassured him in a calm, composed manner.

Relief mingled with confusion as the realization dawned. Lizzy wasn't talking about his hard-on at all. He gave himself a mental shake.

"That's a relief," he muttered, his shoulders relaxing as the adrenaline rush wore off. "I was worried about my honor."

"Isn't that what I'm supposed to say?" Sleepy amusement threaded her words.

"Lizzy." His tone grew serious, his gaze intense despite the darkness. He didn't care. He needed her to know he meant this. "You don't ever have to worry about me."

CHAPTER THIRTEEN

Lizzy's eyelids felt heavy, and she blinked a few times to shake away the lingering haze of sleep. When exactly had she drifted off? She couldn't remember. Hadn't she decided to stay awake all night, hyperaware of the presence lying next to her, warm and undeniably masculine? She risked a glance toward Tuck, but he didn't stir, the strong lines of his face softened by the peacefulness of sleep. The steady rise and fall of his chest mesmerized her, and she found herself matching her breathing to his. So, this was what couples did. They crawled into bed together, their bodies casually close, and surrendered to this drowsy intimacy.

No, surely they engaged in far more vigorous activities, and with fewer layers of clothing. An image of tangled limbs and bare skin pressed together sent a shiver racing through her as she became acutely aware of her position, nestled securely against Tuck's solid form, his arm draped possessively over her, holding her close, his warm exhalations whispering through her hair. How had she ended up like this? She attempted to inch away, but he made a low groan as he tugged her back, unwilling to relinquish his hold.

Suddenly, she became aware of a firm pressure against the

side of her leg, insistently pushing into her upper thigh. Her cheeks flushed with sudden heat. It was . . . well, him.

She understood the basics of how sexual congress occurred between a man and a woman. She'd seen livestock breed in the country. And at balls and various social events, newly married friends would be teased, or, in their new pride, drop hints. At nineteen, armed with a list of rumors, she had approached Georgie, who'd laid out the entire process of fornication in plain terms. It had sounded embarrassing, sticky, and invasive.

But this?

Lizzy held herself perfectly still. This felt like none of those things. Not even embarrassing, which was a surprise, and she had an unexpected yearning to explore further, to delve into the unknown. What if his hands were to wander to other parts of her body? What if he traced the contours of her rib cage, caressing her breasts with his big rough hands?

Her nipples tightened at the thought. Would he tease them with his thumb, tracing circles around each one before applying gentle pressure to the tips, much like she sometimes did in the bath when she luxuriated in the warmth and liquid ease? She paused, still waiting for embarrassment to catch up and find her.

Or worry.

This whole affair could ruin her.

And yet nothing came.

If this was the natural way of men and women who were allowed to share a bed, then she was willing to entertain such intimacies—but only if the man in question was Tucker Taylor.

As if on cue, he shifted his weight. Before she could stop it, he'd half rolled her with him. Glancing down, her hair formed a curtain framing their faces. His initially drowsy eyes snapped into sharp focus, their sudden intensity striking her like a physical blow. Three realizations dawned simultaneously. One was that Tuck had a small mole to the left of one eye, a little punctuation mark to his gaze. Second, she had a sudden and indescribable urge to kiss it. Third, those big rough hands were gripping her backside, holding her firm against him. And the hint of hardness she'd felt earlier? Now was front and center, pushing right into the softness between her thighs.

"What's going on?" he said roughly. "Where'd *you* come from?"

She tried to wriggle free, or at least get her breasts off his chest, and only succeeded in nestling herself more firmly in place, because he wasn't releasing his grip.

"I came from *my* side of the bed," she ground out, realizing that the more she moved, the more she rocked against his . . . his . . . excitement. "I woke up and you were grabbing me and before my next conscious thought, you hauled me on top of you."

"A likely story." He had a half grin, but his eyes were serious. "Except for one critical fact. I'm not the cuddling type."

"Ha! Tell that to your octopus arms."

"I'm serious. I've had old girlfriends complain that I don't hold them enough."

She didn't want to hear a word about former lovers. The idea felt like rolling in a field of nettles. And she wasn't going to have him pretend that she was the reason they were currently in such a compromising position.

"Let go of me." She shoved, but he'd immediately released her when she spoke. This meant that she flew off with more force than intended, tumbling from the side of the bed and landing on the floorboards with a forlorn thud.

Wonderful. Now people in the rooms below would think she was the type to have amorous congress in an unclean Bristol inn.

"Jesus, Lizzy. Are you okay?" He was at her side in a moment and it took all her strength not to pinch his nose.

"My pride is injured more than my body," she replied stiffly. "Now if you wouldn't mind, I'd very much like you to get yourself situated so that I might have the room alone to dress."

"Situated how?" He frowned.

"Please get ready, sir." She clenched her teeth. "And then see yourself out."

"What are you mad at me for?"

Her hip throbbed and she needed space and time to gather her wits. "I am not angry, Mr. Taylor, I am simply requesting a moment. One which does not come with the pleasure of your company."

"I didn't want to . . ." He caught himself, swallowing back whatever he was going to say next. "Fine. I'll take care of what I need to and then get out of your way."

A half hour later, they were outside the inn, awaiting the coach. Lizzy was sure it would be another arduous day, made all the more uncomfortable by the incessant thoughts flooding her mind—memories of Tuck's muscles and arms, and the sensation of being hoisted onto his broad, solid body. The mere contemplation of what it might feel like to reach, touch, stroke, and explore sent a cascade of wicked thoughts through her mind. And the unhelpful fact that he currently stood a mere two feet away heightened the intensity of these musings.

The nose-picking naval officer emerged, strutting like a rooster and accompanied by a striking woman in a red dress—not conventionally beautiful, but utterly unforgettable. As she walked past, she wiggled her fingers at Tuck and murmured, "Morning, America."

When had Tuck forged an acquaintance with *that* woman?

A nettling sensation pricked at Lizzy. She never felt possessive of a man, preferring the company of her female friends. This new feeling was remarkable and unwelcome, perhaps stemming from her protective instinct after rescuing him. And if she found herself flustered by the other woman's knowing gaze, one could attribute it to her current state of discomposure, far from home. Emotions were certainly running high.

They boarded the coach, and she forced herself into a torpor to mask the perplexing thoughts swirling through her mind. She didn't stir again until midday, once they'd arrived in the Cotswolds and the coachman made a stop in a village known as Tree by the Hill. Lizzy couldn't discern which tree or which hill, as the landscape was dotted with many. While the horses were being watered, she seized the opportunity to slip into a shop that piqued her interest: Hill Booksellers. How ideal. Purchasing a book would provide her with an evening activity that didn't involve tossing and turning in bed, tormented by ponders of whether or not Tuck would reach out to her once more.

Tuck, having the good sense to understand she didn't want him near, hung back by the stagecoach, watching the driver load bags for the new passengers.

A bell tinkled overhead as Lizzy stepped into the space, her eyes straining to adjust to the dimness. It was perfect—a hodgepodge bookshop, the type she adored, with its overfilled bookcases and old-paper smell. Dust motes danced in a shaft of light, drawing her attention to a thin green volume on horse breeding in the case in front of her.

Unusual topic. She impulsively reached out and opened it, slamming the cover shut immediately. The images inside the book were decidedly not equine. There'd been a woman with her plump thighs indecently splayed before king and country and a man knelt between them, face buried in her most private part. He was kissing her. There.

She peeked again. The woman's head was thrown back, her eyes closed but her mouth opened in prayer or ecstasy—maybe both. Lizzy glanced around, but the only other person in the shop was an elderly man dozing behind the counter. She bit the inside of her lip and flipped to another page. And another. And another. Dear God. She had a vivid imagination but had *never* pictured any of this.

Was this an accident at a publisher's? Or did an entire world exist of filthy books being cloaked in the veil of respectability? Whatever the reason, there was nothing for it. She was going to have to purchase this book. At the very least she deserved to understand what Tuck already knew about, the myriad activities that men and women performed together alone in the dark. She paused.

Or during the day.

In her mind, intimacy, as she understood it, was secretive and silent, something that happened once the lamps were out and the household inhabitants slumbered. But what nonsense. People must do these things whenever they feel like it, provided they have the space and willing company.

Here she was, no longer a child and not even a green girl. She was a woman with one foot into spinsterdom, and she knew nothing. Invisible flames shot out her ears. She hated not understanding things. And so she wouldn't, not for a moment longer.

But she couldn't saunter forward and purchase this title. What if the seller opened it to check the price? The best thing to do was to use her money as a solution. She grabbed a pamphlet titled *Poetical Essay on the Existing State of Things* by a poet she'd never heard of, Percy Bysshe Shelley, and then William Wordsworth's

popular *Guide to the Lakes*. Perfect. Suitably dull and noncon-
frontational. She placed the so-called horse-breeding book on the
bottom of the stack and made her way to the shopkeeper for payment.

Her heart pounded so loudly she assumed the gentleman behind the counter would wake to it. But in the end, it took her
considerable throat clearing, two polite *yoo-hoos*, and a great deal
of knocking about to get him to stir.

The bookseller yawned, sleepily glanced at the titles, and
mumbled, "Ten shillings."

Before he'd even gathered his wits, she'd paid and was out the
door, walking hard and fast to the coach.

"What happened?" Tuck asked the moment she returned.

"Nothing of interest." Lizzy averted her gaze. Why should she
reveal her secret? It was none of his business. Except . . . he did
appear to be knowledgeable, and she wanted to know about the
business of lovemaking. She fought the desperate urge to fidget,
but tension thrummed through her like harp strings tuned too
tight.

"You're excited or guilty about something," he observed after a
moment. "And I'm not sure if that makes me curious or nervous."

She gnawed the inside of her cheek. How did he read her so
easily? Most days it was as if she lived wrapped in a cloak of invis-
ibility. No one could ever tell what she was thinking or cared to
look hard enough to decipher her moods.

And yet, Tuck had done so with a two-second glance.

"I found something, and I believe it will be of great use in
terms of furthering my education. And it's on a subject that you
appear knowledgeable on."

"That's unlikely. Hockey isn't a thing yet, and you don't seem
all that interested in ice or skating."

"It's about intimacy."

"Wait." He did a double take. "Are you saying . . . ?"

"I have just come into possession of a research guide to intimate relations."

"What? Like a sex book?"

She smashed her finger to his lips. "Do not discuss here, thank you. We will return to this topic tonight at the inn in Birmingham."

The stagecoach was even more full than before, and Lizzy barely registered the bored faces. When they arrived at the evening's destination, the Queen's Goat, it felt as if everything moved more quickly. Washing. Eating. And it was almost as if time had skipped from the previous night to now. Except she had her book.

"Are you ready to unveil the big surprise?" Tuck sat in a chair by the table, his long legs extended and crossed at the ankles. "You're as jumpy as a bean."

Lizzy removed the book from her satchel and handed it to him before crawling onto the bed, tucking her bare feet under her nightgown.

"Breeding for horses? Okay. Unexpected?" He opened the cover and froze. "Hold up." He flicked through the pages. "Jesus." Finally, he glanced at her. "You found this in a bookshop?"

"I was as surprised as you."

"And you bought it."

"I want to learn. We are to be married. I understand it's not in the traditional sense, but am I still to remain ignorant of all that goes on between a man and a woman? You, I imagine, are familiar with the activities in those pages, are you not?"

He handed the book back. "No comment."

She clicked her tongue. "Omission is admission. I want to

learn, and with a book and your experience, I can understand, at least."

"You want to know about all of that?"

"Imagine if I'm having a social call and a married friend begins to ask me about our intimacies. It will raise suspicions if I have not a clue as to what is being asked."

"Do women talk about these things here?"

"Whyever not? Do women not speak to each other in your time?"

"Of course, but it feels like you are all more formal. I thought maybe it was more proper to not."

Lizzy laughed at that. "If I had to make a wager, I'd imagine women have always, and will always, discuss such matters."

"But you don't want to actually do any of these illustrations in real life."

She coughed.

"I'm serious. I'm trying to get clear on what you mean by lessons."

The temperature of the room had increased in a matter of seconds. Her nightgown, which covered as much skin as a normal dress, felt far more sheer.

Because the thought hadn't occurred to her the way it clearly had to Tuck. She hadn't imagined actually being the person to experience such things. She hadn't even allowed her mind to process that idea. And now she wasn't sure she'd ever be able to stop. The idea of Tuck with his head between her legs—what would that even begin to be like, and would it be enjoyable?

"Don't look so worried," he said soothingly. "I'm never going to do anything you don't want to do. But you are handing over a sex book saying that you want to learn. I want to be on the same page with our team goals."

She mouthed *team goals* as a silent question.

"You are on my team, remember?"

"And you'll answer questions if I have them?"

"To the best of my ability."

She reached for the book and opened it to the first page.

"Hold up. I'm going to need a drink."

"Now? How come?"

"Because, Pocket Rocket. Don't take this the wrong way. I have control. You can trust me. But I'm not a masochist." At her look of confusion, he sighed. "I don't get off on torturing myself. And if I sit here and watch you read that book and wait to have a question? It's gonna hurt. I'll have a drink. Or six. And be back in an hour. If you have any questions, you can ask them before bed. Once I'm drunk enough to deal with this."

Before she could say anything else, he was out the door.

It didn't take long before she was engrossed. There was a section where it discussed a woman touching herself. Lizzy's eyes opened wider. The instructions were straightforward. Take two fingers and place them in her mouth, give them a gentle suck. She could do this. Right now. No questions. No assistance. She did as the book instructed and then lay back upon the bed, feeling delightfully wicked. She had time. Tuck had said he'd be gone an hour, and besides, she'd hear his heavy boots before he entered the room. Positioning the book on her chest, she opened her legs as the picture showed and pushed up her gown.

Her sex responded to the air in the room, to the sensation of freshness against her delicate skin, which was more sensitive than usual. Of course, she'd touched herself there, but as a matter of utility, washing and such. It always felt pleasant, but nothing she'd considered exploring more. But when her wet fingers slipped inside her cleft, the sensation surprised her. She was wet, and as she swept over the slippery skin, her backside clenched as her lower back bowed up. The book first suggested discovering a small hard pearl and to explore what motion might suit the lady best: circles, diagonal caresses, or whisper-light taps. She started slowly, around and around, so curious to discover at every pass a low, aching pressure that intensified, spreading from between her thighs to her navel.

She played. There was no other word to describe this. It was as if her body were a new thing. A wild thing. And it had a secret power to feel so good. As she found a rhythm that worked, the book fell closed and she pushed it to one side before using her other hand to open herself up more, stretching the skin slightly to increase the rich sensation. Her hips began to rock. What would it be like if someone else were to touch her like this?

She imagined Tuck's thick, strong fingers here on her delicate, wet softness. The tight ache intensified, and all she could think was *more* as she increased the pace, the pressure, the friction. A soft moan escaped her lips and she bit down to keep from getting louder. How was it this good? And the idea of him coming and watching made the wetness increase.

She was gasping now, her hitching breath the only sound in the world; her thighs began to tremble and she had an urge to be filled deeply. It wasn't enough, but when she eased a finger inside, the pressure helped. She put in another finger. Still not full enough, but it was something. One finger bumped against a small rough patch. As if on cue, her eyes rolled back, her heels digging into the mattress. She kept the pressure as her fingers' pace increased faster, faster. God. Yes. She rolled her head to one side, her body rigid and expectant. This was good. So good. What was she supposed to do with all this feeling?

Stop?

How could she?

No. She needed to keep going. Just a bit more. It kept getting better. How? How could it get— Oh God.

What was happening? She pressed harder and half levitated off the bed as a wave hit her with such force that she yelped. The most immense feeling she'd ever known churned through her, as if she'd turned into pure gold and was melted down rich and warm. And then she felt as if she wouldn't be able to inhale another breath. Slowly, so slowly, the sensation ebbed, like a wave pulling back and returning to the ocean.

Her eyes flew open. Boots. The loud footfalls were coming. A knock sounded at the door.

"It's me." Tuck's voice was low and rough. "Can I come in?"

"One moment," she cried out.

She tried to smooth out her hair and put on a face that wouldn't reveal that she had been shaken to her core. How could she ask about what had happened?

"You may enter."

He stepped in and froze, locking his gaze with hers, and she had an out-of-body sensation, as if he knew exactly what she'd done and how she was feeling.

"I was getting ready for sleep," she said as primly as she could manage, given that she was still half panting. "I don't think I have any questions after all. I'm going to turn in."

"I see." And the answer put her on edge. Because she suspected that he did in fact see. That he could read in a glance every strange thought. And she had nowhere to go to reflect on the experience. He'd be in bed next to her. The bed where she'd just made herself feel so many things. She felt as if she'd unlocked a secret power inside of herself and wanted to know more.

He removed his boots with more ease than he'd done before.

She put her head on the pillow and tried to close her eyes, but they wouldn't entirely obey. Peeping through her lashes, she watched him place the boots against the wall. Then he removed his jacket and hung it on a hook. A neat man. He didn't throw his things about willy-nilly. He filled the water basin and cleaned his teeth. She could watch him do that for hours. His teeth were so straight and bright and perfect.

He briskly splashed water over his face, the motions efficient and practiced. As he turned around, she shut her eyes tight, feigning sleep.

He blew out the lamp and crossed the room in a few slow steps, the mattress yielding to his weight.

He settled in beside her and she couldn't resist the temptation to peek.

He was watching her, a steady, unreadable expression on his face. "I knew you weren't asleep."

Her lips quirked. "You are a remarkably hard person to fool, especially for a man."

"Men are fools?"

"Most assuredly yes. But you're unexpected. You take time to understand, instead of assuming you know everything about me based on some preconceived idea of what a lady should be."

He paused, watching her. "Your face is an open book."

"Or perhaps you're my ideal reader."

He was closer. How'd he get closer? Had he moved? Or had she? Maybe it was the two of them, coming together like a knot being slowly cinched.

"I made myself a promise downstairs." He smelled as if he'd sat close to the fire. It was nice. Cozy, even. "I was going to wait the full hour. I wouldn't come back earlier. I would let you have space."

Her laugh was husky. Had she ever laughed like this? "You've been practically attached to me at the hip since I discovered you."

"I can't seem to stay away." He reached out and smoothed back a lock of her hair.

She arched into his touch like a cat.

"You are very close."

"Oh, no, this isn't close." He slid his hand to the back of her head. "This is close." He leaned in. Their foreheads were touching. "Closer still." His breath was warm on her skin, but for some reason it made her shiver. "Are you okay being . . . close, Lizzy?"

He said her name in such a way, as if it were precious, as if she were valuable to him. Without knowing the destination, they'd arrived at some sort of crossroads. One word from her, a single no, and they'd head down a safer road, one that was well trodden and well lit. But with another word, they'd just as easily take a more dangerous path, one that came with sharp curves ahead, where she couldn't see what was coming next.

All her life, she'd taken the dull, safe paths. Until the day Tuck had arrived. Now she kept feeling uncertain of what was before her, but rather than being terrifying, it was as if she was waking up to herself, aware of her wants, her desires, for the first time. And understanding they mattered. They weren't instincts or sensations to overcome through diligence and prayerful reflection as she'd been taught her whole life.

"This is your idea of close?" She wrinkled her nose, half impressed and half aghast at her forwardness. "I'm very confident we could be closer."

"Is this a dare?" His voice dropped an octave, the provocative question curling her toes. "Because I could get a hell of a lot closer."

"And . . ." Lizzy's breath caught in her throat. "Is that what you want?"

He remained statue still. "I'm much more interested in what you want."

Her gaze flicked to his mouth. "Close sounds interesting." All either of them had to do was reach out a fraction, and their lips would touch. The scent of bay rum from his hair oil mingled with the faint trace of woodsmoke from the downstairs fire.

"And are you interested?" His voice had such a rough timbre, it sanded away her resolve.

She'd never been kissed, and the idea hadn't truly captivated her until this moment. But now she longed to be read like a map, for Tuck to learn all her secret valleys, deserts, seashores, and shadowed woods.

"I—"

A deafening crash shattered the tension as the room's door banged open, sending them flying apart.

CHAPTER FOURTEEN

Tuck thrummed as he drank in the sight of Lizzy, those perfect-ten curves barely concealed beneath that oh-so-innocent nightgown. She set his blood on fire. It took every ounce of his self-control not to sweep her into his arms and tell her all the ways he could make her body sing. That, and the drunken idiot who'd ruined his chances to make a move.

He'd bodychecked the stumbling, bleary-eyed intruder back out into the hall with a growled "Get out," before slamming the door and facing Lizzy.

Her cheeks flushed a delicate pink, her chest heaving with each ragged breath. The charged atmosphere between them was palpable as her lips parted, as if to speak. He couldn't do this. Panic surged through him. He couldn't bear to hear whatever she might say, rejection or encouragement. Either would set them down a new path.

"I'm going to grab a little fresh air. You better get some sleep." Jesus, his voice sounded strained, even to his own ears. Without waiting for a reply, he turned on his heel and left. He needed distance, a chance to regain a hold over his emotions. Only then could he face her, to accept whatever fate had in store.

And shit. He tugged at his pants with irritation. He needed to deal with this hard-on that was going to rip through his breeches if he didn't find release. He stalked through the pub downstairs, ignoring the inviting gaze of a woman at the bar who'd be more than willing to assist him for the right price. He was only captivated by a single woman, the one he knew he shouldn't desire, as it would only complicate an already complex situation. Clenching his jaw, he resolved to keep his feelings in check. Despite the intense pull he felt toward Lizzy, he couldn't afford to let his heart deviate from his ultimate goal. He would find a way to beat the odds and get home—he had to.

Without a word to anyone, he made his way out back. He needed privacy, and the only place he could find was some out-of-the-way corner in a barn. It was quiet and no one was around. The stables in the back were empty, and he entered the furthest one on the right. Bracing his forearm on the back of the stall, he let his head fall forward and tried to breathe through it.

"Fuck," he muttered after a long pause. There wasn't a choice. He needed release.

With quick jerking movements, he had himself free, his hard shaft rising to greet his hand. He gave himself a rough squeeze, frustrated, angry almost that he had to be here, that he couldn't bottle up this need and throw it far out into some great internal sea. But the extra pressure felt good. How long had it been since he'd been this worked up, since he'd wanted with such urgency?

Maybe never.

Earlier, it had been enough to send him to a second and even third whiskey knowing Lizzy was upstairs flicking through pictures and descriptions that would surely do more than raise questions. She'd be excited. But he hadn't imagined that he'd come back to find her pink-cheeked and hazy-eyed. Her nightgown bunched at her knees. And the room filled with the scent of her desire. He knew now how she'd smell if he pressed his face between her thighs. It was imprinted on his mind, to be carried to his goddamn deathbed.

When the telltale slickness of precum sheened his tip, he brushed a thumb over it, letting the slight wetness caress his length. He wanted to be brisk and utilitarian with this act. Just get it over with and get back to regular life. But his mind kept wandering to her eyes, nose, lips, all the micro gestures she made with her face, how he could read her thoughts in a glance, and when he'd entered the room, she'd wanted him. He'd been one drunken idiot away from knowing how her tongue tasted, if she liked to be kissed hard, teeth knocking, hands tangled in hair, or soft and sweet, a tease of lips that heightened the tension, drawing out the pleasure.

This time when he slid his hand to the base of his cock, he let it brush his sac, already drawn tight, aching for release. He bit the inside of his lip and clenched his ass. Nearly there and it was good. Better than usual. Like his body was finding new pockets of pleasure to draw from. Outside, beyond the walls, two men were singing, their words slurring together off-key. A cat mewed in the rafters. He couldn't stay here long. He had to finish.

What he wanted was to be the one reaching under that white nightgown, running his hands up her curves to the wet silky center; he'd watch her while he touched her there. His rhythm grew uneven. His breathing was rough. Wanted to see those blue eyes darken, her pupils dilating until they swallowed the world. He'd use his free hand to run a thumb over her lower lip, and she'd be as likely to turn on a dime and suck it in.

He grunted as his orgasm struck like a tornado on a clear day. He ground his teeth and milked out the finale in slow, tight strokes, lost in the idea of her sweet mouth opening wide.

It was short work to clean up and then head to the pump near the back entrance to wash his hands and splash water on his face.

The joke was on him, because taking matters into his own hands, so to speak, had the opposite effect to what he was hoping. It didn't take off any edge; it merely served as a whetstone to sharpen his desire to the point where he could barely talk to her the next morning at breakfast and feigned sleep the entire day in the coach. That night he took his dinner downstairs and when he went up, she was already asleep, or did a good job of pretending.

But the next day no one else was in the coach. Just Lizzy.

He was preparing to fake sleep again when she broke the silence.

"Are you upset with me?"

He glanced up sharply. "Not at all. I've been tired."

"I don't believe you. You pretended to be asleep all day yesterday."

"What made you think that was pretend? I *was* asleep."

She glared. "I thought we weren't going to lie to each other."

"I . . ." He wiped his hands on his breeches. "Fine. How did you know?"

"Your mouth falls open when you sleep, and you twitch."

"You pay attention."

"You're big and constantly in my presence. Of course, I've noticed some common gestures, but what I cannot figure out or explain is why you are avoiding me. So, let's hear it."

He didn't want to lie. He had in fact promised the opposite, but there was no chance in hell he'd admit that he came so hard he saw stars in a barn stable and now couldn't shake the desire to see how much better it would with her.

He'd approach the truth from another perspective. One he hadn't expected to share, but that now felt as good as any.

"I was recently unwell. Last year I started to feel off, fevers and fatigue that would come and go. Night sweats. I'd often fall asleep without eating dinner. I went to a team doctor, who looked me over and found a lump in my armpit. It didn't take long for tests to give me a result—it was cancer. It's called Hodgkin lymphoma. The good news, if you can call it that, is that my diagnosis happened in my time, not yours. With treatment I have good—really good—chances of being okay. Once I cross the five-year mark without it coming back, I'll be even better."

"I'm sorry you had to endure that."

"It sucked, not going to sugarcoat it." He sat back and crossed his legs, resting an ankle on the opposite knee. "But compared to many, I'm a lucky guy. I can afford great medical care. And I live in a time where a terrible disease is treatable with available medications. But there is one catch, and I want you to know about it before anything else happens."

This caught her attention. Her shoulders went back and she held her head stiffly as if expecting bad news to land with a blow.

"Go on," she said simply.

"The treatment I had. It hit my whole body hard. This is good because it killed the cancer, but the bad news is that it messed up other things. I'm likely not going to be able to father children."

The quiet stretched in the carriage. All he could hear was the rhythmic noise of the wheels on the road.

He had to speak. "I'm sorry."

"For what?" She wrinkled her nose. "I'm waiting for you to finish. Tell me what's the matter."

"Oh." He blinked. "That was it. Not being able to have children. It's not for certain, but the doctors have said it's unlikely, especially right now."

"Ah, I see, and you presumably want them someday?"

"I'm not sure, to be honest. Probably not. But I wanted you to know before we got married."

She burst out laughing. "Why on earth would I mind?"

"Well, now that you put it like this, I don't know." His ears went red.

She stopped and mashed her lips together, trying to look serious. "I'm truly not making fun. I'm surprised. Did you think I was going to use this marriage as an opportunity to have a baby?"

"No, but I still wanted you to have the information before commitment."

"You are very dear, Tucker Taylor. I must say this before we go any further. While I adore children, there is no part of me, and I mean none, that has a maternal bent. I quite like the notion of being an amusing aunt, but the idea of having my own?" She shook her head. "When I see my future, my great desire is for freedom. I have not had the opportunity to taste it yet. But that's what you are giving me. And that's what is precious." A dark look crossed her face. "You might think I'm a monster for that. Many would."

"Not wanting to have kids? Nah. Not at all. Where I come from, I know quite a few couples who don't have children. Most by choice. It's one of those things that is personal. I would never judge you for not wanting them. I only wanted to ensure you had the ability to choose, just in case."

"In case of what?"

"If I can't find my way home again. You must have thought of that too. It's a possibility."

She set her jaw, a fierce determination on her face. "We can't think like that. You got here. There must be a way to get you back. We simply need to find the path. And now, knowing about this cancer, I am even more committed. You will get home and have access to the doctors you need."

"Lizzy . . ."

"And if we can't find a way back, we will make one," she said resolutely. "I'm very resourceful, you know."

"I do." If anyone could tear through the fabric of the universe, it would be her.

"I have some questions of my own." She folded her arms. "You have been avoiding me. You promised I could ask questions and I have not had an ability to do so. When you say you cannot have children, does it mean that your . . . I'm not quite sure what to call it . . . What do you prefer?"

"What do I call it?" He glanced at his crotch. "My cock, I guess. Or dick. I don't know."

Her smile was slow, catlike, even. "From the speed of your answer, it appears you do in fact know quite well. And so I will use *cock*. It feels somewhat violent, but Dick is the name of a man who is a servant in my London home, so I refuse that term wholeheartedly."

"Reasonable." This woman had the ability to skate past his defenses and shoot to score.

"Well, we were discussing your cock and how it doesn't work and—"

"Hang on, Pocket Rocket. I said I probably can't have kids."

"Right. Because of your broken cock."

If she said *cock* in that uptight British manner of speaking one more time, he was going to throw her onto his lap and teach her a thing or two about using her pretty mouth in such a way. But he fought off the impulse. "Whoa, whoa, whoa. I never said a single word about my cock being broken. It works fine, by the way. Better than fine."

"But you said . . ."

"I didn't say I was impotent. Jesus. Look, it means my swimmers don't swim quite—"

"Who is swimming where?" She looked alarmed. "There was nothing about swimming in my book."

What a mess.

"Let me rephrase." As he swallowed, trying to figure out a way not to confuse her more, the coach halted.

"We're picking up more people?" Lizzy asked blankly as the door swung open. Inside stepped a narrow-shouldered slip of a woman, followed by a man with a neat low ponytail and the telltale red coat of a British soldier.

"Oh, Jameson. We have company." Tuck looked closer and saw the new woman couldn't be over twenty, buried in a dress and bonnet that were so large she was almost lost in them. "How do you do? I'm Mrs. Jameson Horatio Darling."

The man—Jameson Horatio Darling, presumably—gave a short nod before refocusing the entirety of his attention on the young woman.

"We are newly married." The new Mrs. Darling passed over her bags and allowed herself to be arranged on the bench as if she were a mannequin or something.

"Dear Jameson takes care of my every need. Why, I only need to think of a thing and *poof*—there it appears. We are going to be joining his regiment now that our honeymoon is at an end, but oh my, I wish it wasn't over. The last two weeks have been magical, haven't they? I've been in positive raptures for every moment."

Dear Jameson picked up her hand and pressed a fervent kiss to the palm. "I'm your devoted servant in all things, madam."

It didn't take long before Tuck and Lizzy had the entire history of the most happy Darlings, from meeting at a ball to a few of the most magical walks in the history of human creation to a letter dear Jameson penned that was the paragon against which all future love letters of the world would be judged and found wanting.

"I do make some pretty verses," dear Jameson offered. "My wife says I have quite a gift for rhyme."

"Wife!" Mrs. Jameson Horatio Darling squealed the word. "Is there anything so wonderful as being a wife? I should think not, am I correct, Mrs. erhm . . . Mrs. . . ." She trailed off, not at all seeming to mind that she'd never requested a similar introduction. Turning to Tuck, she dipped her head. "I'm so sorry, sir, when I'm around my dear Jameson, I'm afraid I'm in such raptures that I forget to see other men at all. Why, recently I was walking down the sidewalk and I bumped directly into one, mistaking him for a cart."

"Pardon, I am failing to see how you could walk into a cart in the absence of seeing a man," Lizzy said tersely.

"My eyes are full of stars and moons for the one I love, Mrs. . . . I'm terribly sorry, I simply must get your name, sir."

"My name is Lizzy Wooddash, and this is Mr. Tucker Taylor."

"Ah, an unusual name, sir. And I thought the two of you were also in such a blessed conjugal union as me and my dear Jameson."

"We are to be married," Tuck offered, remembering the reminders that Jane and Georgie had issued in the shed. He didn't want them thinking unwell of Lizzy for his company.

"Ah." Mrs. Jameson Horatio Darling glanced between them with a knowing look. "To Gretna Green, is it?"

When neither of them confirmed nor denied, she threw herself against her husband. "Dear Jameson, they are eloping! Isn't that marvelous? Of course, we had the banns read and did it in a church and everything quite by the book, but your choice is a choice indeed."

"To be sure." Lizzy's voice was strained to the point where another gush from the beaming bride might send her hurtling out onto the moors.

Tuck took her hand in his; it was cool but soft. He hadn't done this before—sat and held her hand. "We can only hope to be a fraction as happy as you."

"And so you shall." Mrs. Jameson Horatio Darling perked back up at the thought. "Because while you can never hope to be as incandescently blissful as myself, given that I am the one fortune has favored with such a stallion, even having a scrap of this happiness should quite suffice."

Lizzy's eyes and mouth both opened wider and Tuck gave her hand two warning squeezes.

"Yes, thank you for the warm wishes. We are feeling very fortunate ourselves, are we not?"

"If I rapture any harder, I shall be face-to-face with angels," Lizzy deadpanned.

The coach went silent for a moment before Mrs. Jameson Horatio Darling pealed with laughter.

"Dear Jameson, what rhymes with *angels*? I demand a pretty little poem at once."

"When I am away from my angel . . . I find the world in despair and my poor heart grows painful."

The girl squealed and clapped her hands while kicking her feet up in what appeared to be a full-bodied response to his literary prowess. "See! See! He can just do such things with no practice or advance notice. My own personal Shakespeare. My clever little husband."

"Pretty words flow easily when there is a muse as lovely as you, my rose."

"Sweetheart, look, a bird." Tuck pointed out the window and tugged her close, whispering in her ear, "You are not allowed to kill them or throw yourself from a moving coach."

She made a noise in protest. "I promise neither."

"Just keep looking at the birds."

A few were flying by, nothing special or out of the ordinary, but having Lizzy pressed up close made it more interesting.

"The moors have a certain charm, don't they?" she murmured.

"Is that what these are?" The landscape was bleak, devoid of trees or cheer.

"This feels more romantic to me than . . ." She inclined her head toward the couple busy cooing. "Out there, I can imagine feelings get very stark, almost painful. There are no distractions to your thoughts, so it's you and your ugly heart against the horizon."

"Ugly heart? That doesn't sound very poetic."

"But it's true." She pressed her lips to his ear. "Real hearts aren't happy all the time. And they aren't perfect. They get angry, envy, hunger for more, and still crave. But we are all beautiful in our ugly little ways as well. At least that is what I think."

CHAPTER FIFTEEN

Gretna Green. They had arrived.

Lizzy stepped out of the stagecoach and paused. For a moment, she half expected to wake up and discover that the events of the past few days had been nothing more than a vivid dream. However, as her feet touched solid ground and she felt Tuck's hand in hers, it confirmed the reality of the situation.

"Thank you," she murmured, quickly shaking herself loose and lifting her dress hem from the muddy road.

"I've never been to Scotland." Tuck lifted their bags, ready to take them to their final destination, the Jigging Stallion. "I kind of expected more kilts."

"We are only two miles over the border." She glanced around. Everyone seemed more or less to look like people in England. "Does that fact disappoint you?" she asked, following him into the inn.

"My mom's maiden name was McLaughlin—Scottish, obviously. At Christmas, she covers the house with tartan—no surface is free of it."

"Are you close to your mother? You don't speak of her." Lizzy couldn't help but wonder about Tuck's family. It seemed so strange for him to have a father, mother, and sister somewhere out there, lost in time. A pang of unexpected sadness hit her as she realized she'd never meet them, never see where he came from, never understand what he meant by his mother covering the house in tartan.

"We talk on rare occasions—like her birthday or a holiday." Tuck's jaw tightened, his words measured. "Not as much as she'd like, but . . ."

When he fell silent, she gently nudged him with her elbow. "But?"

"But nothing. I'm busy." There was a hardness in his tone that made it clear additional questions would not be welcome.

Once they settled into their room, Lizzy's mind raced. Tomorrow they would be wed.

"The river seemed pleasant," she said. "I'd very much enjoy a walk and some fresh air, if you don't mind."

He nodded, seemingly as desperate to escape the confined room as she was.

Outside, the streets of Gretna Green were quiet, nothing like the illicit stories Lizzy had overhead whispered about the corners of drawing rooms or at balls. Tales of young lovers racing to the border, outraged fathers in pursuit, horses foaming at the mouth, eyes rolling, as they were pushed past their endurance.

Women walked laden with baskets for shopping, and a few children raced past brandishing a paper boat, seemingly intent to drop it into the creek. The buildings were painted white, and low hills were covered in lush grass. It felt more like the sort of place one would go to rest than to give themselves over to forbidden passion.

"Why exactly is this a place for eloping?" Tuck asked, echoing her thoughts. "In my time, we have a city known for fast weddings. It's called Las Vegas. I guess I was expecting more of that sort of energy."

"Las Vegas?" She frowned. "Oh, that's Spanish for . . . let me see. The meadows! How lovely. It must be very green like this."

He gaped at her. "You speak Spanish?"

"Badly. My French is passable. My Spanish is worse. My German is abominable. But I've tried to study when I have the time and find the books. One of my dreams is to travel. This is the first time I've ever been outside of England, so you are helping me realize this."

"You are full of surprises, but also no, Las Vegas is no meadow. It's a desert. People come from all over the world to gamble there, and you can get married in a drive-through." He didn't even wait for her to ask. "It would be similar to you pulling up in a carriage to be wed."

"It sounds very convenient."

He shrugged. "I guess it saves time."

"Are you very rushed?" she asked.

"In my time? Ha! There is no time. Everything happens quickly and people are always searching for the fastest ways to do most things."

Lizzy turned to the creek and watched two ducks float past. "That sounds exhausting."

"I didn't realize how tired I was until I stopped. Days here feel much longer." A distant look crept into his eyes and a silence grew before he finally glanced over. "Off topic, but I've wondered—why do blacksmiths marry people here?"

"I don't know all the rules and laws, but at some point, England changed the laws so that people under the age of twenty-one couldn't marry without parental consent. There isn't a similar law in Scotland, so young lovers flee here to be handfasted. In this country, you are considered married if you declare it so in front of a witness. And apparently the clever blacksmiths around here saw an opportunity to make some extra coin by serving as the official witness. It doesn't have to be a blacksmith, though. It could be a fisherman, or even a horse saddler."

He mulled it over. "A fisherman could give you a bass for the wedding dinner after."

"So practical."

"But smelly."

A huff of laughter escaped her. "To be sure."

A piercing cry shattered the peace, followed by a sickening splash that sent ripples across the water. Screams erupted from the riverbank, a chorus of terrified children. Lizzy's heart leapt to her throat as she saw a boy thrashing in the water, eyes wide in panic. The current's hungry grasp pulled the small figure toward the shadow of the bridge, threatening to swallow him in darkness.

Lizzy's gaze darted to her skirts; blast it, they were too heavy and would weigh her down, but she had to act. As she lurched toward the water's edge, a strong hand clamped gently on her arm.

"Watch the others." Tuck's voice was raw with urgency. "Don't let anyone else tumble in." His gaze locked with hers, concern mixed with determination. "And, listen, if something happens to me and I disappear . . ." His lips pressed to the place where her mouth met her cheek, warm and fast; scruff seared her skin.

Then he was sprinting with purpose, throwing his jacket and kicking off his boots before diving into the churning waters. The current moved swiftly, and it took him only a few strokes to reach the boy, who was about to go under.

Lizzy felt her body go limp with relief. Tuck knew how to swim, thank God.

He locked the child under one big arm as he made his way back to the shallows, hauling him up onto the bank. "Grab him!"

Lizzy reached down and seized the sodden, crying child as his friends pressed in.

"Jamie! You all right, Jamie?"

Jamie coughed out river water and gagged, but a red flush returned to his freckled cheeks.

"Och, you are going to be in for it when Maw hears you got too close to the water," said a girl whose red curls were identical to Jamie's—more likely than not a sister.

Tucker climbed out. "Is he all right?"

"He will be, thanks to you." She reached out and touched his chest. "You're breathing hard."

"I was scared," he said simply. "Why the hell do kids in trouble keep crossing my path?"

She frowned, not understanding his cryptic comment.

"Never mind, I'm rambling." He turned to the cluster of kids with a stern glare. "You. All of you. Unless you learn how to swim, you have no business playing near the river, got it?"

The kids all stared, eyes like dinner saucers, before scampering away.

"You were a hero," she said, watching them flee. "Things could have gone much worse for our young friend Jamie if you hadn't been here." She tugged at his clothing. "But we need to get you dried off before you catch a cold."

When they returned to the inn, Lizzy draped his sodden clothing across the furniture to dry. She avoided even a peek at Tuck changing with quick efficiency in the corner until he was standing beside her, clad in nothing but breeches and an untucked white shirt open at the neck.

His expression was stricken. "My phone—you know, the device with which I could take photos—it's gone. It must have fallen out of my pocket in the water."

"Shall we go back and look for it?"

He shook his head. "Nah. It's the river's now. And the battery—never mind. It's just that it . . ."

"It was a connection to your life."

"Yeah. It's funny. I never took many pictures. My sister sent me a lot of them, though. Things about her day. What she had for breakfast or was reading. A museum. Even a tree she thought was pretty. I barely looked, at the time. But now I miss them."

"Because you miss her."

The casual dress, his bare feet. It unlocked her reserve somehow. Made it feel permitted to ask the questions that had been swirling in her mind since the river. "Before you dove in," she said quietly. "You said in case you 'disappear.' At first, I thought maybe you couldn't swim. But that wasn't the case."

"Right." He hooked a hand on the back of his neck, a faraway expression settling on his features. "The night I disappeared? There'd been a little boy and a dog. I . . . I was driving a car—the point is, the road was icy. They ran in front of me and I didn't want to hit them, so I swerved. I went off the road and ended up flipped over in the pond and getting trapped in the water. The ice blocked my exit when I tried to swim up. Then the world started to churn and everything went black. When I entered the river, I wasn't sure if I'd—"

"If you'd return to your time," she said, finishing his sentence.

"Yeah." He walked to the window and drew a small crown in the dust on the glass. "Can't say it didn't cross my mind."

"D-did you want to go back?"

He was silent for a moment. "Not like that." His voice was low, determined. "No."

"How come?"

"Goddamnit, Lizzy." His rueful laugh seemed to ease the remaining tension from his body. "I think you know."

"Your heroic actions led you to me." She took a step forward, then another, until she was so close that if she put out a hand, she'd be touching him. Her lungs burned as she struggled to draw in a full breath. "But you don't want to remain here forever."

"I can't." He reached out then, cradling her face, his fingers bracketing her cheek while his thumb settled just beneath her chin. Goose bumps broke out down the backs of her arms. She leaned into his palm, savoring his wide-eyed gaze that searched her face for unspoken truths. "But I also can't leave without . . ."

They were close, dangerously close. The rise and fall of his chest mirrored her own. Could he hear her pounding heart? "Without what?"

"This." His lips crashed against hers, hunger fueling the slant of his mouth. As his arms wrapped around her, pulling her flush against the hard planes of his body, she gripped the silky strands of his short hair, anchoring herself as the world fell away.

It wasn't until her back bumped against the wall that she realized in some vague part of her brain that they had been walking backward. Now there was no room to do anything but give herself over to this push and pull, give and take. Raw need passed from his lips to hers, leaving her aching.

"Am I doing it right?" she murmured into his mouth.

"You're perfect." He pulled back, and his breath ghosted across her cheek. "Would you like more?"

"Yes. Teach me."

"That's a good girl." This time, he opened his mouth, coaxing her to do the same; she responded and, with slow, almost aching deliberation, he stroked his tongue against hers.

She arched in surprise at the sensation, her back bowing as their tongues began to explore against each other, slowly, curiously, before becoming insatiable.

A guttural sound escaped him and it awoke something slumbering deep within her. Teeth knocked together and she pulled back not to end it but, as if in some strange trance, to put her mouth all over him. She kissed along the edge of his jaw, so hard and a little prickly in contrast to his lips, and then forged a path to his ear. When she sucked on the edge of his lobe, he groaned again, not in the back of his throat this time, but loud. She inhaled his deep, complex scent.

"Is this nice?" She'd never known that it was possible to shiver from warmth. "Do you really like when I do that?"

"Jesus, Lizzy." His chuckle was nothing more than a husky rasp. "You sure you haven't done any of this before?" He grazed her lips once more, as if committing her mouth to memory, and then took a deliberate step back, putting space between them. "Enough now. That's enough."

Was he talking to her? To himself? To both of them?

Her body screamed no—this wasn't nearly enough—but she knew what he meant. Through the haze of desire, a flicker of reason remained. To surrender to these flames was to risk everything for a blaze from which neither would emerge unscathed.

"Yes, enough," she agreed, trying her very best to act as if she meant it. "Thank you for that."

He turned his head, surprise flashing on his features. "For nearly taking you against the wall?"

The blood drained from her head, the room's edges blurring

into shadows as the implications sank in. Was that where their mad dance was leading them? Weakened, she sank onto the bed, a heavy sense of fatigue dragging at her bones.

"I meant thank you for ensuring my first kiss didn't happen in front of the blacksmith."

"Anytime." Tuck grunted, then grabbed his still-wet jacket and boots and crossed the room in three steps. "I'm going to get a drink. Tonight, I want to sleep."

Because tomorrow they were getting married. Because even if the ceremony wasn't genuine, it was going to be real. And he clearly didn't want to think of that or any future consequences. He'd rather run away and blot it out.

She nodded, forcing any small bubble of hurt to stay deep within. They were both trapped by their circumstances. A few stolen kisses didn't mean anything; it was merely instructive. She'd been curious how a kiss would feel, and now she knew. This was a good thing.

Tuck left the room, the door quietly snicking shut behind him. She fell back on the lumpy mattress and pressed the heels of her palms into her eyes.

When had he started shifting from Mr. Taylor to Tuck in her thoughts?

And how had those kisses felt like coming home, except it was a new house where you want to explore every room, not simply remain in the foyer?

She let out a soft huff of frustration.

This marriage of convenience was turning out far more complicated than expected.

CHAPTER SIXTEEN

The anvil wedding drew closer with each passing moment. Lizzy had ordered a bath and used more of her precious soap than usual. Her heart raced, each beat a frantic flutter against her ribs, despite her best efforts to remind herself that this was to be her one—and only—wedding, a superficial ritual that would ultimately grant her freedom. It didn't mean anything. But she couldn't shake the silly impulse to look pretty for the occasion.

No, not just for the occasion. For him.

She wanted to look pretty for Tuck.

That was why she scrubbed herself until her skin went a rosy pink, cleaned her teeth twice, washed her hair, and sat by the sunny window brushing it out until it dried in shiny waves. She donned a high-waisted white muslin gown and swept her waves into a neat twist, wrapping a single ribbon around her hairstyle in a simple bandeau à la Grecque.

She frowned at her reflection in the room's cracked mirror. Her face was distorted but her eyes matched her blue shawl and held a hectic brightness.

Never mind.

She would simply stop looking. The expression was nerves. Not from repressed excitement, but from what her family would do when they discovered what she had done. At least they wouldn't ever learn her husband was an American hockey player from the twenty-first century. That would send Mamma, Mr. Alby, and her brother straight to the grave. It was quite bad enough that she'd be introducing them to Tucker Taylor, a Baltimore dry-goods merchant.

But it wouldn't be for long.

She left the inn, and Tuck was waiting in front of the blacksmith shop as planned. He'd come back to the room last night and she'd pretended to be asleep as it took him three tries to get off his boots before he then walked into a wall. It appeared he'd had quite a lot more than one drink, and when he lay down on the floor— no blanket, no pillow, just a coat under his head—and began to snore, this day she dreaded couldn't have come quickly enough.

But the man waiting had on fawn-colored breeches, a royal blue coat, and shiny boots, and didn't look like a man who'd spent the evening in his cups. He was beautiful. There wasn't another word for it. His face and form weren't cold, remote, and perfect like one of those Greek statues in the British Museum. Yes, he had impressive height and an angular jaw, but the true secret of his look hid in the collection of small so-called flaws: a wide mouth, close-set eyes, the odd dark hair on his knuckles, the pockmark on his cheek, and the broken nose. It made him more accessible, more human somehow.

And infinitely more fascinating.

As she neared, he stuck out his arm, a few buttercups in his hand. "Here." He offered them awkwardly, avoiding eye contact. "It's a wedding, so I suppose the bride needs to carry flowers."

"Thank you," she murmured, taking the posy. A few stems were threatening to snap off, as if he'd been holding them too tightly.

"I like what you did with your hair. You look . . . nice."

"Y-you too," she murmured.

"I clean up okay." He glanced down and flicked away some invisible lint. "I have the rings as well." She studied him. His voice was rougher than normal and he was so pale that his copper-penny eyes almost seemed to glow.

"Are you all right, Mr. Taylor?"

"One rule for this marriage." He turned to face her fully, holding up a finger. "When we are done with this . . . event, I need you to promise not to call me Mr. Taylor ever again."

"You seem to have a specific dislike that overrides any politeness I intend in the gesture. Does this all truly have to do with your father?"

"Yes," he said after a short pause. "I guess it does."

She waited for him to go on, but that was all he was willing to offer for the moment.

"Very well, Tuck. Are you ready?"

His gaze searched her face. "Are you?"

"Yes." And as she said the word, she tasted no lie. The realization calmed her. This was what she wanted. "Once we do this, we can go to London and research a way home for you."

She might have imagined the glint of disappointment in his eyes, it was there and gone so quickly.

A deep voice boomed from the blacksmith's doorway. "How long are ye two gonna be standin' out on the street haverin'?"

They whirled around to see a broad man wearing a leather apron stained with soot and sweat.

He wiped his brow with his hairy forearm before continuing. "Ye've come to Gretna Green. Yer here at me shop. I've got to put a shoe on a horse afore long, but if you can be quick about it, I've got the time." The blacksmith turned and swaggered back in at such a pace they had no choice but to follow quickly.

The heart of his shop was the forge, a fiery spot where the smith shaped metal on a solid anvil surrounded by an assortment of mystifying tools. The air smelled of burning coal and heated metal. Finished products lined the shelves—horseshoes, tools, and intricate ironwork—showcasing his skill. It was a busy but organized space, much like the aura of the man himself.

"First things first." The blacksmith wiped his sooty hands on his leather apron. "Ye have my payment?"

"Yes, right here." Tuck handed over a guinea.

The blacksmith gave it a small bite before examining it. "Don't see many of these anymore."

Georgie had money stowed away all over her house like some kind of dragon. She didn't part with much, so it was no surprise that some of her currency was on the verge of being outdated.

The blacksmith took their names and beckoned them to stand on either side of the anvil before clearing his throat. "Do ye, Tucker Taylor, and do ye, Elizabeth Wooddash, declare ye wish to be joined in marriage?" He gave them both an expectant look. "This is the *I do* part."

"Oh, right." Tuck nodded. "I do."

"I do as well," Lizzy whispered before immediately wanting to cover her face. *As well.* Why couldn't she do the same as Tuck, speak the words loud and confident?

"I now pronounce you husband and wife."

The only noise was the crackle of the fire.

The blacksmith gave them a look that indicated he was beginning to find them both feeble-minded. "That's it. Our business is done. Be fruitful and multiply and all that."

Within a few seconds, Lizzy was blinking out in the Scottish sunlight, Tuck, her husband, next to her.

"That was quicker than I expected," he muttered, a trifle dazed.

"Yes, remarkably efficient."

"All the more time to shoe the horses," Tuck rejoined, sending them both into peals of laughter before he paused, frowning slightly. "Shit. I didn't give you the ring. It was over too quickly." He reached into his pocket and pulled them out—two plain gold bands. "Do we just do it here?"

"I—I'm not sure." Lizzy glanced about the bustling village street. "We should wait," she decided at once. "I feel as if we're already attracting enough attention." To be sure, most women who passed by gave Tuck a lingering glance. She didn't want those same women watching her exchange rings outside of a blacksmith shop. They might think she was desperate. And right now the only thing she was desperate for was a hot meal. She'd skipped breakfast and needed her belly full so that her brain could think.

They ordered at the inn and waited, uncertain in each other's presence.

Lizzy spoke first. "You spent the evening down here, I presume?"

He gave her a blank stare.

"You were, after all, very inebriated last night."

A whisper of regret crossed his features. "I was, yes. And no. I didn't stay here. I bought a bottle at the bar and went outside. I found a hill at the edge of town and sat drinking and looking at the stars. At some point I fell asleep, and when I came to, sheep surrounded me. I don't know who was more confused, but I took it as my cue to return."

"Remember, Mr. . . . ." She shook her head, correcting herself. "Tuck. This isn't real. You aren't signing your life away to me.

Imagine we are two actors in a play." Her smile went rueful. "A Shakespeare one. Two dirty jokes strung between bits of plot."

He blinked. "We're not real."

She couldn't tell if he was asking a question or making a statement. So, she decided to answer. "We're not real," she repeated with all the conviction she could muster. Because those kisses last night were the realest things she'd ever known. She still tasted him on her lips and smelled his scent on her clothing. "But we are legal."

His lips quirked. "You're ruthless."

"I prefer practical."

"And once you get rid of me, tell me how you see yourself living your best life."

A serving girl brought out their meals. As she stared into her soup, something deep inside her cracked at the thought of him leaving. Was this the power of a few kisses? Did some tendrils of connection forge into each other so that the idea of separation couldn't be without a whisper of pain? "I—I will live at the Woodlands. I will wake and sleep when I choose, pay visits or entertain at my liking, and I will try to write a book."

He cut another piece of chicken. "Why do you hedge?"

She wrinkled her brow.

He took a bite, chewed, and swallowed. "You said *try*." He waved his fork. "A small green wise man once said something to the effect of there is no trying, only doing."

"Green?"

"Forget it. Just know that one thing you're missing out on during this time is Yoda." His expression grew serious. "I want you to do something for me." He smiled at the alarm that must have appeared on her face. "Nothing big. It's quite easy. I simply want you to repeat these words . . . 'I will write a book.'"

"I just said that."

"No. You said you'd *try*. Say *I will*."

"What nonsense." She wiped her mouth with her napkin, casting her gaze anywhere that wasn't at him, watching with his intense expression. "Lizzy. Do it."

"Fine." She set her hands on the table and took a breath. "I will write a book."

"Good girl."

A hot rush of pleasure coursed through her. Why did she like those two particular words so much? She wasn't a pet—his or anyone else's. But the simple affirmation had an undeniable effect, filling some small corner of her soul that she didn't know was missing, a gasping little relief to hear such open praise.

"Now slower, as if you mean every word, like you are making a vow to yourself, to the universe, and to anyone else who might be listening."

"I. Will. Write. A. Book." It was as if she'd studied her whole life to master the art of being invisible, and he was here demanding she frame a canvas of her ambitions and hang it on the wall for everyone to see.

He noticed. "How does that feel?"

"P-powerful."

"From now on, every time you say 'I'll try to write a book,' stop and say it again without the *try to* part. You want the freedom to create your own future. That's not someone who tries. That is someone who takes action and can make it happen. That's why I meant it when I said I want you on my team. Believe in yourself and you'll be unstoppable."

It was at that moment, in a dim bar on the Scottish border, that Lizzy realized she'd fallen a little in love with Tucker Taylor. Her husband. Not enough to cause her great danger. Nothing to derail her from their plans. But enough that her heart cracked open a fraction. And that was far more feeling than she'd ever intended. Because for the first time, she believed that maybe she could take on the stories in her vellum notebook and turn them into a real novel.

"I will get you home," she said, and not only for his benefit. She would get him home for her too—because this crack in her heart? It was too much. She needed to get it patched up and repaired as soon as possible. All his "good girl" talk aside—flirting and fun was one matter. Feelings? True sentiment? That was too dangerous. She had a plan, and it was already going to be a challenge to execute it.

Feelings and freedom did not work hand in hand.

"To achieving our goals, Mrs. Taylor." He raised a glass.

"My name." She blinked. "Oh. I've lost my name."

He froze. "I'm sorry, I was teasing. But you don't ever—"

"Elizabeth!"

Lizzy went very quiet, not bothering to turn. She knew that voice. It was the same condescending tone she'd heard her whole life. The voice that reminded her that she was a burden, that she was a failure, that if she couldn't play by the rules, then the best thing she could do was make herself as small and useful as possible.

"My God, Elizabeth," a man's voice ground out. "It really is you."

She turned slowly, and there was her older brother, Henry. He looked horrible. As if he'd been in a saddle for days. Dark bruises haunted the hollows under his eyes, eyes that were positively murderous.

"Sister, are you dicked in the nob? What have you done?"

CHAPTER SEVENTEEN

"Henry!" Lizzy gasped. "What on earth are you doing here?"

"I believe that's my line," the man replied with deadly calm, "although I'd phrase it much less delicately."

Tuck glanced between them. The same brown hair. But the eyes were different. His were more hazel than blue and his features were sharper, as if he were a bird of prey.

"Henry?" Tuck was just about to register the name when Lizzy spoke again.

"My older brother. Henry Percival Wooddash. Henry, take a chair and I'll introduce you to my husband."

Henry slumped before doing a quick internal rally, a gesture that was startlingly familiar. "I came here to keep you from ruining yourself."

"Which I didn't do."

They were whispering as if they thought that would keep the conversation under wraps. But it was more akin to stage whispers, where anyone with curiosity could listen in on the circus.

"Hey there." Tuck stood, unfolding himself out of his chair. He was a good six inches taller than her brother. "My name is Tucker Taylor and I'm a dry-goods merchant from Baltimore—"

"Not an American as well." Henry looked as if he would combust in three . . . two . . . one . . . "A challenge!" he exclaimed. "I'm issuing you a challenge. For kidnapping my sister—"

"Henry! Stop this instant," Lizzy exclaimed.

"—and ruining her. And thinking you'd be a welcomed member of the Wooddash family, with our impeccable reputation."

"What is a challenge?" Tuck had benched weights heavier than this guy.

"It's when you take a pair of pistols to a quiet glen with the aim of shooting each other in a respectable fashion," she explained quickly. "And don't listen to such nonsense. Henry doesn't even own guns."

Tuck tried to take it all in. This dude was going to shoot him for marrying his sister? And do so wearing those neck ruffles? The past was way more hardcore than he gave it credit for. It wasn't all tea drinking and top hats.

"I should be able to procure some in this town with little difficulty. I can't be the first aggrieved family member to be forced into such desperate measures."

"Henry, I won't say this again. So, sit. Both of you." Lizzy hadn't so much as raised her voice, but she might as well have screamed. "And then I will speak. If you do not listen to this command—and let me be clear, this is not a request—then *I* will find dueling pistols first and fire one directly into your nose to prevent you from sticking it into our business. I am of age, of sound mind, and now married. We stood over the anvil and exchanged our vows. The blacksmith was the witness. It is done, and the only thing you need to do now is congratulate us. After that, we shall make a plan for how to deliver the news to our parents."

"You've changed, Elizabeth." Henry's tone was heavy with accusation as he reluctantly took a seat.

"You say this like it's a bad thing," Tuck said, not caring how much the guy seemed to hate him. He was acting like a murder-happy little brat. "Everything and everyone changes. So don't waltz in here and make threats to my wife."

Tuck wasn't prepared for the possessive sensation that flared within him by speaking those final two words.

"How did you find us?" Lizzy asked.

"I had business to attend to in Portsmouth. I decided to surprise you at the Woodlands and—"

"Surprise? Is that what we are calling it?" Lizzy gave him a skeptical look. "'Spy' is more like it."

"Georgie might be deemed respectable, but we all know it's only because of her income." He sniffed. "I was seeking assurance that your visit wasn't marred by questionable activities; one can never be too careful."

"Heavens, Henry. What questionable activities? Music? Books? Conversation? The Woodlands is a refuge. There's fresh air, plenty of room to move around, and freedom from judgment."

"Must I truly dignify that with an answer?" Henry gestured toward Tuck. "You forsook the season to retreat to the countryside for your whimsical notions of writing and indulging in female companionship. Mamma and Father, against my sound counsel, indulged you for a month, and what transpires?"

"Mr. Alby is Mother's husband. That man is *not* our father," Lizzy ground out.

"*That man*, as you call him, is father enough for my needs. Remember who kept Mamma from sliding down into less-than-desirable economic circumstances after Papa's passing. Her marriage to Rufus Alby secured our place back in the best of society. But you? You just love to bite the hand that feeds you, don't you, sister?" Henry barked out a bitter laugh. "And now

you go and marry this . . . this . . . American with unknown connections and reputation. Did you ever pause to think what this
would mean for our family? Georgie was meant to be a chaperone. How did she allow this to happen?" He slammed back in his
seat. "How am I to solve this problem?"

"Listen, my man." Tuck leaned in, balling his hands into fists
under the table and digging them into his thighs. As much as
he'd love to check this guy, getting red-carded here would only
make the situation worse. "My *wife* isn't a problem. She's one
of the smartest, kindest women I've ever met and if you are so
concerned over reputation, then I suggest you stop acting like an
asshole."

Lizzy's eyes widened as their gazes locked.

"I'm not going to step in and tell you all how to end this. All I
can say is that it's a damn shame you haven't taken the time to
get to know your sister. Because if you did, you would realize that
she never does anything without a reason."

Henry's mouth opened and closed rapidly like a fish out of
water.

"I'm not going to duel you. I'm not going to fight over a woman.
She gets to choose what she wants to do with her life. Not me. Not
you. Full stop. We're married. This has happened. End of discussion."

"Well . . ." Henry huffed; his chest puffed out before deflat-
ing. "I rode the last three days to get here." His haggard features
spoke to the truth of his claim. "I tried to prevent this, but failed.
You've both made your bed, and I welcome you to lie in it. If
you"—he directed his withering tone at Tuck—"think you're going to be seeing a shilling from our family with this stunt, I can
assure you that I'll do everything in my power to stop it."

"While I find your conduct utterly deplorable and unbecoming as a gentleman, I'll have you know that Georgie is giving me a dowry and—"

"I don't need to be paid to want to marry your sister." Tuck dropped his voice low and leaned in. "And I'm going to advise for the last time that you discontinue any conversation that doesn't include a congratulations and maybe a passing comment about the weather." He gestured to the window, where rain had begun falling.

"What did Georgie say when you arrived?" Lizzy asked.

Henry's grin was cold. "Let's say she wasn't the most congenial host."

Tuck settled back, reading the situation. The guy's pride had taken a hit and he wanted retribution. In a tight game, the primary focus had to be on the puck. Sure, there could be a soft focus on other factors, knowing the shooter's usual "tells" or having the muscle memory to react to situations you've handled before. But right now, Tuck had no prior knowledge. His attention needed to zero in on the words coming from the brother's mouth—that was the puck. Tuck had to observe, wait for the play, and be ready to step in and make the save.

"You didn't even send word," Lizzy retorted. "You no doubt showed up on her doorstep with a scheme to catch the unattended women in some form of mischief."

"To which you exceeded my worst nightmares."

"Were you horrible to her?"

Henry made a face. "I think the real concern should be how horrible they were to *me*. After I went to sleep with the stated intention to begin pursuing you in the morning, she and her wretched friend Jane locked me in my bedroom. It appears they thought that would trap me, but I climbed down the drainpipe. I got my horse and was en route before dawn."

Tuck winced inwardly; those ladies wouldn't be too happy with how things turned out.

"You appear supremely pleased with yourself."

"You orchestrated the stunt, sister. I was merely a player in this affair. Naturally, I'll need to apologize to Father for letting down the family. Nevertheless, the repercussions should squarely rest upon you."

The guy was making the case for how to throw Lizzy under the bus as soon as possible.

"Our plan is to return to London tomorrow," Lizzy explained. "I wasn't trying to cause more disruption than necessary."

"You're never trying to cause disruption," Henry snapped. "And yet somehow you always do. You have a rare talent for always making bad decisions. On that note, I'm going to retire. I don't have the appetite you do for ruination." He cast a scornful look at her half-empty plate. "Tomorrow we will begin the journey home."

"Fine," Lizzy said through clenched teeth.

"Fine." He pushed back his chair and stood.

"And one last thing, Hen?" Lizzy's voice had turned sweet.

Her brother froze. "I've told you never to call me that."

"I don't mean to ruffle your feathers." She tucked her arms against her torso, waving her elbows like little wings. "You have no business challenging anyone to a duel. You know you are a terrible shot."

Henry's features contorted.

"Rest well, Chicken."

Boom.

Whatever happened, Tuck had no need to make a save. Lizzy had clearly taken possession.

Henry glanced at Tuck. "My only consolation is that you will be punished for this by being forced to endure her company."

And with that he was gone.

Lizzy exhaled. "Did that just happen? Or did I dream it?" Her hand rested on the table, looking small, pale, and alone. Tuck's gaze lingered on it, mind racing. Should he reach out to offer comfort and reassurance? Would that make her feel better?

As if reading his thoughts, she frowned, balling her fingers into a fist and sliding it onto her lap.

She had her pride. And he respected it. But he didn't want her to feel alone. Sure, he bickered with Nora. Sometimes they both got too busy with their own lives and didn't talk much, but both of them knew they could count on the other if the going got rough.

"Well, he seems great." Tuck's deadpan observation earned a rueful giggle.

"That's Henry for you."

"What was all the chicken stuff? He couldn't deal with that."

Her smile was small but victorious. "My entire life Henry has enjoyed pointing out my every deficit and shortcoming. His favorite hobby is to remind me that I'm nothing but a burden. It's gotten worse over time. And I have very little recourse except he hates when I call him Hen. I couldn't say Henry when I was very small. I would use that nickname and he loathes being equated to a chicken. No sense of humor at all, really."

"His confidence isn't great."

"No. I imagine not." She poked at her plate. "I believe he has always been scared. Of what? I'm not sure. Perhaps the whole world. And how he chooses to mask it is by being terrible. I'd pity him if I were a better person."

"You *are* the better person. The best person." He gestured at her lunch. "It looks as if you are finished. I'd ask if you'd like a walk, but the rain is really coming down out there."

She glanced at the window with a longing expression. "Honestly? A walk in the rain sounds lovely. Impractical but lovely."

"I'm not going to melt, Pocket Rocket. If you want to go out and sing in the rain, I'll keep you company," Tuck said.

"Sing in the rain?" Lizzy made a face. "You are a strange one."

She'd put her hand back on the table. This time he didn't hesitate to take it and give a gentle squeeze. "Takes one to know one. So before we go and disappoint your entire family, want to have a little fun?"

His fingertips traced her skin. Lizzy's eyes widened at the unexpected touch, but they quickly melted into a playful glint. "Very well, let's embark on some more bad decisions."

CHAPTER EIGHTEEN

The rain showed no signs of relenting, but Lizzy refused to yield to the elements. She pressed onward, her arms swinging with purpose as rivulets of water streamed down the back of her neck and into her dress. At her side, Tuck's long strides easily kept the pace, his measured steps falling in time with her hurried ones. She didn't have the faintest notion of where she was going—she simply needed to move, to escape the weight of expectations that pressed down around her. Soon they were off any path and making their way through one of the many sheep paddocks on the outskirts of town.

"Henry had no business going to the Woodlands to spy on me," she seethed, half to Tuck and half to herself. "He may spin a tale about urgently needing to attend to business in Portsmouth, but in reality, his true motive was to discover me in some compromised position. He hopes to use this as another wedge to ingratiate himself to our stepfather and leave me on the edge. It's not fair and it's not right, but Hen has done this my entire life. He always schemes to position himself in a favorable manner that places me at a disadvantage. When we were children, my brother would constantly remind me how difficult it was for him to study subjects like numbers, history, divinity, Latin, and so forth. He'd say it was a good thing that I wasn't a boy, because I could never do it and be successful. Mother and Papa, and then our stepfather, highly valued his education even if he didn't demonstrate more than average aptitude. They expected me to defer to him as some type of genius.

"Of course, I don't want to give the impression that I was not afforded any opportunity. Their expectation for me was to be accomplished. This means my value was connected to how I could embroider, converse in French, play the pianoforte, paint with watercolors, and exude whatever spell bewitches a man. Unfortunately, I would have probably done better at school. Instead, I limped along a failure."

"That's not true."

Lizzy looked up at Tuck, her hand on her forehead as if it could shield her from the deluge. Maybe he hadn't heard her correctly, as the rain was making a great sound on the field stones. "I don't indulge in false modesty, sir. If I say I'm not skilled in an area, I am not skilled in it—"

Before she could protest, he swept her off her feet and began walking. As her back met the trunk of a weeping willow, she gasped out, "What are you doing?" The dipping, downturned branches formed a small shelter around them, like an enchanted fairy ring.

Tuck braced her against the tree and stood between her legs, his big hands gripping her bottom as he looked down at her, a muscle feathering in the place where his jaw met his temple.

"You're so smart, Lizzy," he growled. "But sometimes you're so smart that it also makes you a little stupid." She shivered as he dipped his head, his breath warm against her throat. "Trust me, you have no problem bewitching a man."

Her hands, which had been pushing against his shoulders,

did a sudden reversal, even without conscious thought; she was now gripping him, driving him closer.

"All I can think about is doing this to you," he rasped, skimming his tongue along the curve of her neck before drawing the skin between his teeth for a soft nip. "This and nothing else."

His low grunt sent a shock of pleasure coursing between her thighs in hot prickling dots.

He gripped her more thoroughly and jutted into her again with a slow rock, rolling his hips with enough pressure to make her insides warm.

"Want you." He rocked again. "I fucking love that you don't have anything on under this dress. Just you." His hips canted. More pressure against that small aching spot she'd recently discovered in the inn. Then, her attention to it had been gentle, curious, and grew into a frenzy. This methodical grind scoured away her inhibitions and exposed something new, vulnerable, and intoxicating.

"All I do is want you. I'm your husband, Lizzy. And I'm at your mercy. So don't tell me what you can't do. Tell me what you want, right now, because I'll give it to you."

"Release." Where did that half sob tear from? "Don't let me think anymore."

He hiked her skirts to her waist, nudged her legs apart.

"Open for me," he ordered. And God help her, she did. Was he going to make her his wife in truth here against a willow on the edge of an out-of-the-way Gretna Green sheep paddock?

But he wasn't removing his breeches; he sank to his knees in the wet grass. Using his thumbs, he gently parted her cleft and looked directly into her center.

"Tuck." In some vaguely sensible corner of her mind, she knew that she should ask him to stop, that she shouldn't be doing such wicked things anywhere, let alone outdoors, but she'd promised not to lie. And in this cocooned world of stooped green branches, stopping was the very last thing that she wanted.

"Look at this goddamn perfect pink. Fuck, I can see your slick right there in the slit. You're so wet. Is that all for me?"

Their gazes locked. Despite the cold rain, she burned.

She didn't know why he kneeled or looked at her like a man starving. "What do you want?" Her question was a half whisper, half plea.

"To taste you." He nodded at her exposed center that he still held open. "Can I?"

"D-do people really do such things? It's not just in books?"

"If they see a pussy like yours? They'd beg to. Do you want me to beg, Lizzy?"

Someday she might want exactly that. But at this moment, she wanted . . .

She just wanted.

"Do it. Please."

He pressed his mouth to her center, and everything fractured. Her scalp tingled and she was delirious, fighting and losing the battle to keep herself upright. His mouth demanded release, rolling over the sensitive bud, and when he groaned, the sound vibrated to her very core.

She was warm. So warm. Too warm. But she didn't care. If she was going to burn, she wanted to ignite. Her thighs tensed. Quivering.

When he eased a finger inside, she gasped at the unexpected fullness. He pulled back and stared, his lips shiny from her want.

"Is this too much?" His voice was hoarse.

"More," she choked out. Somewhere above, or in another world, thunder rumbled.

He curled his finger inside her, and the tension built; her knees threatened to buckle again at the deep fullness, and when he did the beckoning gesture again, her body obeyed. He kept coaxing, and shivers increased until he gave her a slow, hard suck and pushed his tongue deep inside.

Time stopped.

A surge of pure sensation set her free. It pounded and pounded and pounded like a wave, but she wasn't drowning. It was as if she were flying.

Tuck stood and was holding her face between his big hands. "Lizzy? Lizzy, are you okay?"

The flames within her still burned. She wanted to kiss the palms of his hands and then both of his eyes. But instead, she simply stared at his concerned face, then rested a hand on her forehead. "Hello there."

"Jesus." He lowered her arm and repeated her gesture. "You're warm."

She bobbed her head, her thoughts as vague as a dream at dawn. "You set me alight."

"No, Lizzy." Worry had eclipsed the desire in his gaze. "I'm serious. I think you've spiked a fever."

The next thing she knew, she found herself in the bed at the inn, though the details were fuzzy. She vaguely recalled Tuck carrying her on his back. Her memories were like half-formed pictures, with him removing her shoes and arranging pillows. However, amidst it all, she kept imagining a talking raven at the window, leaving her in a state of mind that hardly suggested reliability.

She slept in fits and starts, and occasionally there was low talking. Tuck. Henry. Once a man she didn't recognize who lay a warm fabric over her chest—a poultice. The heavy smell of mustard made her nauseous but her head ached too much to move. A cup was held to her lips. She swallowed, coughing when it wasn't water. It was white wine, which did little to mask a bitter flavor—willow bark. She recognized the taste from Mamma's small medicinal cabinet, the tinctures and salves she could make if a doctor didn't need to be called.

Sleep hit hard and fast after. When she woke again, the sun was still shining, but she felt like she'd lost time.

Rubbing her eyes, she pushed herself up on her elbows. Tuck was leaning back in a chair at the side of her bed, staring into space. His hair wasn't long enough to be disheveled, but he was pale, his eyes puffy from lack of sleep and framed by violet half-circles.

"You look about as bad as I felt," she said, wincing when her voice came out with an unfamiliar deep huskiness.

The chair slammed down with a thud. Before Lizzy could clear her throat, Tuck was leaning over her, hands bracketing either side of her face.

"You're awake."

She yawned. "Yes. I believe my little nap helped. I feel much better."

"Little nap?" Tuck narrowed his eyes, searching her face. "You slept twenty-four hours. If you weren't awake in the next five minutes, I . . . I didn't know what I'd do." He pushed off the bed and bent over, hands splayed on his knees. "I didn't know, Lizzy. I didn't have a plan."

"You don't sound yourself." She stretched. Her body felt warm and relaxed. Besides being a little hungry, she was fine.

"Because I was fucking terrified. I am still fucking terrified.

You spiked a fever so fast. By the time I got you back to the inn, you were barely making sense. I tried to get a doctor, but he was out delivering a baby, so they sent me an apot—an apoto—"

"An apothecary?"

"Yeah. Whatever the hell that is."

She settled back on her pillow, puzzled. "How do you get medicines in your time?"

"The pharmacy—a place where a pharmacist dispenses medicines."

"Sounds like an apothecary. It's quite common for them to pay house calls. It happens to me from time to time when I have one of these spells."

"Your brother said you're susceptible to fevers."

"Yes. During times of stress or great excitement it's not uncommon for me to become feverish for a day. Strange, isn't it? And how did you end up speaking to Henry?"

"I fetched him because I wasn't sure how sick you were."

"Did you think you were at my deathbed?"

His throat worked as he swallowed. "You got sick so fast. I didn't have any way to check your temperature. I couldn't get you pain relievers or fever reducers down at a grocery store; I felt useless as hell. Then I found the apothecary and the first thing Henry wanted him to do was to cut your arm open."

"Henry swears by bloodletting. I'm not as convinced that—"

"I let them know that if anyone cuts my wife under the pretense of healing her, then they would be the ones bleeding." His voice was fierce and protective.

"Tuck." She reached out a hand.

He stared intently at it, his jaw clenched in determination as he reached into his pocket and carefully retrieved their wedding rings. With a sense of solemnity, he pushed hers on in a simple gesture. Then he slid his own into place, sealing their union.

"What on earth?" She blinked at the ring, dazed. Though the physical weight was light, the moment felt heavy with consequence.

They were truly married.

"I feel better having you wear it," he continued. "I couldn't help much when you were sick. When I was first told I had cancer? It sucked. But I had a team of medical professionals. If you get sick here? You get some guy who shows up and wants to bleed your arm into a bowl. What the fuck?"

"Tuck," she repeated. "Wearing the rings . . . What does it mean?"

She wanted him to make sense of this moment. He had a remarkable way of distilling things down to the core of the matter, and right now she could use a little of his forthrightness.

"It feels stupid, but maybe it can help protect you. I don't know. I hate that I've been so useless."

Frustration flared. "What if you stopped making this situation about you and listened to the person who was actually sick and has things to say?"

That certainly caught his notice.

"You're right." He dragged the chair back and took her hand between his. "How are you feeling?"

"I'll live to annoy you another day."

"You don't annoy me. Even if you do, I like it, which defeats the purpose."

"I remember the smell of mustard."

"When I wouldn't let them bleed you, he said he would apply a poultice. All it looked like was a smelly cloth."

"It would help keep the infection from my lungs."

"Then he gave you a drink with some kind of bark and laud-a-mon?" He winced. "It felt like I was in some sort of *Harry Potter* outtake watching someone make potions, when magic isn't real."

Who knew what he was rambling about half the time, but she did realize what the apothecarist had given her and why she had slept so deep and long.

"Bark? That would be willow bark. It brings down fevers. And laudanum is to help bring sleep for rest and healing."

"Never heard of it."

"It's also called opium."

His eyes widened. "The doctor gave you opium?"

"It's very common. I hear friends in London swear that rubbing laudanum on their baby's gums helps them rest."

"It's amazing humans keep surviving."

"All right, Mr. Everything-Is-Better-in-the-Future. We make do here, and clearly must get plenty of it right for so many of you to have made it."

He looked abashed. "Are you really going to be okay?"

She squeezed his hand. "Yes. This happens, like I said. I was so distracted that I forgot to prepare or think of it. But eloping and Henry appearing. Also preparing to announce the news to my parents. I should have expected my body would react."

"And you are sure it's not how . . ." He looked away. "Nah. Forget it. I'm being stupid."

"You aren't at fault here." She kept the amusement from her voice. He'd think she was making fun of him, but it was nothing close to that. She found his anxiety that their intimacy might have harmed her rather endearing.

"What you did to me beneath that tree? It burned, yes. But in a different way. And if we do it again, I wouldn't take laudanum—I'd want to feel every single thing your mouth does."

He patted her hand, gaze averted.

"Look at me," she said. He turned slowly, his face a mask. "You didn't hurt me. You aren't to blame."

"I'm to blame because I'm taking you to your parents' house, and I know they will hurt you there. Henry keeps reminding me of this."

"I've long become accustomed to the fact that my wishes and my family's wishes have not been aligned. It shall be unpleasant. But my life without you? That would be far worse."

His gaze locked with hers, still unreadable.

"We are helping each other. We've become friends, haven't we?" Even as she spoke the words, they tasted wrong. This wasn't a lie—they were friends. It was just avoiding all the other words they were or might be, words that were more confusing and complicated and better left in the ether.

"Friends." His voice held the same careful, neutral tone. "Who need each other to achieve our goals."

"Precisely."

Why was he still staring like that? And why was she? It was like playing one of those silly parlor games where you wait to see who will blink first. It wouldn't be her. She wasn't going to add to his worries about returning to his home by demanding his attachment like a spoiled child.

There was an undeniable spark between them, but like a flame, their connection needed tending to grow. If she didn't actively pursue it, their bond could remain as it was—a small glowing ember, safe and contained. Nothing dangerous. No one would be burned by the heat.

They would not play with fire.

CHAPTER NINETEEN

The carriage clattered against the cobblestones as they entered London's city limits. When Tuck had flown over, he'd landed in Heathrow but hadn't lingered. His priority had been to see Nora, so he'd ignored all the advertisements for the palaces, West End shows, torture museums, and double-decker bus tours and jumped on a quick commuter to Bath. Now, almost a week after leaving Scotland, the sheer magnitude of the city, even in this time, sank in as they traversed the busy streets. It far eclipsed the towns and quaint villages they had passed on their long journey back from Gretna Green.

Night crept in, and lamps flickered, casting a glow down twisted lanes. The scene brought back memories of the labyrinth from Nora's old picture book of Greek myths—the one with the Minotaur art that gave him bad dreams, even when he was the older brother pretending not to care. The air was thick with the smell of decaying wood and mud.

"That's the Thames," Lizzy mentioned casually, as he coughed into his fist. "The river's not particularly close, but when the wind blows from the south during the summer, you can enjoy that distinctive blend of brine and fish all over town."

"Good to be home?" he inquired.

"London's complicated." She glanced out the carriage window, fidgeting with the pearl button fastening her glove. "The city's never felt like a place where I belong. And the atmosphere in my stepfather's townhouse—well, let's just say it is nothing like the Woodlands."

When she turned back to Tuck, her tight smile didn't come close to reaching her eyes. "But," she reiterated for the third time in the past hour, "all shall be well. I'm not the least bit troubled."

Tuck studied her like he was gauging the morale of a teammate. Lizzy's flushed cheeks and distant expression hinted at a different truth, as if she were gearing up for a high-stakes game.

Henry had ridden ahead from Gretna Green, the little weasel practically vibrating with excitement to be the bearer of bad news. Although Henry's three brain cells failed to perceive it as such, his early departure served a purpose. By leaving a few days before them, he gave Lizzy time to gather her strength for the impending confrontation. Henry had cheerfully insinuated it didn't matter, as she'd just be arriving for her funeral. But having him break the news was a hell of a lot better for her than showing up unannounced with a new husband and saying, "Surprise, surprise." This way, her parents would have a head start on processing the event.

"Tell me about the part of the city that you live in," he said, to keep her talking.

"Mayfair." Her voice was high, strained. "We've now passed Wembley and Notting Hill, and are into Marylebone. This is where I was raised."

"You've mentioned your family is well-off?"

"Though we're more fortunate than many, it's not sufficient enough for their ambition. While we now reside in Mayfair, it's not within the most prestigious enclave, like Grosvenor Square.

That's why you can see my purpose in this world is to secure an attachment to a gentleman from such a quarter to aid our climb. Wit, humor, kindness—basic decency. All those traits in a partner are negotiable if the address is right. Mayfair, you see, is not merely a neighborhood; it's a ladder we're all required to climb. The option of avoiding marriage and preserving my independence has never been truly viable."

"I'm sorry," Tuck said sincerely. "We should all have the right to choose our own paths in life. When you were talking just then, it made me think how marriage is no longer the measure of a woman's worth in my time. Except . . ."

"Yes?" Lizzy leaned in, curious. "What is it?"

"I went to a wedding before coming out here to England. It was for a teammate—Jason Burns. The bride wore a traditional white dress, which I guess symbolizes purity. Everyone kept going on about how thin she looked. Her father 'gave her away,' and she took her fiancé's last name. To conclude the ceremony, the minister, also a man, granted the groom permission to kiss the bride. Even with all of this, they called it 'her day.'" Rubbing his forehead, Tuck confessed, "It's pretty strange when you really think about it."

Lizzy nodded thoughtfully. "It's hard to notice pitfalls when you hold the advantage. But to think that even hundreds of years in the future, so much remains the same? How utterly wearying."

The carriage slowed. Lizzy shook her head as if refocusing her thoughts. "What are your parents like?"

Tuck frowned, memories of a less-than-perfect family surfacing. "My dad always worked; he's an air-traffic controller and, uh, well, explaining the finer points of that job would be complicated. Suffice it to say that he is rigid, detail-oriented, and life-or-death decisions are part of his job. Everything has to be by the book, and if anyone in my family wanted to go in a different direction . . . he didn't always take to it easily or kindly."

The carriage stopped. He didn't have time to explain about Nora or why his little sister had wanted to get so far away that she left the whole damn country. Because one lesson he'd taken to heart from Dad was to triage and focus on the biggest problem first.

Right now? That was Lizzy's family.

He climbed out of the carriage and peered up at the four-story townhouse with its rows of symmetrical windows and pale stucco exterior. The double doors were carved with wooden rosettes and framed by simple Greek columns. The vibe was very much "Don't touch anything with your filthy fingers, peasant."

A curtain twitched on the second floor.

"I'm sorry in advance," Lizzy said, reaching out to take his hand.

"What for? If your family is weird, that's not on you."

"But I'm sorry nevertheless." She squeezed his fingers and then, as she tried to withdraw, he held on.

"We go in together," Tuck asserted. "As a united front, no matter what happens. In hockey, there's a saying—speed is hard to defend. If we work together, they won't know what hit them."

A footman opened the door and bowed to Lizzy. "Welcome home, miss," he said, before correcting himself. "My apologies, *Mrs.* Taylor. Right this way."

Lizzy nodded her greeting and they strode inside. Their footsteps echoed on the polished marble of the grand entrance hall as they passed a sweeping staircase. They walked by a room with overstuffed armchairs and sofas gathered under ornate chandeliers, which cast a warm glow on gilded mirrors and silk-draped windows. They passed a formal dining room, and then a library.

All the decorative touches added elegance, but the atmosphere remained impersonal, like a model home, or even a museum—no personal items anywhere.

They paused before closed doors. "They await you in the drawing room," the footman said, his tone carrying a hint of pity.

"Thank you, John," Lizzy replied solemnly.

"And congratulations, miss. I mean, missus." With a conspiratorial wink, he retreated down the wide hall.

"Ready to face the music?" Tuck asked.

Lizzy made a face. "Maybe we could slip down the servants' stairs and ride back north? I hear summers in the highlands are so warm you can sometimes remove your coat for a whole hour."

He brushed his thumb over her ring. "I've got your back. I'm here every step."

"Elizabeth," a deep, unfamiliar male voice boomed. "Enter, if you please."

Tuck had imagined a firing squad, the parents and brother standing in the middle of the room ready to take aim. Instead, they casually lounged on various fancy furniture.

"That's him, Father." Henry waved in Tuck's general direction. "That's the American."

"Sir." Tuck stepped forward, hand out. "Tucker Taylor, pleased to meet you."

Lizzy's stepfather gazed at his extended hand but refrained from accepting it. Instead, he meticulously folded the *Evening Ledger* newspaper, resting it against his potbelly before crossing his arms.

"Mr. Alby!" Horror flashed in Lizzy's tone. "You can't mean to snub—"

"I was a naval officer during the American War. I saw action in the Battle of Long Island. The siege at Kip's Bay. Nasty business. Nearly lost my leg. Good men lost their lives. I was twenty years old. I'd never been out of England, let alone across the Atlantic. And for what? Loyalty betrayed by colonists who decided that the king and the rule of law no longer applied to them. We beat back your general on the shores of New York, that Washington who became your president." His voice was thick with contempt.

Cool.

The problem was that Tuck only had the barest grasp of the Revolutionary War. Of course, he knew about George Washington. But specific battles? Nope. Not a one. Paul Revere rode around saying "The redcoats are coming!" in Massachusetts. That's all he had.

Shit. Why hadn't he taken Nora up on her offer to go see *Hamilton* when she'd invited him to fly to New York to see it on Broadway? That would have been the CliffsNotes version at least.

The man had deep-set heavy-lidded eyes, a red nose, and spidery red veins in his round cheeks. He might not be one of the most powerful men beyond these walls, but in this house, he was the king. How to play it? Tuck wasn't going to make peace or earn respect by rolling over and submitting. But if he picked a fight, he'd just be giving this dude a reason to let his temper unleash.

Better to be unpredictable.

"I don't know much about the war, sir. It was over before I was born."

"Your history doesn't matter to you?" Mr. Alby's voice was calm, but Tuck noticed his jaw tighten a little.

"I prefer to be more future-looking."

So far, so good. And also, true.

But an awkward stillness filled the air, carrying a weight that felt like anger.

"A future that you decided to rob our Elizabeth of securing. A future that you claimed even though you have no right. A future that will be darkened forever because my stepdaughter, a Wood-dash, no less, has been prevented from securing a marriage with a member of one of the families we had envisioned."

"Sir, I haven't gone to war, and I'm not looking to start one here in your home. I understand that our elopement to Scotland must have not been what you imagined for your stepdaughter's future. But Lizzy made a choice. It was different from what you would have chosen for her. But it's done. And I'm here. And I'm not going to ruin her, or be a nuisance to you and your wife. I'm not even going to ask you to give me a chance. But I will work harder than any other man and I'm not going to quit until she has everything she wants."

"Rufus, my darling dove—" Lizzy's mother deployed one of those sugar-dipped voices that she probably believed was calming but in reality was about as soothing as a needle in a balloon factory. "Do exercise prudence. Provoking your temper will only be at a detriment to the well-being of your tender heart."

Tuck resisted the urge to scoff. That dude was less dove and more deranged dictator. But then he caught the subtle glance that mother and daughter exchanged. Maybe this was also part of the game.

"Mr. Alby. Mother. Hen . . . ry." Lizzy stepped in. "You might have fallen asleep at night with dreams of little old me marrying into a great family in Grosvenor Square. Except no one ever wanted me there, and I didn't want them. But I want this man. I need him and he needs me. We are married and it's legal and binding and the best choice is the simplest—accept it."

"But what's next?" Lizzy's mother stood, wringing her hands. "Shall you abscond to the colonies? Oh, Lizzy, what will Lavina Throckmorton have to say about such a libertine lark? The very thought makes my head ache." Lizzy's mother whirled to address Tucker directly. "And will my precious progeny reside above a Baltimorian mercantile shop?"

Tuck cleared his throat. So far telling the truth had seen him in good stead. "What matters is that I am here to support your daughter, not be supported *by* her. So instead of debating what doesn't matter, why don't we all agree on what does. Your daughter is extraordinary. And I'm very grateful that I found her when I did." His lips pressed together firmly, the hard thump of his heart thrumming in his ears. The gravity of his words lingered in the air, and there was no denying it—he knew he'd meant every word.

The trouble was, he had no idea what to do about it.

CHAPTER TWENTY

Lancelot had embarked on a quest for the Holy Grail to elevate himself in the eyes of Guinevere. Romeo had scaled Juliet's balcony despite her relatives wanting him dead. Tristan had evaded the gallows to rescue Isolde from a leper colony. Tucker Taylor? He stood in front of her family and declared that she, Lizzy—the underloved, overlooked daughter—was extraordinary.

Extraordinary.

She's been called other words: wallflower, bluestocking, spinster, ape leader? Yes.

An obligation? Unnatural? On the shelf? Of course.

But here, in front of her family, a man—her *husband*—had stood and declared for her.

Who was he? With every other eligible man she had ever met, she'd instantly known that she wouldn't want to spend her entire life with them. But Tuck Taylor had ended this record with a single word.

She steadied her stance, locking her legs to prevent any sign of weakness. No, she wouldn't entertain the notion of a wobble. With chin held high, she maintained her composure and preserved her dignity.

And it wasn't for the benefit of her family; it was for herself. She refused to shed tears in Tuck's presence, unwilling to reveal a vulnerability that suggested she could be swayed by a kind word acknowledging her inherent worth. The prospect was mortifying. For so long, she had crafted a narrative of her own value, apart from others' judgment. Along the way, she had either forgotten or ceased to believe that someone else could genuinely see her as deserving of love, not merely as an accessory for securing a dowry, supporting aging parents, or managing a household.

"We've had a long journey," she remarked, inwardly relieved that her voice maintained its steadiness. "I suggest we retire upstairs to freshen up. It would also provide the added benefit of allowing you all to indulge in gossip and conjecture without the burden of our observation."

Nodding to Tuck, she took his wrist and led him out the door. Together, they had achieved a rare coup, an occurrence so infrequent that she couldn't recall experiencing it in living memory.

Her family was stunned into silence.

She didn't allow her lips to curl until they entered her childhood bedchamber on the third floor.

"You seemed to enjoy that," he remarked as the door shut.

"Au contraire, I enjoyed *you*. You were very nice to me down there. That was a tough audience and you were brave."

"I don't believe in being nice. I prefer kind."

"Aren't they both very much the same in meaning?"

"Nah, not as much as you might think. Folks often toss around *nice* and *kind* like they're similar, but let me break it down for you. *Nice* is when you're coming from a place that is all about pleasing others, trying to be likable, doing the crowd-pleaser thing. It's self-centered, all about you. Now, *kind* is a different story altogether. It's about putting others first. *Nice* is trying to act in a certain way to get something. What do I want to get from your family? You are the only thing I care about here."

It wasn't a declaration. She knew that. He needed her just like she needed him. This wasn't a fairy tale with a happily-ever-after, and yet it wasn't nothing. Why couldn't a few stolen moments of happy-for-now be enough? It was more than many ever got.

"Kiss me?" Before he could do more than arch his brows in surprise, she added, "For kindness, of course. Also, because you are my husband for the moment. And we are alone. And you are a skilled kisser and right now I could use some skilled kissing to drive out my other thoughts."

His gaze darkened. "You asked for it."

He approached, and she instinctively lifted her chin, readying herself for the sensation of his lips on hers. But instead, he grasped her shoulders and turned her around to face her dressing table mirror, pressing her back against his firm chest.

"Look." His voice was warm against her ear. "I want you to look at that person right there—I didn't say anything that wasn't true downstairs. In fact, I held back.

"*Extraordinary* is a weak word when you're fire." He flicked his tongue under her earlobe before taking it between his front teeth and slowly pulling down until it released.

Her gasp hitched in her throat, morphing into a soft moan. Their eyes locked in the mirror's reflection, revealing a wild intensity in hers, highlighted by the vibrant flush on her cheeks and the rhythmic heave of her chest.

"I don't believe for one fucking second that your family doesn't see it." He blew gently on her wet skin, bracing her waist when her knees trembled from the tingly sensation. "They know. And they fear that if you're unleashed, you'll be able to do anything you want and do it well. That terrifies them. Nothing scares the mediocre like watching someone step into their power. But to me? It's sexy as hell."

She turned to ask what he meant, but he wasn't in the mood for conversation. At least not any that could be had with mere words. His lips met hers like a question—and *she* wasn't in the mood for teasing or games. She reached up, drawing him down to her, and gave him her answer. Yes. Yes. God help her, yes.

The kiss started gently, cautiously, but gentleness wasn't what she craved, not now, not after this evening. She clenched her fists in his shirt, tugging him closer. She sensed a tide pulling at them. His hunger had an intensity that made her clutch onto him as the only stable truth in a volatile world. His insistent mouth parted her lips, sending thrilling tremors along her nerves. A soft groan escaped him, low in his throat, and then his tongue slipped inside her mouth. Nothing was gentle. But she felt safe.

Her fingers ran over his short, coarse-cropped hair, reaching the back of his head and drawing him nearer. He was her husband, but that fact wasn't what made this feel so good. It was that he was hers. In a way that she couldn't explain. That she couldn't admit except when they were body to body, in this give-and-take that didn't allow for half-truths or secrets. She could either embrace desire or reject it, but not both.

"I love the way you taste," he grated.

"Tuck," she whimpered.

"That's right, darlin'. Moan my name," he breathed into her mouth. "And while I love these lips, there's somewhere else I can't stop thinking about kissing, how you tasted against that tree. I want my mouth there again."

He braced her lower back against his hand and sank down, bringing her with him until they were on the thick carpet of her floor. He'd likened her to fire, and right now every inch of her skin blazed. He couldn't draw her any closer, yet she had to have more, needed to feel every part of him. She wished he could witness her blood coursing through her veins, the chaotic turbulence he'd ignited within her body.

She wanted to discover what else he was capable of. A hairpin slipped loose, releasing a cascade of curls. Her skirts were hiked up past her knees, but she paid that no mind. In that fleeting moment, nothing else in the world mattered except the weight of Tuck pressing down on her, the roughness of his jaw grazing against her cheek. It was exhilarating, yet not enough. She craved more. Each kiss felt like a beginning and an end, and she clung to every fleeting moment like a dragon hoarding its treasure.

He broke away, his hands braced on the floor on either side of her head. "I'm sorry," he ground out, eyes closed. "I shouldn't have— I can't have you on your bedroom floor for your first time."

"It's all right." She licked her lips. They were so swollen. "I suppose it's my fault."

His lids flew open and he stared at her with confusion. "It isn't. Not at all."

"Oh, but I'm afraid it is." Her mouth crooked in the corner. "Because I'm so extraordinary. How are you meant to help yourself?"

This time, he didn't groan from hunger, but annoyed amusement. "Goddamn. How are you this good?" He nipped her neck.

She gasped. "I've always been a quick study."

He hummed his assent, deep in the back of his throat. "Gifted and talented, baby."

There came a knock at the door.

They exchanged a surprised glance, eyes wide.

Lizzy cleared her throat. "Who is it?"

"Your dearest mother." Mamma's voice had lost the earlier sweetness from the drawing room; it was sharp now. All business.

Hell's bells. Just because Lizzy was a married woman didn't mean she should roll about on her bedroom floor the moment the door clicked shut. Had she lost her wits? She glanced in the mirror, attempting to tidy her loose hair, but it was futile. Her eyes appeared glazed, her lower lip slightly swollen, and her complexion flushed.

She grabbed a handkerchief off her desk, and gave Tuck a glare that meant she was deadly serious. "Follow my lead," she whispered. "And play along."

She walked to her door and took a shuddering breath as she opened it.

"Y-yes," she whispered, pretending to dab her eyes. Better to look like she'd been up here devastated and getting some small comfort from Tuck as a reason for her dishevelment, and not that she had almost given up her maidenhead on the rug.

"Compose yourself, my dear," Mamma admonished as she strode into the room. "You know better than anyone how Mr. Alby is—especially when it comes to the Americans. What, pray tell, did you expect from him?"

"I—I'm sorry for upsetting you." Lizzy blew her nose for good measure.

Tuck watched the show with barely disguised confusion.

"Upset me?" Her mother's laughter rang out, genuine. "Oh, my dear, I truly didn't think this day would ever arrive. Do you have any notion of the countless sleepless nights I've endured, pondering your future? Each of these lines"—Mamma gestured to the creases beside her eyes—"is a testament to you. And as for my gray hairs, don't get me started. But now, my dear, you are married. It may be unconventional, but such matters can be rectified with good manners. Cousin Georgie wrote about your dowry. And the Crawfords' ball is in a few days' time. Good news is all around!"

"You can't be serious." Lizzy dropped her hands to her sides—too surprised to keep up the fake-crying ruse. "We can't attend that."

"You not only can, you will. I have had a dress made for you in your absence and I'm confident Henry will be able to outfit Mr. Taylor."

"Mamma, come. Be reasonable. A ball at the Crawfords'? That's the lion's den for the ton."

"Then you better be ready to roar, my darling little lioness." Mamma's smile was tight but deadly. "Because we have one chance to do this right. You were in the south on holiday when you fell madly in love with this . . . this American man of business and married in a whirlwind romance. Of course, we are all in raptures, and Mr. Taylor is very respectable in his trade. What is your line of work again, sir?"

"Dry goods. I'm here expanding trade contacts in teas and ceramics," Tuck said by rote.

Lizzy smashed her lips to prevent a smile. Jane and Georgie would approve.

"Ah. Yes. Very well then." Mamma's eyes glazed and she gave her head a small shake, refocusing. "While the circumstances may not be entirely ideal, there is no denying that a fortuitous path opened for us. Oh, Lizzy, marriage. It shall grant you the privilege of knowing your place in society is secure. That is what truly matters for a woman, my dear. Why, you might even have the unparalleled bliss of cradling a son in your arms one day, and my, there is no joy in this world quite like having your own little boy."

"I can't begin to imagine," Lizzy rejoined crisply. Mamma

loved rhapsodizing over the pleasure of mothering sons as if she'd never had a daughter.

"And remember," Mamma continued, "a lady's proficiency in household management is how she achieves her significance, as does preserving our family's position."

But Lizzy couldn't afford to waste time attending balls. They needed to start collecting clues—anything that might help Tuck find a way back home. The more days they frittered away, the greater the risk of arousing suspicion. Others might come with ties to trade and America, especially from near Baltimore, or someone might try to question Tuck about the latest war activity, only to discover his implausible ignorance. Someone might even start whispering "imposter" or, more dangerous, "spy."

She'd have to get him back home, fake his death, and move on. "Mamma, I don't want to—"

"Attending the Crawfords' ball is not just a nicety, but your duty as my daughter. Society will be eager to catch a glimpse of the newly wed Mrs. Taylor, and your absence would undoubtedly raise eyebrows. You know how Lavinia Throckmorton, Araminta Wentworth, Millicent Harrington, and the others are—they'd love nothing better than to sink their teeth into another piece of gossip. It's crucial to present a gracious and charming presence at the ball to dispel any rumors that may begin circulating about the gentleman's background and the haste of the wedding. We wouldn't want anyone to question your marital bliss now, would we? Not when I worked ever so hard to remarry a man like Mr. Alby to keep us all in comfort and ensure we will be able to continue dear Henry's climb."

"Of course not." Lizzy was tempted to bare her teeth, hiss like a cornered alley cat. "I can think of little more that I'd rather do than please you."

Mamma's smile was small, but her eyes were tired. She'd battled for their position in society as long as Lizzy could remember. "What a stroke of luck that your greatest joy is in perfect harmony with my wishes." With that, Mamma swept from the room, leaving the scent of orange blossoms wafting in her wake.

"What am I missing?" Tuck muttered after the door closed. "I mean, I don't know all the cool waltzes, but I'm confident I can get you around a room without crushing your toes. I'm quick on my feet. What's the problem here? And don't you dare try to say it's related to you not being good enough in some way, because—"

"It's not, thank you very much," she said, bristling. "But some fights are my fights, not yours, and I want the space and trust to fight them."

"And you are welcome to it." Tuck threw up his hands. "But I still don't know why you are so against—"

"First, not one person in my family has expressed curiosity about my happiness. The entire focus is on their reputations. As long as Mr. Alby can view me as civil, obedient, and passably sweet, he can continue to view me with contempt. And Mamma, I know she loves me, but she's always loved my brother more." Lizzy's admission cost her something, a toll she would be able to review once Tuck was gone and all the accounts came due. "Second, it's a risk to you. You don't know the ton."

"I don't have a clue what you are talking about. A ton of what?"

"Not what—who. It's French. *Le bon ton* signifies good manners and etiquette and consists of royals, aristocrats, and the wealthiest, best-connected members of the upper classes. Imagine fashion leaders."

"Like celebrities and influencers," he mused.

"They do have great influence," she agreed. "The ton possesses its own codes, hierarchies, and an exclusive membership, emphasizing a sense of belonging, and loyalty."

"I think I get it, sort of."

"Our family isn't at the top of the order there. No titles among us. The prince doesn't know I exist. So, the knives shouldn't be extra sharp. We are more in the middle. My stepfather made a fortune in shipping wine after his time in the navy. People drink in good times and in bad, I used to hear him say. He had hoped I could land a baronet. They come with a hereditary title that can be passed to sons. Mr. Alby wished to leave this world having secured the right for his lineage to be addressed as *sir*."

"I can't help him, but if you want to call me *sir* behind closed doors, I'm not going to say no."

"There is no time for fun and games." She began to pace, needing to expend some of the energy bottled within her. "The moment you've been introduced to the ton, the clock will start ticking. It's a matter of time before you draw suspicion—it won't be through any fault, there's just too many ways to make a mistake. No one will dream of you coming from the future, of course. But the last thing we need is to have anyone suspect you as fake. Given my country's tension with yours, that could lead to dangerous consequences. I'm not willing to risk your safety, or mine, for that matter. Our best chances are to be as little noticed as possible, but when you step into any room, people will notice. You're too much. The height. Your face. The build. And then the accent."

"What's wrong with my face?"

"Don't take this the wrong way, but it is possible to be too handsome. You do not have a look that will go unnoticed."

"I guess you'll have to protect me, then."

She scoffed. "And as for what just happened, the kissing and the rest of it."

"I know." His answer was clipped. "We need to stop. It's a distraction. What's happening is normal. We have been forced together by fate or chance and there is natural attraction. But while it's normal, I can do better."

Lizzy blinked. Her brain was saying *no* but her mouth couldn't form the words. She had been about to say "we need to wait until the house goes to bed," not "we need to stop this altogether."

"Can we request another room?" he asked. "This is a big home. I don't want to be an inconvenience, but my guess is there is space."

"You don't want to sleep with me?"

"This isn't the road to Gretna Green. We don't need one bed. That's skating on thin ice. We're going to be friends, not lovers. Right?"

"Correct." His logic made sense in her brain, even as her body demanded she reject common sense and return to the floor to tumble him in quick order.

"Friends shouldn't know what the other person's mouth tastes like." He crossed his arms. "Don't look at me like that."

"Like what?"

"I don't know. I can't read that expression. Ever since I was a kid it's been what I can do. Playing hockey. Focusing. Reading people. Put those skills together and I'm a natural goalie. But what you're thinking in that head right now, I can't figure it out."

For a smart man he was quite thick.

Her head was no mystery. It was a swamp of wanting, mixed with a thousand half sentences trying to find a way to ask him to kiss her again.

"I'm trying to be the good guy here." His voice was strained. "You don't deserve to have me pawing you until I leave."

She sighed inwardly. He hadn't done anything she hadn't wanted. And rather than simply ask her, here he was telling her how she felt. What she wanted. What she was allowed to have. The exhaustion of the last two weeks sank in, and she glanced at her bed. Sleep would help clear her head, and suddenly she wanted space.

She went to the wall and pulled a discreet cord.

After a moment, the door opened and a servant entered.

"Please take Mr. Taylor to the blue room. And ensure that he has a supper tray sent up." She gestured to his travel case. "I hope you sleep well."

Tuck's gaze was shuttered as he grabbed the leather bag. "And you too."

She shut her eyes as the door snicked shut. Listened to the small sounds of the house. The distant voices in the hall. The wind against the panes. The flicker of the candlewick in the lamp near her mirror. So many words were in her head, but maybe he was right. Silence could be a virtue when thoughts were better kept to themselves—not every wish deserved fulfillment, and not every inclination should be explored.

The emptiness of the room loomed, and she tossed her head, refusing to be beaten. She had been managing quite well on her own. And she would persist in doing so. Perfectly well.

Alone.

CHAPTER TWENTY-ONE

A stony-faced servant escorted Tuck to his chamber, also on the third floor but at the opposite end of the townhome—as far away from Lizzy as possible.

The spacious room had one of those gloomy, empty feelings, the way rooms get after hardly ever being used. From the shadows emerged a four-poster bed, its polished mahogany gleaming in the lamplight. Two large windows, draped in beige and indigo, overlooked the street. Everything else in the room that wasn't wood was navy—the thick rug, the lace doily on the table beside the bed, and even the ornate wallpaper. And the furniture, like the bed, from the desk to the wardrobe to the chairs, was all built from the same dark wood. No paintings. No personalization. Just deafening silence, as if it was only ever disturbed when maids entered to dust.

He ignored the bed altogether. For once, he sensed sleep wouldn't come easily. He hated to toss and turn and rubbing one out wasn't going to help—not now. Even though his stolen moments with Lizzy had left him turned on. Christ, if electricity had been invented, he could probably power half of London. But that wasn't the point—at least not the only one. He wanted her, but he wanted to hold her more, to feel her body folding into his, to enjoy what it was like to lie there and listen to her breathe.

So instead of spending the night in an empty bed with the absence of Lizzy, he dragged a chair to the window to stare out over the dark London streets and gather his thoughts.

When he'd had the accident back in Hallow's Gate, losing control of the car, trapped in that frigid water, lungs burning, unable to see a goddamn thing—his life had never flashed before his eyes. There'd never been a moment when some grand comfort enveloped him in peace.

There was only bewildered fear, and a determination that he wouldn't die, not like that.

He wasn't embarrassed to admit to panic. Fuck. He'd been under ice. It was the only logical emotion. Death had come so damn close before retreating in the jumble of darkness and indescribable noise, combined with a dizzy, nauseated loss of balance—up went down, left turned right. Before he could unscramble his brain, sunlight warmed his skin, cattails bobbed overhead, and an apple core smacked him in the face and his life changed.

In all that chaos, only Lizzy's big blue eyes had made any sense.

It wasn't that he accepted being in this world. But what was the option? To walk around every minute mumbling "I can't believe this happened, this is wild"? He was here now. And that meant he had to deal with life as it was, not as he wished it would be.

He wasn't meant to be in 1812, but under different circumstances, he might be meant for Lizzy. They had chemistry. He sensed they both wanted more.

Dust motes floated in the air, directionless. Stuck in the past with a wife he'd caught feelings for—genius-level decision-making. Looked like he was on his way to being the Einstein of cluster-fucks.

He stood and cracked his back. There was no one in this whole damn city able to shoot two pucks toward his head, a ritual he'd made Regals' forward Gale Knight perform before every game to silence his mind.

The only other way he knew to tamp down his thoughts was to sweat.

Not the same as a hundred-mile-an-hour rubber biscuit flying at your face, but it'd do.

He ripped off his shirt and started doing reps of single-leg, opposite-side reaches, slow and controlled to focus on balance and ankle stability. Then the half kneel to double jump. Coach always said "reload to explode." Gotta always have the power to be ready to make a second jump with the same leg. Squats. High reps for endurance. He groaned. These routines sucked, but he'd be glad he did them come a 5–3 power play in the third quarter. Because he'd play again. Because he'd get home. Jane had seemed sure of it. Lizzy believed. And they were both smarter than him. He had to trust the process.

Life had to return to normal eventually—to a world that made sense. In that world, his job was to soak up the electric charge of the crowd without getting overwhelmed and to keep an eye on game plays while maintaining a laser focus on the puck. If he ever let one in, he'd have to let it go, funneling all his energy into stopping the next one.

After busting out lunges, side planks, sit-ups, and push-ups, he was breathing hard, sheened in sweat.

Good. That was good.

This next game was a whole new challenge—a fancy ball. He

wiped his hand against his damp brow, catching his reflection in the mirror. "You're not exactly Prince Charming material," he muttered. Couldn't tell a waltz from a Texas two-step to save his life. A high school PE teacher had tried to teach him ballroom moves once, and it had been a disaster. He'd gotten a C, the only time he'd ever tanked a grade in that subject.

But tonight wasn't about stressing his nonexistent dance skills. It was making damn sure Lizzy didn't regret having him there. The twenty-first century might be light-years away, but he could still sharpen his mental game. Being around Lizzy Wooddash meant finding that delicate balance between being on high alert and staying cool. Just when he believed he'd nailed it, memories of how she tasted—sweet on her tongue, salt between her legs—would hit him like a freight train. This week's mission: master the art of being in her presence without getting lost in fantasies of peeling her down to her silk stockings.

The intense workout did the job, and he collapsed into a dreamless sleep. When he woke up, it was light out and he was starving. Top priority: determine the breakfast situation. Pulling the door open, he almost collided with Henry, who appeared to have been skulking in the hallway. "Fancy seeing you here."

Henry made a face. "I was about to knock." He peered over Tuck's shoulder as if he could take in the contents of the room. "I'm going to assume you are not prepared to be outfitted in appropriate evening dress for a ball?"

"Define appropriate." How was this stuck-up clown related to Lizzy? They had similar eyes, but where hers were curious and intelligent, his were clouded in judgment and disdain.

"Let's start with the basics." Henry pointed to Tuck's feet. "Boots won't do. Gentlemen may not enter a ballroom in boots. You could break a lady's foot at worst or ruin the floor at best. And you'll need better-quality knee breeches and stockings. Those are hopelessly out of fashion."

Tuck prayed that neither Georgie nor the ghost of Edward ever heard the slander.

"Gads." Henry pinched his nose. "Of course, it's going to be up to me to manage all your colony ill manners so you don't show up like a barbarian and undo the inroads this family has made."

"What kind of roads are we talking about?"

"The Wooddash family lacks one of the ancient names. My father's grandparents were not nobles, nor did they possess grand country estates. Across generations, we've diligently nurtured respectability and wealth. Both Lizzy and I hold a duty to perpetuate that progress. She has chosen to attach her fortunes to a person of obscure identity and no social standing; thus the responsibility falls on me." His smile was tight and humorless. "Thank you for this weight. Nevertheless, you require proper shoes and anything but buckskin. Not for your sake, but for mine. Now get dressed and fetch a hat. We are going out."

"Why for your sake?" Tuck inquired, attempting to tie his cravat as best he could. He struggled on a good day, and this was definitely not that. "I'm not quite grasping your thinking."

"Make haste, Taylor." Henry beckoned him to follow. "I'm not about to ruin my prospects of marrying Olivia Abbot Davies, who has a dowry of thirty thousand pounds."

"That's good, I take it?"

"My dear man, you know it's very good," Henry exclaimed. "Considering you'll be lucky if Father bestows upon you a shilling, I can see your envy. I've been courting her throughout the season, offering charming compliments, always observing her ribbons and such. She possesses a robust constitution and will undoubtedly secure me my heir and spare. Moreover, she speaks little and thinks even less. What more could a man desire in a wife? And with my position and society connections, she'll have no complaints."

"Lucky Olivia Abbot Davies." He shuddered to think of Lizzy surrounded by men like her brother.

"Indeed." If Henry registered Tuck's sarcasm, he didn't let it show. "Now let's go to my club."

It FELT LIKE a lifetime later, but was realistically only a few days. Tuck waited in the wide marble foyer staring up at the stairs, willing Lizzy to appear. It wasn't that his desire to attend the ball had increased—if anything, it was the direct opposite. But he'd spent the past days at Henry's club or in the empty house as she attended dress fittings or made social calls, and he missed her. He missed her gaze, the way she'd look at him with a combination of fondness and exasperation. He missed her smell, like a summer garden.

He missed the fact that being around her made him come up with dumb shit like thinking she smelled like a garden.

This fact should bother him a lot more than it did. In fact, it didn't seem like the worst thing in the world that he had a wife who lived in a different time. But he wasn't sure what this meant either.

He fidgeted with his tailcoat, double-breasted with a high collar that scratched his neck, stopping above his waist in the front and hanging down his back. Henry had found friends—if that's what the smug pack of bastards could be called—to loan him clothing. Tuck was dressed for a ball, but he felt so far outside of himself that he had to rock in his low-heeled buckled shoes to keep grounded.

Where was Lizzy?

Then she was at the top of the stairs. Tuck knew next to nothing about fashion, but her pale blue dress only made her eyes deeper, like a mountain lake that he knew would be too cold to swim in, but it didn't matter because reason had no place here. He would jump, and he would endure whatever discomfort because, for real, if he had to drown, it might as well happen here in Lizzy and all her lace and feathers. He'd never seen anyone look this beautiful, and it almost made him angry—not angry at her—just at the world that this person could appear in his life and be so totally unable to stay by his side.

"Hello," she said softly, taking another step down. Her cheeks were bright.

"You look beautiful," he blurted, voice more jagged than he wanted.

She looked startled, but her eyes measured him. "Y-you too."

He glanced down, smoothing his silk waistcoat. "Guess I don't clean up so bad."

She lost her footing on the next stair. Her mouth formed a silent O of surprise, and then he was rising to catch her, grunting as her weight made an impact, but he could still steady her.

She stared up at him in shock, pupils dilated, still in his arms as if they had nowhere else to be for the rest of tonight. She didn't just smell like a summer garden now; it was as if she were the full Garden of Eden and he wanted knowledge.

"Please put me down," she whispered.

He cocked a brow, let his gaze travel leisurely to her mouth and linger. "And if I don't?" He wasn't serious. But he wanted to see what she'd do.

"I wouldn't want to make a spectacle. So maybe I'd purse my lips. And then when you got close, I'd . . ." She arched up, snapping her teeth.

"Christ." He startled, settling her back on her feet. "You're a wild animal."

"Don't test me."

Henry had left from his club and her parents had departed separately, no doubt to avoid having to talk to him. En route, he squared off with her.

"I want to ask some questions."

"Very well." She sniffed. "Go."

"Do I need to bow? Henry discussed bowing, but I wasn't really listening."

"Yesssss . . ." she said slowly. "But only sometimes, and when in doubt? Make it small. You aren't a metronome."

"What else should I know?"

"I enjoy dancing. We *will* be dancing. If you don't know the steps, I'll tell you what to do. I can take the lead."

"This I believe. But—"

"But nothing," she continued with a wry smile. "Tonight, you will dance, make little bows, nibble delicious food, and make small talk."

"How small?"

"About things of teeny-tiny significance. The ballroom's flower arrangements. The crispness of the biscuits. The temperature in the room. Nothing at all. Mouths moving, pushing air. You will chuckle at every word I say and keep fetching me drinks. That's enough that my friends will be wildly jealous of my very handsome, witty, and wonderful husband, and ensure no one will engage in malicious gossip."

"Your friends will be there?"

"More like acquaintances. Georgie and Jane are true friends— people I can go to and be honest and myself and they will answer me in turn. The friends here are city friends. We have a laugh but don't have a great deal in common. I worry sometimes that they are forced to pay social calls because of my family."

"Why is that?"

"Oh, my stepfather has investments, of course. He is a true gentleman. However, he has a small business everyone intensely cares about, and that is the paper, the *Evening Ledger*."

"I saw him reading that when we met."

"It has the most prosaic content (shipping and trade, legal notices), the useful (news and events), and the popular (society gossip).

"Mr. Alby has no doubt already printed a joyful announcement on our marriage. If I had to make a wager, I'd say it went out today to spin my failure into a success."

"I'm a failure?" That was a new one.

"You're not part of the ton. So some people find it odd and unpleasant when a surprise tumbles in, much like a body down the stairs."

"Are you saying I was an unpleasant surprise?"

She yelped as he flicked the underside of her chin gently with his thumb.

"The paper. Do you ever write for it?"

The smile left her face. "I used to ask. A few times I begged, I'm not proud. But no, Mr. Alby was adamant that I not write. He said a husband wouldn't want a wife who thought she was too clever. I disobeyed, naturally."

He nodded solemnly. "Obviously."

"When I was twenty, I drafted up a short satire. Nothing earth-shattering. It was called 'The Grand Society of Peculiar Pretensions.'"

"I'm impressed already."

"My nom de plume was Sir Jestington Jotsworth. Clearly false."

"Sure."

"But that was part of the humor. The stories followed a certain Lady Serendipity and her aristocratic cadre. It poked at eccentricities and was generally preposterous, but in the spirit of fun. It became popular. Mr. Alby would even read excerpts at dinner. Mamma and Henry often ended up in stitches."

Tuck's heart twanged as her eyes took on a faraway look, remembering a moment when she had caused joy for her family, even if they didn't know—she had, and that warm memory had lingered.

"Anyway, Mr. Alby found out eventually. I was careless and left a draft out on my desk while I had breakfast. A servant brought it to my stepfather and let's just say he was no longer amused. I was forbidden to write, and to punctuate the point, he sold my pony."

"What!"

"I had a white pony named Petalwhisk. I loved her and so he sold her as my punishment for going against the family's wishes."

Slow, strong rage gathered in Tuck's gut. How could anyone purposefully cause this woman pain, let alone a parent? And to sell a girl's fucking pet because she wrote some smart stories?

She giggled.

"This isn't funny."

"No. It's not. I've lived it and I know indeed how bleak it feels. But you . . . I believe you growled."

"Huh."

She giggled again. "You did. You growled sitting there."

The carriage came to a halt. "We're here."

A stream of people poured into a well-lit townhome. The footman hadn't even opened the door and the sound of the people outside still filled the space.

"No growling allowed in there."

"We'll see. Depends if anyone thinks about hurting you."

Her gaze found his. "You act as if we'll be among beasts."

He took her hand in his; even if it was small, it was still strong. How many years had this woman walked among these people and never been allowed to be her full self? He liked holding her hand. He liked it so much he wasn't sure he'd ever be able to let go.

CHAPTER TWENTY-TWO

The Crawfords' ballroom gleamed with mirrors strategically positioned to catch and amplify the dance of five hundred candles. Beyond the mirrors, glass, crystal, and polished metals worked in concert to light up the space, each reflective surface sparkling for the evening's festivities. In every gap, hothouse flowers burst in vibrant colors. The blooms not only added pops of natural beauty but also carried a sweet fragrance, masking the exertion from the lively dancing. Excited waves of chatter flowed and ebbed through all corners of the room.

"You'll relax if you have a glass or two of punch," Lizzy murmured, nodding toward a bewigged servant in a coral-colored velvet jacket making his way in their direction, a silver tray gripped tightly between his gloved hands.

"I'm going to need something that hits harder than kiddie punch." Tuck tugged his cravat for the third time in as many minutes, peering up at the musicians on the balcony.

"It will be fortified with rum, brandy, and wine. I can assure you that it's no beverage for children." She had to lean in to speak. There was noise. Gossip. Laughter. Music. Heavy breathing.

The dancers whirled in muslin and taffeta to the cotillion, everything gay, light, and airy until you looked closer and realized the dance floor was a battlefield, and each glance carried the weight of intrigue. Henry flew past, red-cheeked, sweat sheening his forehead as he appeared to gulp a breath and disguise it as a chuckle.

"Dancing is hard work," Tuck observed. "I don't know why, but I never pictured it to be so strenuous."

"Oh, yes, my legs are always sore for days after a ball. But if a woman wants to dance, she must say yes to whoever asks. If you tell a gentleman no, that's it—you are not able to dance the rest of the night unless you're willing to risk your reputation."

"That's bullshit. What if you don't want to dance with the person?"

"Then you get to be called Lizzy Wooddash, and welcome to what is known as my life."

"Not anymore." He fixed her with such a stare, too perceptive by half. It felt as if the room grew degrees hotter as people turned in their direction with curious stares, as if to say, *Yes, that's him, the American from Baltimore. I heard she married him after a courtship in Southampton. Indeed, it's all very sudden. He is in a trade of some sort. Dry goods or something equally dull.*

If Lizzy strained her ears, she'd be able to hear the cogs turning in their brains, gazes cast toward her middle, rooting out any telltale sign of pregnancy. Alas, all they were going to notice was the poached salmon with dill sauce and fruit tartlet she'd enjoyed for lunch.

"Go on, ask me another question. I'm positive you have them. And that keeps me distracted from the fact that we are clearly a topic of minor interest."

"People have been staring since we entered. What is that card women keep pulling out of their bags for men to sign?"

"Bags? Oh, you mean their reticules. Ah, yes, those are dance cards," Lizzy remarked, crossing her arms with an air of authority. "Returning to my earlier point, that's the proper manner to request a dance."

"Okay, I get that. And then who are these people on the side watching and not talking?"

"Chaperones. Silent guardians of virtue, observing like undercover agents. Their presence ensures that while love is in the air, it's kept strictly within the boundaries of propriety."

"And so everyone stands around and gossips if they're not dancing?"

"It's a perilous business. Conversational choices could secure alliances or lead to a polite but firm dismissal. One must choose words as if crafting a masterpiece. And on the dance floor, restraint is the cornerstone of your choreography. Be close enough to converse or flirt, but avoid scandalous contact as if your reputation depends on it—because, rest assured, it does."

"Why is there chalk all over the floor?" He pointed at the heavenly bodies, the sun, moon, and stars drawn across the wood.

"That's very fashionable. Of course, by the end of the ball it will all be gone, but that's not the point, is it? It's there now and rather lovely. Plus, it helps people not to slip."

"And what's over there?" He pointed to a space hidden by screens and palms.

"That clandestine hub? That's the women's retiring room, a den of more gossip and strategic retreats. Light refreshments are the snacks of espionage. The retiring room is where social maneuvers unfold like a covert operation."

"Do men ever, I dunno, take one of the ladies' fans and go somewhere quiet to wait for them to come to them? That's what I'd do."

"You're not the kind of man who would ruin a woman. Present

company excluded, of course." She took another sip. That was when it hit her, and she realized with a jolt of alarmed observation that she'd drunk too much punch.

"Don't look now," Tuck muttered, "but there's a man across the room who has been staring at us for more than ten minutes."

Lizzy glanced over to spot a man with dappled silver hair and pointed sideburns. He noticed her gaze and quickly busied himself with examining his fingernails.

"I said don't look," Tuck admonished.

"I never promised to obey. I've seen the man before, though. He is a history scholar of some type. I believe he is at Oxford. Or is it Cambridge? I can't recall the specifics or his name. But if you'll excuse me, I must take leave to freshen up."

Tuck jerked in alarm. "You can't leave me here."

"Well, I can't take you into the women's dressing area either." She petted his head. "You must be brave. And do not put your name on another woman's dance card because I'll become quite jealous. If anyone is going to have the pleasure of you trodding on their toes, it should be me."

He snorted. "Very well. I'll try to memorize a few steps while I watch."

Lizzy made her way to the ladies' room. It was already half full of acquaintances needing to freshen up from the dance. It didn't take long for them to turn their attention to her.

"Married? Lizzy Wooddash—or is it Taylor now?" Cornelia Witt said, turning to adjust a curl in a mirror her lady's maid held. "Isn't this unexpected? What secrets you keep! Everyone is quite abuzz."

Cornelia was Lizzy's age but had been married since she was eighteen and had already given birth to two children. Though amiable at social functions, their connection lacked intimacy. Nevertheless, they found pleasure in brief exchanges.

"I was wondering about your rush to wed until I laid eyes on the man. My goodness. American or not, who gives a fig about his reputation when he's got a form like that?"

"Where is he?" inquired Dorothea. "I am curious."

Theodosia, her twin sister, pointed toward a large potted fern. "If you peer through the foliage, you'll have a splendid view. His chin is by far the most distinguished in the room. It could cut precious jewels."

"Goodness. Let me see again too!" Cornelia laughed, craning her neck.

"You know what they say about men with big chins, don't you, Lizzy?" Dorothea said.

"I thought that was regarding hands," Theodosia added. "Or feet."

"Well, it feels like a silly debate because his hands and feet appear sizable as well."

"Poor dear." Cornelia turned to Lizzy with a knowing look. "Was the wedding night difficult? After mine, I couldn't cross my legs for a week. Frank had been so shy during our courtship. I didn't expect him to bed me like a castle he needed to storm."

"Got you with the battering ram, did he?" Dorothea fanned herself faster, shoulders shaking with merriment.

"I'm still a bit mad for it even with two children," Cornelia continued. "But you, Lizzy. You waited so long. What's he like?"

"A bit quiet," Lizzy said carefully. "But he notices a lot."

"Perfect qualities in a lover." Theodosia's comment earned knowing nods from the others in the room.

That wasn't what Lizzy meant, but she knew better than to try to make a correction. These women all assumed she had carnal knowledge of her husband. And of course they would. It wasn't the normal way of things for women to fake-marry men from the future to ensure a life of happy widowhood.

"It's . . . it's . . ." The women were hanging on every word. Damn it all. Why must they be so nosy? "It's a very tight fit, but perfectly adequate." That seemed about right based on what she'd read in that book from the Gretna Green trip, plus the length of Tuck against her. Even if he'd had it clothed, she knew it wasn't going to go in with one fell swoop.

"Oh, darling." Dorothea handed her a glass before filling it with champagne, the yellow bubbles popping up to a head of foam. "Drink up. It won't be so uncomfortable if you're foxed."

"Don't listen to her." Cornelia poured her own cup. "You get used to it. And the better it gets, the easier it is. Why, sometimes my muff gets so wet that Frank falls right in when he comes to tup me."

"Honestly," Theodosia chastised her, scandalized. "We have a new bride in our mix. What will she think with all this muff and tupping talk?"

"She will think, *I am glad to know such honest and forthright women.* Plus, she has a muff and gets tupped, don't you, Lizzy?" Cornelia's voice was thicker and held an edge of a slur. She was tipsy in a happy way.

Lizzy beckoned to a servant. "Please see to it that Mrs. Witt there gets a glass of water. As big as you can manage, thank you."

"Oh, poo," Cornelia said. "One should enjoy oneself at a ball. On the way home tonight, I might let my husband do a bit of a bum fiddle and—"

"I have very satisfying tupping," Lizzy blurted, ears burning.

What if Mamma entered during all this talk? Did she ever discuss her muff or tupping with other women? Unlikely. Mamma had probably only ever been tupped twice in her life, to make Henry and then herself.

"Have you tried riding a dragon like St. George?" Cornelia asked, giggling behind her hand.

"I—I don't think so?" Lizzy realized she had never needed to bother with that book at all, not when these ladies were willing to give her a Cambridge-style education in the finer points of bedroom antics.

"Here is how you must proceed." Cornelia leaned in conspiratorially. "Tonight, when you return to your chamber, straddle him. Let him take you that way. He'll recline and admire your bouncing charms, then shower you with praise fit for a queen. How else do you suppose I acquire all my better jewels?"

"Sounds like quite the adventure." Lizzy's voice squeaked. She hadn't been intimate in most ways, let alone riding dragons with her modest assets. She doubted she had large enough charms for any significant bouncing.

Occasionally, talking to her married acquaintances felt tedious, but now she had to admit that maybe she'd been overly prejudiced. Of course, they couldn't ever discuss carnal relations with an unmarried woman who wasn't even related. But now she'd entered into the secret club.

"Of course, you could gallop along like you're on horseback, but that's missing much of the pleasure." Theodosia glanced over her shoulder to ensure no one else was entering their space. "For me, it's best when he's either propped up by pillows or we're on a couch. That gives you the best angle to pleasure yourself. I use the back of the couch or his shoulders for support, and while it can take time to find your perfect spot, when you do, it's off to the races."

Lizzy gulped her champagne, grinning at the bubbly sensation that spread across her tongue, then buzzed down her throat. "One more, if you please."

"For courage." Dorothea clapped her hands.

"For courage." Lizzy held out her crystal flute as Cornelia refilled it.

"Tip it back and go get him," Theodosia said.

Lizzy wasn't ever going to be close friends with these three social butterflies flitting from one event to another, delighted to see and be seen, but a new enjoyment had been unlocked. Except for the fact that she was very much still a maiden.

If her husband was going to make her a widow, she'd better be certain to bed him first.

CHAPTER TWENTY-THREE

"Tucker Taylor." A high, thin voice spoke behind his back. "Southpaw. Spent a year in Montreal before getting traded to Texas. Played forward in high school but was a goalie at University of Michigan. Decent scorer but far better between the pipes. Last time I saw you play was in 2019."

Tuck turned slowly. He wasn't losing his mind and hearing voices, right? The slight man who Tuck had seen earlier, the one Lizzy had pegged as a scholar, beamed at him. The guy wasn't tall, around five-five, with bushy brows and graying temples.

"Do I know you?"

"Of course not." The man chuckled. "But I know *you*. When I learned that the Wooddash girl had wed a gentleman bearing the distinctive name of Tucker Taylor, I couldn't help but find it a remarkable twist of fate. As I'm sure you've observed, your name is rather uncommon for this time. However, I dared not entertain high expectations. Upon discovering you were American, I resolved to obtain a ticket to the Crawford ball by any means necessary, and here you are now."

Tuck opened his mouth. A dozen questions lined up but none could make their way out.

"Who? How? When? Where?"

The man glanced around. "This isn't the place for a lengthy conversation." He slipped a folded piece of paper into Tuck's hand. "Come to this address tomorrow. Bring your wife, if she knows. Are you planning to stay?"

"Stay," Tuck dumbly repeated.

"Here, at this time? Nineteenth-century England does have some things going for it. The days are longer, aren't they? There's more time to think—less hustle and bustle. Of course, there are no pizza delivery services, podcasts, or plane rides, but we can't have it all."

"Where do you come from?" Tuck blinked.

"Same place as you. Well, England through birth, EU on my passport. But I taught Celtic studies in California. Berkeley."

"England left the . . ." Tuck slammed his mouth shut. "I didn't expect to meet anyone else this ever happened to!"

"Indeed, you are my first fellow crosser, but rest assured, others have come before us, and others will come after. Some must make it back to their time and others must choose to stay. And, of course, some get sick and die. There are some very nasty things here—cholera, for instance. Stay well away from that. Oh, and don't get the clap without modern medicine. I've seen it once. Not pretty. We are all much better off having a nose."

"What's your name?"

"Ezekiel Fairweather." With a flourish, he swept an arm across his waist and inclined his head. "Friends call me Zeke, and I do think we will be friends, Tuck Taylor; indeed, I do. I never played hockey myself, but I wish I'd gotten a crack at it. I was quite mad about the sport while I worked stateside. I went to as many games as I could—the Mighty Ducks were my team."

"I . . ."

"It's a shock, of course. But tomorrow will be informative. Where did you enter?"

"A pond. In a farmer's field. It was a car accident."

"A pond?" Zeke hit the *p* hard. "How marvelous. Mine was a spring in Oxfordshire. I had been doing research into the Rollright Stones nestled on the outskirts of the Cotswolds hills. There is quite a collection of megalithic monuments spanning nearly two thousand years through Neolithic and Bronze Age development. I had an idea that I had been toying with and wanted to put to the test. So, I entered the water during Beltane, a Celtic and also Druidic holiday that people now refer to as May Day. I dove in, laughing to myself, half thinking I was mad, and then the world churned and all direction disappeared. I crawled out of that pond laughing no more. It was 1809."

"Three years ago?"

"Three years ago. And it was a different season too. There are details I don't begin to understand, but I have many theories. Also, how many of us are there, who have crossed and slipped into the fabric of their new world? It's just simple, dumb good fortune that I recognized your name." Zeke's gaze was far away before he shook his head. "I look forward to meeting with you tomorrow, Mr. Taylor. Much to discuss. And tell me—do the Regals still have Gale Knight as their center?"

"Sure do." Tuck glanced around the ballroom, so incongruous to any discussions about his teammates.

"He's young, but I believe he's a once-in-a-generation player."

"That's what he likes to say."

"Ah, yes. He is cocky, isn't he? But it's true. And is he still a ladies' man?"

"That's the rumor."

"You never were, though."

"What can I say? I'm an enigma."

That was his go-to with the press. They loved it. Ate it up with a spoon. And from the way Zeke was grinning, he liked it too.

Zeke bid him good night, and Tuck slipped out onto the balcony, head too full to think, when Henry slunk out. Lizzy's brother's smile was polite, but his eyes were not. "I've been looking for you everywhere, man. Lizzy's in her cups. You better take her home before Father notices and we all catch it."

"Where is she?"

"I managed to get her to the carriage. She danced the whole way. It was unseemly. If my fiancée's family noticed, it would be the end of that, I can assure you."

"Fiancée. Congratulations are in order after tonight?"

"No, no." Henry pressed his lips together. "Not quite. At our last rendezvous, I may have pressed a bit too forcefully on the topic of her dowry. Father provides for me adequately, but I find myself eager to plan investments. Of course, they will benefit Olivia too, for my rise will only mean hers, but she did seem to want to play the coquette a bit. You know women, they don't want to seem overeager in front of a prized buck."

Tuck responded with a noncommittal murmur before striding back indoors, his gaze sweeping through the bustling ballroom. The grand space was alive with a kaleidoscope of colors as women floated past in an array of elegant dresses adorned with jewels and feathers and holding delicate fans. Every corner seemed to sparkle with opulence and grace. Though numerous eyes followed his movements, inviting him with subtle gestures, none belonged to the woman he cared about.

"Husband," Lizzy breathed a few minutes later as he entered the carriage. "My dear wicked husband. Are you here to have your evil way with me? I tried to find you everywhere, but only ran into grouchy old Henry."

"Lizzy. Baby. I think it would be best if we cracked a window to let in some air."

"You can crack my window," she purred, reaching over to brace her hands on his knee. "Because tonight I will ride on St. George all the way to where dragons live." She burst into peals of laughter.

She was drunk with a capital *D*.

"Damn it." He had so much to tell her and she wasn't in the mood for anything other than . . .

"Jesus. No." He flew back as her hand came near to whacking his crown jewels. "Please sit still. We'll get to your house and you can drink some water. I have a lot to tell you.

"Me too. I've decided something." She slowly blinked. "Me." She pointed at him. "You." She pointed at herself.

"Think you got that backward, Pocket Rocket."

"We are going to have intimate marriage relations. If we do not, I will die not only a widow but also unknowledgeable. And that . . ."

Tuck reached forward to grab her as she half slid off the bench.

"That is a tragedy for my muff, and my muff is not a tragedy, do you understand?"

"I think I get it," Tuck muttered.

Why shouldn't she live a little? She had to deal with so much every day. If hooking up with him could give her some fun, well, he'd done it for way less noble reasons in the past. But he would never have sex with a woman who was drunk. If she sobered up, and still felt the same? Could he risk it? He'd never worried about physical acts messing with his head before. He compartmentalized. That was what he excelled at. If she wanted to have some sex, he could have some sex. What was with the vague fear churning through him? It wasn't as if when his dick slid into her, his feelings would lock into place like some magic spell. That was ridiculous.

As ridiculous as falling into a pond and traveling back in time.

Lizzy was snoring now, loudly.

He scrubbed a hand across his face. He didn't need to sleep with her to know his feelings were something he hadn't experienced before. If this scene were a cartoon, there would be a red alarm on the wall over his head that read, *Danger! Danger!*

He took a deep breath through his nose and released it. Once. Twice more.

A lot was coming at him tonight and he didn't have a clear head to think, let alone make decisions.

The carriage stopped. They were back at the townhouse. Her parents were in the foyer when he entered, holding her in his arms.

"Dear heavens," her mother exclaimed. "What have you done to my daughter? She's as drunk as a Dionysian nymph."

"Madam," her stepfather said, "I believe Elizabeth managed this feat entirely on her own. I saw her in the ladies' room with Cornelia, Dorothea, and Theodosia."

"Goodness." Her mother slumped. "At least she is married and can't ruin herself. Small miracle."

"Exactly." Mr. Alby turned and struck Tuck on the back, right on the kidneys. "Now escort that troublemaker to bed before the servants gossip. I see public intoxication is a trait she can claim from your previous husband." He directed the last snide comment to his wife as they withdrew down the hall.

Not for the first time Tuck wondered how Lizzy had turned out as well as she did in this family. It wasn't merely a lack of attention to her needs; it was the outright disregard that she might even possess a few. He couldn't help but imagine how much further she might have progressed in ambitions like her writing if she'd been surrounded by people who supported her dreams instead of stifling them with ordinary ones that only benefited themselves.

Tuck carried her up the three flights of stairs. He was breathing hard by the last few steps. Lizzy stirred, lifting her head. "You are my husband?" Her fox-eyed gaze was unfocused, drooping sleepily in the corners.

"I am."

"My handsome husband!" She petted his cheek.

"Thanks."

"Who will leave me."

"Shhhhh." He glanced around. Even though he didn't see any eavesdroppers, it wasn't safe to talk in public like this.

"I don't want you to go away." She burrowed into his side. "Don't want you to disappear." She kept whispering it like a nursery rhyme.

They reached her room and he managed to get the door open, then kicked it shut behind him and staggered to the bed, where he aimed to deposit her to sleep it off. She had much to learn in the morning. His head was still reeling from the conversation with Zeke.

He rested her head on a pillow and started to pull back, stopped by her hand on his cheek.

"Don't go." Her voice was soft.

"You are drunk."

"Very."

"Babe. I'm not going to take advantage. Nothing is going to happen tonight. You need to go to sleep and hopefully not feel too bad in the morning."

"Stay. Won't ravage you. Hold me."

He could do that.

First, he removed her shoes and the pearls pinned into her hair. Then he pulled the covers up over her until they reached her chin. She looked young then, all big blue eyes and dreamy innocence.

He removed his shoes and the cravat that threatened to strangle him. He stripped down until he was shirtless and crawled in next to her.

"Yes, yes. Hold me." She burrowed against him, the soft warm roundness of her ass against his dick. He gritted his teeth. It wasn't hard to know there were lines you just didn't cross in life, and messing around with a drunk woman was one of them. But that didn't mean that he couldn't acknowledge this was nice. That he liked it. That he liked it too damn much. He took a deep breath, only to be flooded by her perfume—lavender and other herbal plants, as if she were a secret garden.

"Why can't we do this forever?" she whispered, with less slurring and more clarity.

"You know why."

"What if you stay here?"

He closed his eyes. Tried to imagine that. No more Regals. No more goalie. No more cars. Lights. Toilets. Grocery stores. Airplanes. Modern medicine. No sister. "I don't think I can do that."

"Not for me?"

Fuck. Because the truth was . . . maybe. Maybe he could. Maybe he could spend the rest of his life here in 1812 with the balls and the cravats and the rules and Lizzy. He'd make her believe she was good enough, brew pots of tea, watch her become the writer she dreamed to be.

"Or you could come with me?" He planted a soft kiss on the back of her head. To hell with them all—they could escape.

"To the future."

"Yeah." Dangerous. He was stepping onto thin ice.

"The future you won't even tell me about."

"What do you want to know?" Even riskier. He needed to exercise caution, yet he wanted a deeper connection.

"Let me see . . . What are the top three most useful items you possess that are not present here?"

He mulled it over quickly. "Electricity. It's a game-changer, ensuring there's always light at the flick of a switch. It's not just about brightening up a room; in the cities, it practically banishes the darkness altogether, making nighttime feel like daytime."

"If it's too bright, you can't see the stars." She frowned at him. "I wouldn't like that."

"Okay, okay. There is this thing called a car. Not a cart. A c-a-r. Picture a big metal carriage that doesn't need horses to move. It has four wheels and runs on a special liquid called gasoline. Instead of a horse, there's a powerful engine inside that makes it go. People sit inside them and use a steering wheel to control where it goes. It's like a magical machine that can take you anywhere you want to go, much faster than a horse and carriage."

"You've mentioned this before."

"Travel is more comfortable and way quicker. You don't have to walk everywhere."

"But I like walking."

"People still walk, but for exercise."

"I don't know what that means."

"It's setting aside specific time to move your body in ways to make it stronger and healthier. You do things like running, jumping, lifting weights, or stretching to keep your body in good shape."

"Exercise—that doesn't sound enjoyable at all." Her voice was quieter; she was drifting away. "You have one more chance to impress me." She wrapped her hand around his pointer finger, rubbing her thumb back and forth on his palm.

"Let's see. Cars. Electricity. None of these grab you. What about tampons?"

"Mmmph . . ." she murmured sleepily. "What's that?"

"They're these small cotton cylinder-shaped things used during a monthly cycle. You insert it into your vagina, where it absorbs the flow. I guess it can make things easier."

"You have my attention." She flipped herself on top of him, eyes wide. "Tell me more."

"I mean, there isn't a lot more to say. At least that *I* know about."

"You put these magic tampons inside you and then you don't bleed everywhere?"

"I mean, I don't have first-hand experience. But I shared a bathroom with my sister all through our teen years so, you know, I know enough."

"How marvelous. Although my stomach would still hurt."

"Yeah, but we have medicine for that. Ibuprofen. Acetaminophen. Pills you take to relieve pain."

"I have no inclination to engage in exercise like running in the future, but the idea of using these tampons and these pain pills doesn't seem too objectionable." She tumbled off him and flopped back onto her pillow. "Goodness. I'm pickled, aren't I?"

"If that means drunk, then yes."

"I believe I might have behaved in a way I won't be proud of tomorrow."

"Hey." He rolled on his side, wrapping an arm around her. "You can't be held responsible for wanting to get with such a good-looking guy."

She craned her head back. "We're talking about you, I presume?"

He gave a deadpan smirk. "Don't see anyone else here who owns a dragon you'd like to ride on."

"Never *ever* repeat those words." She pushed a finger to his lips. "As far as you're concerned, they were never uttered."

He nipped the tip of her finger, grinning at her squeal. "We'll see. You were cute."

"It was kind of you to not take advantage."

"Kind has nothing to do with it." He cupped her cheek, forcing her to meet his gaze. "You are safe with me. Whatever happens, know that."

"Safe." Her voice was thick again. "Until you leave me."

As she drifted to sleep, Tuck stared into the night, wondering how he'd ever be able to do that.

CHAPTER TWENTY-FOUR

Lizzy's headache felt like a relentless tempest, pounding against the walls of her skull. All she could recall was being at the Crawfords' ball and thinking more champagne would be brilliant. She had hazy yet horrifying memories of attempting to crawl onto Tuck's lap in the carriage, yet he gave no indication that anything was amiss. When she'd finally woken up, he'd simply placed a glass of water, some toast, and a pot of strawberry jam on the table in her room. She couldn't quite bring herself to face the jam, but the toast helped settle her stomach. Now she and Tuck were crossing Rotten Row to meet a stranger named Ezekiel Fairweather near the park's mermaid fountain at the hour he had chosen.

"Why is this place called Rotten Row?" Tuck glanced around as they strolled. "I expected a dump, but it's pretty."

"It used to be called Route du Roi, or the King's Road. It is hard to believe, but Hyde Park was once a wild expanse on the outskirts of the city. King Henry the Eighth took the land from monks and turned it into a royal hunting ground to use with his friends."

"A way better hobby than chopping the heads off wives, I suppose."

Lizzy let out an unexpected laugh. "Yes, quite."

It felt strange that they could speak of anything else at all, considering they were going to meet another time traveler—someone from Tuck's era, who even knew him in his hockey dealings. Yet, chatting of other matters somehow made the weightiness of the moment feel lighter. It helped her resist the mad urge to seize his hand and suggest they flee London, head back to the Woodlands, and live a quiet life together.

She cast him a sideways glance, noticing his size, the set of his jaw, and the way he frowned when lost in thought. His face didn't seem warm or friendly, except when he spoke to her; then his eyes softened, and he smiled more, as if he couldn't help but find her amusing.

In his presence, she felt a sensation of leaning in, like a sunflower facing the sun. The problem was that she might be falling for him—just a little, maybe more than that. And it was a joke, because one *should* love one's husband; that was a good and lucky thing. Unless he came from another time, and their marriage was false, and then she was a ninny.

"Are you unwell?" He turned and faced her. "Never mind. Dumb question. Of course you are. I'm sorry, I shouldn't have let you come hungover."

"Let me?" She placed her hands on her hips. "Have you forgotten who you are speaking to? I'm not the kind of woman you *let* do anything."

He snorted. "True. And I do want you to meet this guy. Incredible, isn't it, that we didn't know where to begin looking for answers and then an answer found us?"

"What's incredible is that you were recognized. Are you quite famous?"

He considered it. "I guess it depends on the audience. Sometimes I can be out for a day and no one looks twice at me or says anything. But if I'm in the right locations, where people know my sport and who I am, then yeah, I guess I'm famous enough."

This pleased her in some strange way—not that it mattered what the world thought of him, but his success made her proud. She wanted him to be admired. He deserved it. But . . .

Her stomach contracted, churning and twisting.

She wasn't the only woman out there who could see that not only was he a handsome man, but a good one.

"Uh-oh." He took her hand and looped it through his arm. "I recognize this look."

"What do you mean? I'm a bit under the weather due to my overindulgence."

"Well, that's true, but when those two lines appear between your eyebrows? That means there is a worry. What's up?"

Her lips were so dry, and her tongue felt like sandpaper. She mustered a bright tone, despite not having the energy for a smile to match. "Worry? Me? I'm not worried about anything, I can assure you."

His gentle grin faded. "Guess that makes one of us."

"Why are *you* worried?"

"Oh, I don't know. Guess it's the whole going-to-meet-a-time-traveler-and-learn-about-my-fate thing. You know, normal stuff for a Sunday morning."

She bit her lip. "You don't have a woman in your time, do you?"

"What?" He tripped, a look of surprise stamping his features. "Is that a serious question? If you thought that, why are you just now asking?"

"I do not think you have anything formal established or you would have surely mentioned it by now. You are a man of character. However, given that you have just stated you have fame, and also clearly possess good looks, and likely a respectable income, it does seem odd that you'd be unattached."

"In truth? I've been way too busy to think about dating. You know, fighting a life-threatening disease and everything."

"I see." They walked a few more steps. "Most men wouldn't let that stop them, though, would they?"

"Are you asking if I have had opportunities to be in a relationship? Yeah. Sure. Of course. I've dated, but, look, it's a game that gets numbing. Especially in a position like mine when you don't know if anyone ever likes you for you, or what you do when you strap on some skates and get on the ice."

"Women like men who skate for money?"

He chuckled. "When you put it like that, you make it sound dirty. I suppose whenever someone is well known and successful at something, it makes them more attractive or popular. In my era, sports like hockey, which I play, are prominent. But then there are things like basketball, where you throw a ball through a hoop, or football, where you kick or throw a pigskin to each other, or baseball, where you hit a ball with a big stick."

She cocked her head, considering. "And people enjoy doing such things?"

"Yeah, of course. And even more people enjoy watching it."

"I suppose it's like bull-baiting," she said, reaching to make a relatable correlation.

Tuck shook his head. "Never heard of it."

"I'm not privy to the particulars, but as I understand it, there exist venues where individuals convene to witness the spectacle of a bull tethered within a chamber and then assailed by hounds. Wagers are laid on who will outlast the other, and it is deemed quite diverting entertainment. Although I must say, I personally find the idea positively nightmarish."

"Yeah, that's messed up. I'd say that's one example of where the idea of entertainment has moved on to way better avenues."

The mermaid fountain came into view, and there before it waited the wiry, gray-haired gentleman Lizzy had recognized from the ball.

His eyes lit up when he saw them approaching, and he came forward to meet them, walking briskly, arms extended. "Hello, hello." He took Tuck's hand and shook it heartily before turning to face her, clicking his heels and dipping into a full bow.

"Madam Taylor. Pleased to make your acquaintance. I am Ezekiel Fairweather, also known as your humble servant."

Lizzy met Tuck's dancing eyes and tried not to laugh. Mr. Fairweather's manners were very earnest and she didn't want to give offense.

"I imagine you have many questions," Zeke said. "But from what I learned last night, I believe it would be helpful for me to make a summary. Is this agreeable for everyone?"

They nodded.

"Very good, we can stroll about the fountain as we talk. I've always been partial to this place when I visit town. Now, from what I understand, on the night of the winter solstice, in the town of Hallow's Gate, you, Tuck, were driving . . . Pardon me, Mrs. Taylor—I might be using some terminology that is unfamiliar for this time."

"And I must confess, hearing you refer to me as Mrs. Taylor gives me more of a start than the mere mention of horseless carriages."

"Ah, yes. Your marriage is a recent thing, I believe."

"Yes. And while Tuck has deemed it wise to not reveal much about the future, I have been able to glean a few things."

"It is very wise of him to exercise prudence." Mr. Fairweather nodded. "One doesn't know how the future can be affected if information crosses time. Better to share as little as possible. Now, where was I? Ah, yes, you were driving and to avoid hitting a boy and his dog, you overcorrected the car and crashed into a frozen pond. While attempting to free yourself, you emerged here in the year 1812."

"That's about it, yes."

"In the modern world, I was a professor of Celtic studies at Berkeley. In this era, I've been fortunate to pursue similar work as a scholar in Oxford. Crossings have become quite a passion project of mine, and through my research, I've determined numerous likely portals on this island that were well known in ancient times, predating the arrival of the Celts and the rise of the Druid class.

"The indigenous Britons believed in the power of the unseen world. There are over one thousand standing stones across Britain and Ireland, and this number doesn't even begin to account for those over the Channel in Brittany, or Basque Country, or as far out as the Black Sea. When we consider the burial mounds, hill forts, and springs, and we can begin to put together ancient maps that reveal energy pathways or ley lines.

"And of course, these are stories that extend far beyond the boundaries of Europe. There are the stone circles of Senegambia located in Senegal and Gambia, and the Stonehenge of Keishu in Japan, and—"

"Ley lines?" Tuck asked.

"For those who believe in the power of the earth's energetic vibrations, ley lines hold great significance, often referred to as the earth's veins. These lines cross the globe conducting metaphysical energy. But here's where things get interesting. At the intersection point of some of these lines, energy gets concentrated like a battery."

"What's a battery?" Lizzy asked.

"Think of it as a device that can store energy. Where we have these intersections, there is an excellent chance at finding a portal. Take Hallow's Gate. The name of the town is itself a clue. *Hallow* originally comes from the Old English word *halig*, which means 'holy' or 'sacred.' Over time, *halig* evolved into *hallow*, which refers to anything that is considered holy, sacred, or consecrated."

"That old cow pond is a sacred energy storage?" Lizzy said incredulously.

"Precisely!" Mr. Fairweather clapped his hands. "And remember, in ancient times, it wouldn't have been an old cow pond at all but a place of reverence, ceremonies, and contemplation. Time leaches memories, and over centuries and even millennia that which was holy and sacred is often forgotten."

"But if that's the case and the pond was some energy battery or whatever, then why didn't it work when I jumped back in?" Tuck asked.

"Ah, very good question." Mr. Fairweather shook a finger, increasing his pace. "The night you took your crossing was December twenty-first, the winter solstice, or Yule, or, as the Druids called it, Alban Arthan. This is a night of great energy, when the ley lines seem to supercharge. The pond would have been at maximum power.

"We know Druids celebrate what is called the Wheel of the Year, and while they arrived after the first people of Briton, they learned some of their knowledge. The wheel is made up of eight Druid high holidays, times when I believe the energy super-charges through the ley lines. Some you will know, like Samhain, or Halloween in your time, Tuck. But the next one is in a few weeks—Lughnasadh, which has been mostly forgotten. It was said to honor the beginning of the harvest."

Lizzy glanced at Tuck, only to find him already staring at her.

"If I go back to the pond on Lughnasadh, you think that I'll . . ."

"I think there's a reasonable chance you will cross back to your own time. And given the accident and the trauma—I do wonder about one of my theories, the omni-reality paradox. For people like myself, who cross over with full knowledge of their actions, my best guess is there is a straight transference of corporal matter."

"I'm not following," Tuck said. "Can you explain it to me like I'm in kindergarten or something?"

"Certainly, I'd be thrilled to boil down my years of complex esoteric research into a neat little sound bite," Zeke said with a wry chuckle. "In essence, I suspect that a portal can be used a bit like an airport, enabling a person to enter at one location and exit at another. However, my omni-reality paradox theory takes this a step further, addressing what might occur when an individual experiences a traumatic event and crosses unintentionally.

"According to this theory, it's conceivable that the person's body could remain in a state of stasis, such as a coma, in their original world. Simultaneously, their presence in another time period could be a predestined event, meaning that their existence in that time was always meant to occur. In other words, their body might exist in two different times and realities at once."

"Forget kindergarten. I need the preschool CliffsNotes," Tuck muttered.

"It's a paradox," Zeke said with a shrug. "Absurd in nature and yet—"

"Wait." Lizzy held up a hand. "Let's suppose that all of this is true about ley lines and batteries or what have you. And imagine that Tuck enters the pool to cross at the correct date and time. Who is to say that he won't end up in the time of William the Conqueror? Or back when those so-called ancient Britons roamed the island in nothing but furs and mud?"

"Ah." Mr. Fairweather nodded. "That's a question, isn't it? And a very good one. Now, first, it's important to remember that everything I am saying is speculative. There is no independent research to verify these claims, just educated guesses, if you like. But while I have never personally encountered another crosser, I've come across stories here and there of others—and one thing the legends and stories hold in common is the idea of a lodestone. If a person has an affinity for someone in a time, they place their mental effort there. The lodestone acts as a sort of magnet that draws the person to that time."

"But you yourself have never returned?" Lizzy asked. "You suggest Tuck should go off wandering through time and space when you have not?"

"I'm not suggesting he do anything." Mr. Fairweather's tone remained infuriatingly mild. "If he wants to return, this is what I know."

"Why don't you try?" Lizzy swallowed. "I don't mean to sound snappish. I truly am curious. Why don't you return?"

"Because my hands are bound with beautiful manacles." Mr. Fairweather pointed to a ring on his finger. "I fell in love. I have a wife now and two beautiful children. I wasn't born into this time, but it's where I belong, and I'm not willing to risk crossing four people through a portal to the same destination. While I believe in the power of the lodestone, it is a theory, and my reality is that I put my family first. So here is where I landed; here is where I'll remain."

"I don't want to be asking only prying questions, but I do have another," she said.

"Never say sorry when an inquiry is to be made," Mr. Fairweather exclaimed. "I'm an academic. While I have veered very much into the metaphysical world, I do value debate and questions."

"If a lodestone is what is to guide Tuck home, what led you both to this time? You had no prior knowledge of or acquaintance with this period. It sounds as if you, Mr. Fairweather, were far more interested in life thousands of years ago, but Tuck, well, Tuck didn't have a great deal of curiosity in this century."

"True," Tuck agreed with a shrug.

"Well, if I might be so bold, I'd like to suggest that this could well prove the lodestone theory—insofar as it's possible."

"Do go on," Lizzy said.

"I crossed and met the woman who became my wife," Mr. Fairweather said. "I came to my lodestone without knowing or planning." He smiled, his eyes darting between her and Tuck. "Perhaps it is the same for the two of you? The mysteries of fate."

There wasn't much to say after this. Tuck and Mr. Fairweather talked a little hockey. They agreed not to share any news from the future to be safe, but Mr. Fairweather asked if Lizzy would write if they did decide to try the portal and it worked.

The walk back to the townhouse was quiet. Tuck glanced at her again and again, but she pretended to be otherwise focused on admiring a bird singing in a low branch, or a pretty horse and carriage. Anything to avoid focusing on the many confusing things Mr. Fairweather had spoken about.

When they got to her street, Tuck paused. "Don't shut me out."

"I don't know what you mean." She attempted to laugh it off. "No one is shutting anything."

"Can you talk to me? Please?"

"I am pleased we have a viable plan to return you home," she said briskly. "It's coming up soon, so we will need to plan our departure from London. Of course, there is that little tiny problem that this is all going to work based on the loose-knit theory of some man. I'm trying to get my mind around the fact that when you cross you might very well be sending yourself right into the heart of the bubonic plague or the Viking wars."

"You heard what he said about the lodestones."

"I did, but does it feel strong enough to stake your life on it?"

He halted. "What do you want from me? To stay here in 1812?"

She glanced around. The street was quiet. A few pedestrians were out, but no one was close enough to eavesdrop.

But still . . .

"This is not a conversation to have in public." She resumed walking, and he followed.

"Well, it's a conversation we need to have."

They didn't speak again until they were in her bedchamber. The house had been empty when they arrived, which wasn't a surprise. Mr. Alby and Henry were likely at the club and Mother out on a social call.

"Very good," Lizzy said, removing her gloves and laying them on the dressing table. "We learned quite a lot."

"I wouldn't believe a word that came out of Zeke's mouth except for the fact that I have no other explanation for how I got here."

"Yet all he uttered was fraught with peril. What happens if you end up in another, more dangerous time? If you emerge from a pond at the wrong time and the wrong person sees you, that could be your doom."

"He talked about lodestones. My sister is one. I could focus on her. She drives me crazy, no doubt. But she's my closest family."

"As a theory." Lizzy's voice cracked. "As nothing more than speculation."

"Are you crying?"

"Should I be ashamed of tears?"

"No. God, no. It's just . . . I'm not sure I've ever made a lover cry about me before."

"Congratulations to you, then." She swiped at her eyes, willing the tears to dry up. But they kept coming.

"That's not a track record I want. Babe. Come here."

She stiffened as he embraced her. "I'm not a babe. I'm a very confused woman." He didn't release her. If anything, he held her tighter.

"You were meant to be a stepping stone to all my ambitions; instead, you became my rock." She buried her face into his chest, inhaling freshly laundered cotton. "I wasn't supposed to develop feelings for you."

He stopped patting her back. "What did you say?"

She pushed him off in a quick gesture that took him by surprise. "I said I am developing an attachment to you, which is not only a bad idea, but a worse one to say out loud. I should be telling myself it's a passing fancy and that it means very little. But I don't like to lie to myself. And that's not what this is. It's not some silly fancy because you are a handsome man who happens to be around me. Or because there is a novel strangeness about our circumstances. Or because we married. It's as if somehow you became the air that I breathe. And the thought of you leaving, it's suffocating."

"You care about me?" he repeated, searching her face. "More than this just being fun?"

"I won't repeat it." Her face was flaming. "Because when you speak a thing, you give it more power." She pinched her eyes closed and counted to three. "I've told you my truth, and that's enough. You don't have to be polite and make some excuse to spare my feelings. But you can do me the courtesy of forgetting I ever mentioned it."

"That's not going to happen." He moved with speed and precision, his gaze fixed on her.

"What are you doing?" Before the question was finished, she was up against the wall.

"Who said I'd make an excuse?"

"Tuck." It was impossible to take a breath when he was so close, and when he looked so keenly serious.

"Have you never thought even one time that I might care about you too? That I might have been developing genuine feelings ever since you hit me in the head with that stupid half-eaten apple?"

"But that's impossible."

"The hell it is." His warm mouth slanted over hers, and as their tongues tangled, she knew she had gotten it all very, very wrong. Tuck wasn't a stepping stone, nor was he her rock. He was a landslide.

CHAPTER TWENTY-FIVE

Tuck wasn't reckless, and he wasn't stupid. But with Lizzy in his arms, all bets were off; neither of them could be content with just a kiss, not anymore. The countdown that began ticking at their first meeting was running out. She wrapped her hand around the back of his neck and he sank deeper into her mouth—invisible currents surged as if ley lines ran through his veins.

"Tell me what you want me to do to you," he murmured into her hungry lips.

"You could surprise me." Her gasp was hot on his skin.

"I'm serious. I need to know how far you want to take this."

She gripped him harder, her nails scratching gently at his skin. "There are too many decisions to be made and plans to figure out. I don't want to do that here, not now. You understand lovemaking. I don't." Her voice softened, growing almost shy. "So rather than me asking for what I think I want, why don't you give me what you believe I need?"

He smoothed a loose strand of hair off her damp cheek. "You want me to take the lead."

"Please."

"All right, then. We're getting into some trouble." He traced the skin beneath her jaw with slow, lazy circles. "Good trouble."

"More." She wiggled closer.

"You trying to tell me what to do?" He cocked a teasing brow. "Just for that, I'm going to go even slower."

He edged his fingers over the delicate ridge of her clavicle, inch by unhurried inch, traveling toward the swell of her breast. As her breathing hitched, turning into uneven pants, he slowed down even further.

"You love it when I touch you."

She opened her mouth to reply and he nipped her lower lip. "That wasn't a question." Her hips jerked as he slid his palm down, capturing the weight of her breast. With a thumb, he teased her nipple, growling when it peaked even through the layers of fabric. "And you like that."

A hitched gasp.

"Good girl."

Something indigo and intoxicated entered her eyes, making her gaze go unfocused and hazy. The only sound in the room was their ragged breathing.

"Let's get you out of this dress."

It wasn't quick work. She came in layers, the final one was a long white slip. Once he'd slid that off, she wore nothing but a half-corset and stockings held in place by pale blue garters.

Time slowed down as he took in her body. The flare of her hips. The dark triangle of hair. The subtle quiver of her thighs. Her hands fluttered as if she fought an urge to cover herself. So shy.

"Don't hide." His voice was hoarse. "Remember how I kissed you in Scotland, slid my tongue across that sweet pussy?"

Her pupils were so wide they threatened to eclipse the blue.

"I'm going to get another taste. I'm tasting everything today." He ran a hand over the front of his pants, stroking himself for a moment. "Fuck. I'm hard. I'm always hard for you."

Her sharp intake of breath was his reward.

"Your little sounds make me want to do bad things. Climb on the bed."

She obeyed quickly, pushing to the center of the mattress and leaning back on her hands.

"Spread your legs."

She opened them a fraction.

"Wider," he ordered.

She bit her bottom lip, but complied.

"Just like that," he rumbled, nodding his approval. "Do you feel exposed?"

"Very."

"Focus on how that feels—the air on that sensitive skin." He climbed over her and nipped her neck before licking the spot with the flat of his tongue. "Where am I going to touch you first?" He sat back, took her ankle, and brought it up to his shoulder, caressing a hand along her silk-clad calf until he reached her garter and, with a single tug, undid the ribbon. As he rolled the stocking down, there was virtually no difference between the texture of the stocking and the feel of her skin. "You're so soft." He turned to press a kiss to the side of her leg before mirroring the action on her opposite side.

With her legs propped on his shoulders, he reached down. "You know what I'm going to do now?"

Her lashes fluttered, her "No" so soft as to almost not exist.

"I'm going to open you like a present." He reached down and got to work unhooking her short corset until she was naked, her full breasts tapering into dusky nipples.

Fuck. He could barely breathe, let alone think straight. But he had to remain in control. "Stay still for me. Can you do that?"

She gave a little nod, lips parted, her features slack.

"I want to hear you promise."

"I promise."

He bent, his tongue circling her nipple, and she bowed, back arching.

He pulled back with a mock scolding. "I told you to stay still."

She half laughed, half bared her teeth. "But you want to torture me."

"Only in the best of ways. You said you wanted me calling the shots. You're still good with that plan?"

"I must be a masochist."

"Nah. Look at you. You're greedy for pleasure." He bent low again, pausing before taking her hard nipple back into his mouth and laving the peak. "But don't worry, I'm going to let you move later. For now, though, I want you to hold still, keep every ounce of that busy brain focused on me."

"Why?" Her eyes were glazed.

"Because you're mine, and you're never forgetting that." And he sucked. Hard.

This time she held still. God—he loved that this woman would and could do damn well whatever she pleased, and right here and now, it pleased her to trust him. He wanted her to concentrate and quiet her mind because when he began to level up, it would be more pleasurable if she was fully present.

Normally he liked to check in on a new lover. Ask questions. *Do you like this? Harder? Faster?* But this wasn't a new lover. This was Lizzy. *His* Lizzy. All the focus he'd honed, he'd use here, now. Instead of tracking pucks, he tracked her breaths, her goose bumps, her little moans, and her trembles. He wasn't cautious or tentative with his strokes and explorations; he wanted her aching, tight, and hot.

He worshiped her neck, the sensitive sides of her breasts, the inner curves of her arms, the soft span of her belly—and then he had his fingers at her center.

Slowly, he traced an outline around her triangle of hair, letting the soft satin of it caress his fingers. She was so wet it sheened, but he still placed his fingers against her mouth.

"What?" Her brows crinkled.

"Suck," he murmured. The sight of her taking his fingers into her mouth nearly sent him over the edge right there. There was something so erotic, so perfectly fucking filthy about the sight.

"That's it, work them over," he panted. "Make them drip."

Her cheeks hollowed as she sucked harder. It was too good—shit. At this rate, they'd be over before they started.

He pulled his hand back and let a bead of saliva drip down his fingers to the hint of her inner lips, the pink petals just visible. She shuddered as he began to circle in featherlight strokes, slick and steady, working until he found a rhythm that made her teeth latch on her lower lip.

"I'm going to put a finger inside now. Help you adjust first."

She fisted the blankets. He opened her with one hand, lifting her clit a fraction, pulling back the hood to heighten the sensation. Then he dipped his middle finger in, pushing gently and holding, not far, only to where he could feel the ridges of her G-spot. As she began to breathe again, he pressed in while using his thumb on her clitoris, crooking his finger in a come-hither gesture as she pressed a hand to her mouth, moaning into her skin. She was so wet it was time for one more finger, then another. Her stomach rose and fell in short heaves.

"You are doing such a good job holding still for me." Her cheeks went as pink as peach blossoms. "But you want to move, don't you?"

"Please. Please." She was begging now. "Please."

"Let you move or get release?"

"Both. Everything. God, I don't know. It's good. So good."

"Want to know what makes it even better?"

Her brows rose, gaze pleading.

Without breaking his rhythm, he dipped his mouth to her clit, humming with pleasure at her salty, needy taste. It would be best for her to come once now, so she could be relaxed before he entered her. He sucked her clit, then lapped it. The rhythm worked and it wasn't long until she came like a tide, her inner waves crashing over his fingers as he continued to work her, lighter now, ensuring she didn't ebb too fast. He glanced up and her mouth was slack, a loose lock of hair stuck to one damp cheek.

"That was impossible," she murmured. "How was it so good?"

"Oh, babe." He kissed her inner thigh. "We're just getting started."

CHAPTER TWENTY-SIX

Lizzy didn't have time for a single coherent thought before Tuck had fisted off his shirt and kicked his pants from the bed. Where should she look first? The wall of shoulders? The narrow waist? Each of his muscles begged for independent research. He was exposed in all his brutal beauty, unselfconscious as she finally dared to stare at his thick length. When she heard him swallow, a strange, primal hunger caught her off guard with its intensity.

"I don't have condoms—any protection—but I can't get you pregnant," he said.

The reality of what they were about to do settled in, a tingly anticipation that made her thighs twitch. "You shared that information before . . . because of the medicine you took during your illness."

"That's right." He gripped his hand over his shaft and stroked it a few times, root to tip.

The movement was hypnotic.

"May I try? I want to see how you feel."

He took her hand and placed it on his shaft. "Yeah. Grip firmly and jerk it like I was doing."

"Am I doing it right?"

"If you did any better, I'd be fucked before we fucked," he

muttered, his eyes half-closed. After another minute he took her wrist and stilled her rhythm.

"I'm going inside of you now, okay? I'll take it slow, but it will feel better when we start moving together."

"Yes." She licked her lips as he crawled over her, nudging his shaft between her legs.

He pressed his lips against her ear. "Ready?"

"Yes." Her eyes flew open. The stretch was so different from his fingers. It was far thicker, a burning pressure that rose deep, deep, good God, so deep, within her core. And then he was closer than he'd ever been, hip bones flush with hers.

"You okay?" he ground out.

She sucked in a breath, struggling to locate the right words. For she was still herself but not. Her body had always been her body, the lines of Lizzy Wooddash were a clear border, a personal country—but Tuck was here now too. And not just inside her body, but also her heart. He was everywhere and yet she didn't have a need to push him off; if anything, she wanted . . . "Go on, then." The words exhaled out of her.

Tuck's shoulders shook with his surprised chuckle even as he obeyed. His movements were gentle, small pulses. As she acclimated, taking his advice and rocking back in reply, their bodies engaged in a slow, languid dance. Unexpected.

She'd expected a claiming—a man coming to conquer. But as Tuck loosened the tension in her body, she marveled at how she could hold him so completely, her muscles snug and tight. She would be happy to remain this close forever. He followed her lead, adjusting his rhythm to hers. Lifting her head, she captured his mouth as they increased their speed. He drank in her breathless, soft sounds and slid a hand between them, moving with expert fingers.

It didn't last long after that. She couldn't think. Her mind wasn't capable of holding this much feeling, her blood ran thick as honey, and a trickle of perspiration streamed down her breast. How was this intensifying? How was he everywhere?

A whimper escaped as he pressed his thumb on her bud. He muttered a litany of filthy, lovely words and an edge appeared, fracturing her mind. The full, anchored sensation was replaced by a vast open space before the world contracted into a point of pure pleasure.

"Tuck!" His name broke through her lips in a thick sob, and then she lost the power of speech, only managing an exultant moan. He bucked, and wherever she was, he was there too.

Her name was a roar on his lips. She gripped his muscles and gave him everything.

When she regained her senses, he was lying on his back, holding her to his chest.

She lifted a hand and covered his heart, letting it thunder under her palm.

"That was a surprise." She licked her lips. "I didn't ever imagine it would be like that."

His chuckle was thick. "Baby. It's never like that."

"What do you mean?" She raised her head. "I didn't do something wrong, did I? I wasn't sure what to—"

"It was extraordinary." He pressed a kiss to the side of her forehead. "What I'm saying is it's never that good—that was next level."

"What's the level after that?" She propped herself up, hand on chin.

"I'm not following."

"If you say there is a next level, there must be a level after that and one after that, correct? And if this was our first time together, I presume we should be able to go even higher, would we not? Should we try again and see?"

"Right now?"

"I don't have any other pressing engagements on my social calendar today, do you?"

He sputtered a moment before chuckling, warm and lazy. "Beautiful monster, you might honestly kill me."

"All part of my grand widow's plan," she murmured.

"Evil woman." He threw a forearm over his eyes and yawned.

She took the opportunity to admire this big naked male, sprawled out for her discovery. His shaft was still half hard, and she had to admit it looked far more appealing in person than in the sketches from her book. Perhaps because it was Tuck and every part of him felt precious to her. His stomach was smooth but for a trail of hair extending from his navel. A few ridges of muscles rippling. There was a wicked ancient scar on his knuckle, nearly white against his tanned skin.

"What's this from?" she asked, tracing her finger over it. "I've been curious."

He grunted. "When I was a kid, my dad used to make a rink for me in our backyard. He'd build a border and then set in a liner. After that it was just a matter of using a hose to fill it with water—that's like a long, flexible tube that carries water from one location to another, for gardens, to water plants and stuff like that."

"Much more convenient than buckets."

"Very." His lips quirked. "So, he'd fill the rink with water once it was cold enough and it would freeze. Then he'd smooth it all out. It was funny, though, he never wanted my help even though it was for me. He'd say I'd mess it up. He's like that—we call it being a control freak. But once it was ready, he ordered me out there to practice all the time. And if he wasn't at work he'd come out and shoot with me. He used to play hockey too, back in the day—never professionally, but it was a thing for him. But eventually, I don't know, I got better, I surpassed his abilities. I could block all of his shots.

"One time there was a big storm. He told me to get on my gear and go outside and I didn't want to. I was playing a game or something. I just didn't want to freeze my ass off. But he made me, and this isn't a guy you say no to easily.

"We were out there. The wind was howling. It's cold as hell. And he's shooting at me, and I can catch whatever he dishes out; it wasn't a challenge anymore. And finally, I yelled, 'What's the point? You're not that good, so can we go in now?'

"I shouldn't have spoken to him like that, but I was freezing. I threw off my gloves and I announced he could stay but I wasn't. I wasn't ready when he shot—the puck flew at me and I didn't want to break my hand, so I hit the deck and it missed me. He skated up and skidded to a halt, his blade sliced my hand, and then he told me to put away the equipment before going inside. That's the last time we played together." He paused. "I remember how much blood was on the ice."

She had half a mind to crawl through time and find this horrible man. "If I ever saw your father, I'd not be held responsible for my actions."

"If it was just me, I could have taken it. But he and my mom— what they did to my sister. Well, we don't talk much these days. But you don't want all my sad stories."

"Untrue." She lightly pinched one of his nipples and he jerked. "I want to know all the parts of you."

"My sister likes women. They don't approve."

Lizzy frowned. "They'd prefer she be a woman who doesn't like women? That makes no sense."

"I mean she likes them romantically—and exclusively."

"Oh. I see." Awareness dawned. "Like Georgie."

Tuck raised his brows. "Yeah. Like that, I guess. My parents believe it's morally wrong, and so they don't talk to her now unless it's strictly necessary. It's hard on Nora. She used to be close to my mom—and now there's just this gulf. But she can't change who she is to make them happy. That's not love. So she decided to study far away."

"I hope your sister finds her happiness."

"Me too. I want that so much."

"And I hope your father stubs his toe and that his toast is always cold."

"Get over here." Tuck's voice was deep with amusement. He hauled her onto him so she straddled his waist.

"What did I do to deserve you, huh?"

"Something that pleased the fates." She glanced down. "It's growing hard again."

"You have that power over me."

"Like a witch." She waved her hands as if casting a spell.

"More like an enchantress." He braced her hips between his hands. "This time you could take the reins."

She glanced down. "Me?"

"I remember some big talk last night in the carriage. What was all that about wanting to ride St. George's dragon?"

She covered her face. "Oh my goodness. I'd hoped that was a dream."

"It's definitely one of mine, sweetheart."

Perhaps it was too much. Maybe she was too greedy. It was

entirely possible that she wanted more than the world would ever see fit to give her. But that didn't mean she'd stop asking. She eased herself over him, his tip at her cleft. She was still so ready that she took him again easily, her body hungry.

"And now I ride you?"

"Sure, baby." He made a low growl of appreciation. "Let yourself go."

She made an extremely slow hip circle and that was good. Her nipples hardened. Bending forward, she arched and increased the pressure, bringing herself right over his pelvic bone, right at the spot that had felt so good before. She kept the angle to maintain the contact.

"You're beautiful." He never took his gaze from her, the strain evident in his clenched jaw. His eye contact was fierce, lethal almost, and yet she knew she had the lead now. He'd handed her the power and the fact made the muscles coil low in her belly.

"I'm close. So close."

He went taut. "Together. We go together."

He took her hands and laced his fingers with hers, and as she writhed, her body quaking, he flowed into her. The only sounds in the world were his rasping grunts and the wet sounds of their bodies meeting as she rode through the last of her pleasure.

She melted into him, exhausted but beyond blissful. As they lay together, their hearts an echo of the other, it seemed impossible that this connection—more real than any she'd ever known—could eventually become a bittersweet memory. Would this moment resonate through the ages, or become another forgotten tale?

CHAPTER TWENTY-SEVEN

Tuck rubbed the sleep gritting his eyes, and squinted into the twilight seeping into the bedchamber. Odd—it felt as if a sound somewhere within the house had dragged him from sleep, but it seemed all quiet now. He leaned down and kissed Lizzy's temple, then shifted his gaze up to the fancy plaster designs on the ceiling, all roses, grape leaves, and cherubs. In so many ways, this felt like where he was supposed to be—except not. His stomach twisted at the thought of leaving Nora all alone. He was her family.

But why not take Lizzy when he went? Imagine her in jeans, driving his Jeep, or on a date night at a wine bar, wearing a killer black dress paired with heels. The thought of her reaction to everyday activities like grocery shopping or going to the movies made him grin. Damn, it would be so much fun.

And what about her family? It wasn't as if Rufus Alby or Henry would be devastated by her absence.

She deserved happiness, and he could give her that.

Wait.

He froze—ears straining. The faint, far-off sound rose again—the same one that must have woken him up. Goose bumps broke out down the backs of his arms. Somewhere in the house a woman wailed.

Lizzy stirred, her lids flying open. "Mamma," she mumbled, pushing herself up to sit. "Why is she crying like that?"

They rose and poured water from the pitcher into the porcelain basin, cleaning themselves before dressing quickly. All the while, the wails continued. Tuck's guts clenched at the sound.

They crept downstairs. Lizzy's mother was in the drawing room, pacing in front of the fireplace, a letter half crumpled in one hand.

"Mamma?" Lizzy's voice was sharp with worry. "What has happened?"

"There you are! Where have you been hiding away? I've been beside myself with worry."

"You're frightening me."

"A most dreadful accident occurred at the Row this very afternoon. A horse took a fright and bolted and a man died. We know him—it's Frank Witt, the husband of your friend Cornelia."

"No." Lizzy pressed a hand to her mouth. "That's impossible. I saw her the other night and she was so happy."

"And now she'll never see him again. Oh, Elizabeth, it's a most ghastly turn of events. He was promenading with her when a white horse of doom flew into a wild frenzy—something must have spooked it. Frank removed dear Cornelia from harm's way, but in doing so he was run down. He met his untimely demise on the dirt path in full view. I say, an indecorous end for a member of such a respectable family."

"Mamma!" Lizzy looked annoyed if not shocked. "A good man is dead. I think we can leave off dissecting whether or not his end had sufficient decorum."

"Well." Her mother plucked a handkerchief from the sofa and dabbed her eyes. "I imagine it is of importance to his dear mother. The family is making funeral arrangements, but we shall all be calling to pay our respects prior, of course. Poor Cornelia, she will look ghastly in mourning. Remember how washed out she appeared after her father's death? Black doesn't suit her coloring in the slightest. Her figure's remained passable, though, so she should be able to make another match. Although I wouldn't advise Henry to throw over his pursuit of Olivia Abbot Davies."

And her thirty thousand pounds, Tuck mentally added.

"Mother!" Lizzy's voice rose. "Frank Witt, whom we have dined with on multiple occasions over the years and who was quite a kind man, has not been dead a day. I think you can wait to ponder his wife's marriage prospects."

Her mother pressed her lips into a thin line. "You're absolutely right, my dear. Fortunately, Frank's estate should provide for Cornelia quite well. She could choose to remain a widow, I suppose, and no one would question her decision. It's certainly better than being an ape leader." She waved her hands between the two of them. "At least you're saved from that particular fate."

Turning toward the door, she added, "Now if you'll excuse me, I must locate my lady's maid. My puce taffeta has faded to more of a mauve. I need her opinion on whether it would be suitable for paying condolences. Your gray silk will suffice nicely. And someone shall locate a black silk armband for Mr. Taylor."

Then she was gone.

"I'm sorry." Lizzy sprawled into a chair and kicked out her legs with a frustrated groan. "I wish I could say she means well, but that would make me a liar. As a widow herself, maybe she feels entitled to her judgment. I'm not certain she loved Papa, although I recall them being affectionate in their way."

"Her actions don't reflect on you." Tuck knew that from experience. "Our families will behave how they are going to behave, and we have no control over it."

"Try telling that to the ton. She is a ridiculous woman and so I too am at risk to be deemed as such. But then, so are most of her friends. Poor Cornelia. We aren't incredibly close, but she is friendly and amusing and had clearly found a love match with Frank."

He went around to the back of her chair and placed his hands on her shoulders, rubbing the tight muscles. "Your mom talked about apes. What was that?"

"Oh. That." She scoffed, plucking a loose thread from her dress. "It's a particularly charming old adage. As you've learned, women of a marriageable age fit into one of three categories: spinsters, wives, or widows. Among these, only wives or widows are truly accepted. Spinsters, on the other hand, are considered unnatural. Those who persist in their unwed state are occasionally dubbed 'ape leaders,' a term suggesting their ultimate punishment in hell, where they'll be forced to lead apes—a supposed punishment for their controversial lifestyle."

"The fuck? What the hell is wrong with people?"

"That's perhaps a little more inelegant than I'd express it, but yes. Exactly." She buried her face in her hands. "I need to clear my conscience."

"What is it?"

"I'm afraid . . ." Her voice wobbled. "I'm afraid I've been too quick to celebrate widowhood. Before I met you, I had no clear understanding of what it might be like to be married to a person whom I not only liked but also respected. I'd been led to the idea that matrimony could never be an agreeable state, so I ignored the evidence that some people have found it quite fulfilling. One such person is Cornelia, who is now moving from wife to widow, and will no doubt find herself the worse for it. You see, she enjoyed her husband's company, and suddenly I'm struck with the thought that . . . that . . ."

He froze. Waiting to see if she'd say the words—which ones exactly, he wasn't sure, but he hoped they'd have something to do with her not viewing him as a means to an end. Maybe she'd say that this marriage of convenience had become infinitely more complicated.

But she never finished her thought, as Henry wandered through the door.

"What's with all the serious faces? Did somebody die? Ah." He clicked his tongue. "Pardon me. I heard the news at the club. I should go pay Olivia a visit. She was rather close to Cornelia. I'm sure she'd appreciate it if I put in an appearance. What do you think?"

"That you're an unfeeling monster?" Lizzy asked dully.

"I shouldn't say unfeeling, no. When I think of marrying Olivia, I have quite a lot of ideas on how to invest all that money and it makes me quite cheerful indeed."

"Why is my family so insistent on being awful?" Lizzy addressed this question to the ceiling, but Tuck had to agree.

"You should be grateful that our father even allows you and this oversized colonial bear to remain in residence." Henry gave a mocking nod in Tuck's direction.

During one playoff game, a forward on the Canucks got one in the net. Tuck had put his all into blocking, but it wasn't his moment. While he was pushing himself off the ice, the scoring player, in his hurry to celebrate with teammates, plowed through the crease, knocking Tuck back on his knees. Normally, he could shake shit off, but that day? He was ornery. And that player? He was a showboating prick. Tuck had made like a bull and charged after him. The only reason he didn't get off a truly good punch was because he got stopped by a lineman.

He had a sense of déjà vu right now. Henry deserved at least a bloody nose. But Lizzy must have sensed the fact that he was seeing red, because she caught his eye and gave her head a subtle shake.

No. That will make it worse. He wants to provoke you.

Instead, he used the tactic he'd perfected with his dad and made himself a statue, his face nothing but impassive granite, staring ahead. The strategy worked as Henry soon shuffled off. No doubt there was a kitten to kick somewhere.

"We must go pay our respects," Lizzy said. "You'll come with me, won't you? I'm dreading this."

"I'll be there every step of the way."

The next afternoon, Tuck was next to Lizzy and behind her parents as a servant at Cornelia Witt's townhome ushered them into a crowded parlor. The gathering was dressed like a bruise; everywhere were black, gray, brown, or purple outfits. The atmosphere was subdued, yet an undeniable frenetic energy buzzed through the air. It was as though most folks present couldn't help but feel a strange thrill amidst the unexpected news of death. Folks whispered, and tutted, and stared around wide-eyed, registering who was making an appearance.

In the center of the space sat the widow, dully staring out the window, as if outside was another reality, one in which her husband still lived and her life was as it had always been.

"I must go and speak to her," Lizzy whispered to him. "I think it best if you don't. It must all be feeling very raw, and I don't want to remind her of any of my recent happiness. It feels cruel."

"Understood. I'm very good at standing around and ignoring people."

She huffed out a laugh. "Thank you for understanding."

He stood by a potted plant as Lizzy approached Cornelia, giving her a quick embrace before taking a seat beside her. Cornelia took her hand and appeared to be present for a moment. She and Lizzy spoke for around five minutes, heads close together, before Lizzy nodded, they embraced again, and Lizzy took her leave.

For the rest of the hour that they were there, Lizzy barely spoke. They stood side by side until Tuck took to counting the seconds in his head before they could depart. It wasn't until they were back in her room that he felt able to speak freely.

"What happened? It looked as if your conversation got intense fast."

"I'd already felt guilty. After speaking with Cornelia, I am a wretch. She told me how happy her marriage had made her and that if I found even a fraction of the same joy with you, then it would make even the hard parts worth it. Cornelia said she'd always grown up imagining what it would be like to be a beautiful bride, and live a fairy tale, but not what to do if it came to an end. She hoped I had a long time before we concluded our story. And that I should never take anyone I love for granted for even a minute." Lizzy began to pace, one arm wrapped tightly around her middle. "But we can't ever presume we can just grow old together. Or that this strange, sad world is fair or makes sense.

"If we want to ensure you are back in time for the next chance at going home, we will need to leave within a few weeks. That will give us a little time to say goodbye."

"But I don't want to say goodbye, Lizzy."

She wiped her eyes. "You can't remain here. It was a happy idea, but it cannot practically work. What if your sickness returns? There is no medicine in this time to save you and I'll be hanged to watch a doctor cover you in leeches when I know that somewhere else, you could live, but you were dying to be with me. I won't do it; I can't do it. It'll be difficult enough to be a widow as a ruse, but I don't want to know the pain of knowing you are truly gone forever. At least this way I can think that you are out there somewhere."

"But—Lizzy—you'd be such great friends with Nora. You could—"

"I can't live in your time. My place is here. I have my friends— Georgie and Jane. I'll leave London and live at the Woodlands. And while Mamma is difficult, I can't force her to endure the loss of a child. Thanks to you, no one will bother me about spinster-hood. I'll be respectable even if I remain independent forever, and someday I'll inherit Georgie's estate. I have my writing. I haven't been able to focus on it, but I want to; the fact that Jane was able to have success is motivating me to want to work hard."

"You don't want to be with me?"

"We will have a few more weeks. Then we must face reality. I want you to have your dreams, and I want mine."

"What about the dream of you and me together?" he asked.

"That . . ." Her smile was sad. "That was make-believe, don't you know? All the very best love stories end tragically."

CHAPTER TWENTY-EIGHT

The night lay silent, devoid of any stirring breeze. Above, through the shroud of clouds, faint glimmers of cold light pierced the darkness. The stars stood sentinel over Lizzy's solitary stroll. As she unlatched the gate to the cemetery, the frigid metal protested with a loud creak, causing her to startle. Nearby stood the imposing mausoleums of the wealthiest families, their names all too familiar to her. Yet, she sought a more secluded spot, away from prying eyes. Her gaze settled on a simple hand-dug grave, its freshly disturbed earth marked by a modest stone. Dread filled her at the sight, but she pressed on, each step slower than the last, the crunch of gravel beneath her shoes echoing loudly in the stillness of the night.

Finally, she reached that darkest, shadowy corner of the yard. From underneath her black shawl she removed a single red rose and bent to throw it at the bare clumps of dirt. The name carved into the stone read TUCKER TAYLOR RIP 1812.

Lizzy startled awake, beads of sweat coursing down her back.

Tuck glanced up from her stepfather's newspaper that he was reading beside her in the carriage.

"You okay? You've been twitching in your sleep."

"I—I simply had a dream, nothing more," she murmured,

her hand bracing against the brocaded wall for support. "We're nearly there." The rolling green fields of Southampton spread out beneath the unblemished deep blue skies. This was reality; she wasn't in a cemetery, and Tuck was not deceased. Yet, this was the third time she had dreamt this since Frank Witt's passing. It was as though the looming reality of becoming a widow haunted her, forcing her to confront all the careless words she had uttered about it in the past. Despite the tight ache in her stomach and the throbbing in her chest, she couldn't bring herself to plead for Tuck to stay. Not if his health declined again and something unfortunate occurred. She would never forgive herself.

"Hey now." He slid his hand over and took hers. "Your breathing is speeding up."

"I suppose I'm feeling a bit fatigued," she said with a forced cheeriness.

"You sure that's all?" He searched her face. "I'm here if you need to talk."

"You may always talk to me. But I'm perfectly well, thank you."

He appeared as though he might resist for a moment, and her throat constricted with apprehension. If he insisted on having this conversation now, she feared she would break down in tears. And once she started, she doubted she would be able to compose herself before reaching the Woodlands.

"Georgie and Jane will be glad to see you. Last they saw you, Henry got on the chase right after."

"They both sent me letters cursing his name. If he possesses any morsel of wit within his small head, he would be wise to steer clear of the area. Their capacity for holding grudges surpasses that of most."

"It feels like six years since I crawled out of that pond."

"Everything has changed, hasn't it? And yet out there?" She

gestured to the rural scene out the window. "The world continues as it always has. How many others like us are out there, people whose entire worlds have shifted, and yet the sun rises and sets regardless. Some days are warm, others bring rain. The seasons inexorably change."

"You are acting like we are facing death."

"I'm sorry," she said automatically.

"Don't do that. Apologize if you've done something wrong and you want to make it right. But don't say sorry because you think I'm getting annoyed; that's not who I am, and that's not what we are. I respect you too damn much to need you to make yourself small in the hopes that I'll listen."

He didn't pen her sonnets or odes, but something in his plain speech sent her swooning just the same.

She poked out her lower lip. "Please kiss me, immediately. Right here."

He smirked. "I just have to say a few nice words and you want to kiss me?"

"Truthfully? I always want to kiss you. But right now, I want to kiss you as properly as possible."

"Because?"

"I need no reason. But if I am to offer one, it's for my own pleasure and hopefully yours as well. You make me happy."

"In that case? I accept."

He leaned in and she watched him the whole way. She never got tired of noticing the small ways the brutal hard lines on his face eased when he looked at her. Or how his mouth, wide and stern, softened. She put a hand on his cheek, and he closed his eyes for a long moment. His lashes were so dark and thick. When his lips brushed hers, they both released a sigh, the heat from their breath warming her face. She began to pull back, but he grunted his refusal, his hand reaching up to cup the back of her head.

His subsequent kiss was firmer, more exploratory. As she parted her lips, his tongue slid across hers in a languid manner, as if time were of no concern, when in reality, it was slipping away rapidly. It felt surreal that this moment, so intensely real, would soon become nothing more than a fleeting memory. He pressed in and her neck tilted back as he deepened the kiss, taking his time to taste her properly. She clung to his wide shoulders and let him steal everything he wanted, because the great mystery was that for everything he took, he gave her back twofold.

The carriage jolted with a hard bounce and they knocked apart.

"That's enough. I want Jane and Georgie to be glad to see me. Not to pull into the Woodlands with the idea that if this carriage is rocking don't come a-knocking," he said.

She slapped a hand over her mouth as she swallowed back a giggle. "Rocking?"

"I'm serious." He grinned. "I'd never hear the end of it."

The carriage slowed as the large redbrick home came into view. Somewhere a dog's deep bark began. "Goliath knows we are back."

"That means everyone else does too."

Sure enough, as they stepped out of the carriage, Georgie came rushing out the front door. Before Lizzy could even raise a hand in greeting, her cousin enveloped her in a warm embrace.

"My, what a tumultuous time you've had," Georgie exclaimed, checking her over. "Come inside, come inside. Let's have you fed and rested. I'm eager to hear every detail."

"What's the order of events here?" Lizzy teased. "Eating while telling you everything? Or resting first?"

"Let's see if you can manage both at once. You're talented. And you." Georgie released Lizzy and dusted off her skirts while eyeing Tuck up and down. "You've gotten bigger in your absence."

"Nah. If anything, I've dropped weight. I haven't had time to focus on my fitness."

"Hmmm." Georgie gave them both a suspicious glance. "Something tells me that's quite a lie. Lizzy's cheeks are too bright, for starters."

"Cousin!" Lizzy was scandalized, but Georgie was already leading them back inside, chuckling to herself.

"Jane shall be coming to dine and will remain a few days."

"How is she?"

"Consumed by this book. I believe she is almost finished, though she keeps saying that. She claims it's her best one yet, which is alarming given that *Sense and Sensibility* was frightfully good. How about you? Have you been writing?"

"Not a word," Lizzy admitted. "But . . ." She forced a bright smile. "That won't be for long. Soon I'll have all the time and I'm ready to get right to work."

Georgie drew near. "Does that mean what I think it means?" she muttered, out of earshot of the servants carrying in their cases. Tuck was walking at a discreet distance, giving them time to catch up with each other. "You figured out a way to send him back?"

"I'll explain when Jane comes. I don't think I can do it twice." Something in Lizzy's voice caught Georgie's attention.

"I see," her cousin said in a tone that made it clear she likely didn't, but she was willing to be more patient than usual. "Shall I put Tuck back into Neddy's old room or—"

"He can be with me," Lizzy said briskly, though she imagined her cheeks must have been the color of summer tomatoes.

"Hmmmm." Her cousin sent out a few orders before asking

for tea and cakes to be brought into the drawing room. Tuck excused himself to stretch his legs.

It didn't take long for Georgie to be spraying crumbs of cake as Lizzy described encountering Henry in Gretna Green.

"I knew he was a toad, but I hadn't pegged him for a rat," she said, taking a glug of tea to clear her throat. "We'd thought locking him up would be deterrent enough, but the horrible creature went crawling down the drainpipe, did he? Too bad he didn't break his traitorous little neck."

"Georgie! Henry is your cousin too," Lizzy scolded.

"Is blood thicker than water when one is as odious as your brother? I think not. He would have either strong-armed you into a hideous marriage with one of his popinjay friends at his club or he would have made your life an absolute living hell if you remained unmarried. Likely forced you to be a governess to his future spawn. Imagine a nursery full of little Henrys." She gave a full-body shiver. "The very notion will haunt my dreams. Ah, there's Jane now."

Lizzy turned to see Jane walking up the front yard, her arms wrapped around her middle and her thin lips mashed together in thought.

"Is she quite all right?" she asked.

"I'm telling you, it's this book. *First Impressions* is what she's calling it, but that isn't a very good name, is it?" Georgie took a sip of tea.

"It's not so bad," Lizzy said diplomatically.

"It's not so good either. She can do better. And I'm sure she will."

Jane was announced to more exclamations and hugs before Georgie got them all back down to business with her usual pragmatism. Lizzy filled them in on what Ezekiel Fairweather had surmised in terms of ley lines, Druids, and the eight wheel dates. By the end, both their eyes were round. They exchanged a glance.

"You believe it will work?" Jane asked.

"Mr. Fairweather seemed to think so, and while it makes little to no sense to me, it also doesn't make a great deal of sense how he arrived here in the first place."

"And in three nights' time, he will go back to the pond, and if he doesn't come out again, it will have worked." Georgie sat back in the chair. "And what will be the story?"

"There cannot be a body," Jane said with authority. "That much is clear. We'll hatch the little story about Mr. Taylor going down to Southampton Water to go bream fishing near Hamble. He takes out a dinghy and doesn't come back by teatime. A fishing accident. We can organize a search party that bears no fruit. Our Lizzy grieves. We observe a time of mourning. And then . . . she is free."

Lizzy tried to take a full breath. Had her stays gotten tighter? Or was the room just overly stuffy?

"Good heavens, that's quite a plan to come up with on the fly. Remind me never to be your enemy," Georgie remarked.

"We can arrange to have all her belongings sent down from London, and she can become permanently installed here. My goodness, Lizzy. When you used to say you dreamed of being a widow, I must confess it felt rather like a dream that we'd indulge. And now look, here you are, right on the precipice of having everything you wanted. You've made all your dreams come true!"

Lizzy grasped the arms of her chair tightly, meeting the smiling countenances of her two closest companions before promptly bursting into tears.

CHAPTER TWENTY-NINE

The cow pond didn't offer much to the eye. It sat in the center of the field, reflecting the clear expanse of sky overhead. Cattails swayed along its banks, while a solitary duck lazily paddled across its surface. Tuck strolled around the perimeter, his gaze sweeping over the basin, searching for any distinctive features that might hint at its significance as some sort of cosmic ley line battery supercharger, as Ezekiel Fairweather had described. He wanted to give Lizzy some time with her people, so he'd decided to take a short stroll around the Woodlands grounds to loosen up his legs after the carriage ride. But he found himself drawn back here. It was as if he needed to see it with his own eyes to believe it was real.

No matter how hard he tried to perceive it differently, there was nothing remotely magical about the scene before him. It was just a splash of water in a field, blending in with countless others in the surrounding area. There were no mystical signs or inexplicable phenomena hinting at the possibility of being transported over two hundred years into the future in three days' time. Yet, the undeniable truth remained that this was the exact same spot where he had first arrived, sinking into the mud while conversing with Lizzy.

It was wild to think that not long ago they had been strangers, and now she was such an integral part of his life. How could he even consider leaving her behind? The very notion sparked a deep-seated resistance within him. Yet he recognized that the decision ultimately lay with her. He wasn't about to force his will upon her; it had to be her choice. Always hers.

He came to a sudden halt and rocked back on his boot heels. If he managed to cross over and return to his era, how much time would have elapsed? Would Nora have presumed him dead? Held a funeral in his honor? Perhaps there was a stone somewhere with his name etched upon it. The mere thought turned his insides upside down.

He was afraid. That was the truth and there was no point lying about it. But he also was ready—or at least resigned. This wasn't his time. He needed to go back. It would tear him in half to do it, but he had a place where he belonged. He had a team and a career he was committed to. And if the worst happened and his cancer came back . . . he wasn't going to hurt Lizzy, dying slowly while she was unable to do anything to help him, and only blaming herself.

He knew what he had to do. He just was going to need all his guts to do it.

When he wandered back to the Woodlands, Jane and Georgie and Lizzy were all hugging and laughing together out in the garden. Lizzy wiped tears from her eyes as she moved to greet him.

"No, no, stay where you are," he said, holding up his hands. "I don't want to interrupt your fun."

"Nonsense, nonsense," Georgie tutted, swatting the idea away as if it were an annoying mosquito. "You've passed every test we have set for you with flying colors."

"It's truly delightful to see you once more, Mr. Taylor," Jane

said, inclining her head. "And I'm grateful that you've safely returned such a cherished individual to us! I must confess, I seem
to be lacking composure today. I find myself unable to speak with
any refinement, instead constantly lapsing into various exclamations. I attribute it to the overwhelming excitement of the occasion. I'm actually departing to visit my sister, Cassandra, and
our dear mother at Chawton Cottage for a month. However, I've
made a promise to Georgie to swiftly return to ensure Lizzy is
settling in comfortably and not too lonesome."

"I'm sure she'll appreciate that," he said, a little bemused. Of
course he didn't want Lizzy to be some sad, solitary figure—it
was just that it was surreal as hell to imagine her living her life
without him soon.

As if catching his train of thought, Lizzy stepped toward him.
"I find myself quite fatigued by the journey from London," she
said. "If it pleases you, I would appreciate an hour or two to retire
and rest."

"Of course!" Both the women were full of understanding as
Tuck gave them a short nod and escorted his wife back into the
house and upstairs to their chamber.

"I wept in front of them," Lizzy confessed, once they were
alone in her room. "They bore it with kindness, yet I cannot help
but worry that I have caused them undue concern."

"Lizzy," he murmured, hating to see her upset. Yet, deep
down, he understood that every choice moving forward would
carry its own weight, its own consequences to bear.

"They anticipated my joy, my triumphant demeanor, believ-
ing my scheming had succeeded," she remarked with a touch of
bitterness. "It's rather remarkable, isn't it? How everything has
aligned in my favor."

"You had a plan and you've executed it," he replied carefully.

"That I did." She kicked off her shoes and flopped backward on the bed, stretching her arms out to him. "Come lie with me. I want us to hold each other."

"Don't have to tell me twice." He removed his boots and crawled beside her, folding her into a hug.

She fell momentarily silent before raising her head to face him. "I daresay I have a notion of where you disappeared to."

He kissed her forehead; her skin was cool to the touch. "That a fact?"

"You visited that dreadful pond, did you not?"

He hummed his assent deep in the back of his throat.

"You are so predictable." She leaned up and planted a long kiss on his neck, right at the sensitive place beneath his ear.

"It's like that, is it?" He moved quickly, pinning her underneath him. His lips brushed hers, and he flicked out his tongue to tease the seam before pulling back.

She pouted. "Is that all?"

"Thought you wanted to rest?"

She lightly sucked her teeth. "Yes, but that was before."

"Before, huh?" He dragged a hand over her hair, letting the silky strands slide between his fingers. "Before what, exactly?"

"Before you climbed on top of me and made me realize that I can sleep anytime, but I can't do this with you for much longer." Her teasing smile sputtered. "Oh. I didn't want to make this morose."

"Then don't." He made a trail of kisses across her cheek and down her neck and he reached down to bracket his thumbs over her hip bones under her skirts. "We get to decide how to spend our time. And I'm not planning on sitting around watching you cry, unless it's crying out my name."

She arched off the mattress. "You're wicked."

"And you love it." He put one hand under her skirts, getting between her legs. "And *I* fucking love how you are always accessible here to my hands."

"What should I be like?"

He put his mouth against her ear, but didn't touch. "In my time women usually wear panties, but you make it easy."

"W-what are panties?" She gasped as he rolled his fingers over her. Wet. Slick.

He eased the tip of one into her, swirling her center. "They cover up all of this." He cupped her. God, she was so wet for him. He wanted to be inside her and never come out.

"Oh, drawers. All women wear them in your time? The linen itches."

"Sometimes they're made of silk."

"Sounds scandalous."

He slid his finger inside her, deep, and then another, feeling her body adjust, welcoming his gentle invasion. "I'll tell you what sounds scandalous. When you get this wet for me." He pushed in and out, slow and intense.

She shivered, squeezing her eyes closed.

"Oh no, I don't think so." The corner of his mouth kicked up. "Look down and see what I'm doing to you."

She licked her lips before opening one eye and then the other.

"That's it," he growled. "I want you to know who is taking you so good." He unbuttoned his pants with a swift motion, hastily tugging down the flap, freeing his cock. He stole a quick glance at her face and found himself ensnared by the longing in her eyes. "You're going to watch everything I'm gonna give you, right?"

She cast her gaze down between them, bending her legs and letting them fall open to the sides. "I'm watching." Her words came out a whimper.

A snarl tore from him. He charged down between her thighs and devoured her sweetness until she shuddered against his tongue and moaned his name. While she was still convulsing, he crawled up. She barely blinked, utterly focused on his cock as he sheathed it into her. When he reached the hilt, she gasped.

"God, you smell so good," he grunted.

She kept her head angled to watch as he rode into her, raw but reverent. His body felt on fire. "I can't get enough of this. You drive me fucking wild."

She quaked around him, her body hungry to milk him.

"Such an eager little thing. You know exactly how I like it."

She shivered, sending surges from the base of his cock to the pit of his flexed stomach like summer lightning. The smell of their sex hung heavy in the air.

He focused on every sensation, didn't want to miss a moment, not when so few were left. They lit up together—kindling igniting, before falling together, panting and spent.

"I could do that forever." Lizzy jutted out her chin, lazily tracing a finger along his collarbone, her nail gently scratching at his skin.

"You have amazing stamina." He grabbed her hand and kissed the palm. "I've got to work to keep up with you."

"Is that a problem?"

"Nah. I like it. You're a challenge."

She curled into him and whispered in his ear, "I like you so much."

He had bigger words swirling around in his head than just "like." His feelings for this woman were way beyond that. They were huge. But what was he supposed to say at this moment? She was here, and he was about to go to a place far, far away. Leaving was already gonna be tough without making it even more complicated.

"Jane told me about her idea," he murmured into the top of her head. "My death story."

"Where you will go on a forever fishing trip?" She went quiet for a moment, but when she continued, her voice was steady. "What do you think?"

He exhaled a broken laugh. "You mean, is that the death that I'd choose?"

"I suppose, yes. Not everyone gets that, right?"

"You've got a point. And as to my thoughts, a fishing mishap is a little boring. What's the implication? That I got overexcited pulling in a sea bass and tipped my ass out? Then I couldn't swim, so that was it? Lights out? Down to Davy Jones's Locker?"

She gave an exasperated huff. "What else would you prefer?"

"I don't know," he mused, the lingering sensation still coursing through his body, the shock waves slowly fading. "Lightning? What if I got struck by lightning? That'd make for a story, wouldn't it?"

"It certainly would. But then there wouldn't be a body, which poses a problem. I don't believe lightning can make a person disappear, can it?"

"Fair point, fair point. You're always one step ahead of me. All right, then, if we're aiming for a lack of a body, I suppose Jane's plan will have to suffice. There aren't many options that can be believable yet avoid the need for a corpse. But even with this, there will be some who don't believe the story."

"How could anyone ever predict the truth? It is impossible."

"I agree. They'll never predict what really happened. But after seeing your family, it seems reasonable that some folks might be unkind . . . Gossip and say I ran off back to America. I guarantee at least one rumor will be that I was already married."

"It may tarnish my reputation, but it shan't be enough to ruin me. Mamma will undoubtedly require her smelling salts, and Mr. Alby will fume. Henry will feign disappointment, yet secretly he will be relieved, as it means he will once again be the sole heir and progenitor of future Wooddashes."

"You could . . ." He cleared his throat and gave name to a terrible idea that had occurred to him a few days earlier. "You could marry again. You'd have every right."

"Oh heavens, no. Why would I ever do that?"

"Love." He spoke the word; at least it was safe in the abstract.

"No, Tucker Taylor." She burrowed into his chest with a sleepy sigh. "I'm afraid you'll be the only man I'm ever willing to have as a husband."

He rubbed her back gently as she drifted into a midafternoon nap. A twinge of jealousy crept into his heart, whispering that he should feel content; after all, he shouldn't desire to share her with anyone else. And yet he found himself wanting her to experience a life brimming with passion and love on her own terms.

The next two days passed in a blur. When they weren't sneaking up to the bedchamber while Georgie and Jane pretended not to notice, they spent time together as a quartet, enjoying cakes, engaging in gossip (or rather, he listened to Jane, Georgie, and Lizzy gossip while he chuckled), playing parlor games, or enjoying Jane's readings from her book, *First Impressions*.

"No, no, no. That's still not the right title at all," Georgie asserted matter-of-factly. "*Sense and Sensibility* is memorable. You need something similar. Something that will capture the public's imagination."

"I'm not disputing your point," Jane replied, taking a small sip of tea, her brow furrowed. "I simply haven't come up with any-thing better. Tuck, what are your thoughts?"

He sat up abruptly. "Me?"

"I don't believe there's another Tuck in our company," she retorted with a hint of amusement.

"All right, all right. Let's see. You have this Elizabeth Bennet, a spirited and intelligent woman. While at first she can't stand Mr. Darcy, their misunderstandings gradually give way to love. What kept them apart?"

"Her pride after he hurt her feelings at a ball. And his preju-dice to her social position and her family."

"Why not just call it that? *Pride and Prejudice?*" he asked with a shrug.

Jane dropped her teaspoon into her cup. The metal rattled the porcelain, exacerbating the silence. "What did you just say?"

"I mean, I'm not a writer." He held up his hands. "If it's stupid, just ignore me and move on."

"It's not stupid," Lizzy said carefully.

"It's rather clever," Georgie chimed in. "I believe I like it quite a lot."

Jane set down her cup. "*Pride and Prejudice.* Why, I love it." She turned to Tuck, eyes shining. "You just named my book!"

"I did?" He wondered if she'd really use the name. He'd have to ask Nora if he got back if she had ever heard of that one.

Not *if.* He mentally shook his head. *When.* This plan was going to work. All of Lizzy's talk about plague had him a little on edge. The whole "bring out your dead" period of human history was not a time with which he needed to get up close and personal.

He was smashed out of the dark thought by a body barreling into him. It took him a second to reorient and realize it was Jane, who'd thrown herself at him in a fierce hug.

"Whoa, now," he said, half jokingly and half to keep from tipping off the sofa and ending up tangled together with her in a heap on the floor.

"I should apologize for such a frightful lack of good manners," she said, releasing him and stepping back, cheeks flushed and eyes bright. "But you really have done me a great service today."

"If I can be honest, you did all the work," he said. "Me? I just listened."

"Well, thank you, anyway." She reached out and squeezed his hand. "I suspected you were one of the good ones."

"I seem to recall you threatening to bury me in an unmarked grave if I didn't treat Lizzy honorably."

"Pardon?" Lizzy gasped. "Jane! You didn't."

"And we'd do that again," Georgie retorted. "But I'm happy to say, Mr. Taylor—Tuck—you are part of the family now."

Lizzy jumped as the clock chimed another hour. She didn't look in his direction, but he knew what she was thinking. Every hour was the last hour for them. A last meal together. A last lovemaking—fast and urgent as if they could tattoo their memory onto the other.

It was quiet when they left the house. Georgie and Jane didn't emerge to say another good night. "They know I want this time to myself," she said simply.

And while he enjoyed the company of the other two women, he was glad of it. He didn't want any goodbyes or fuss. Saying it once would be enough. They walked through the forest hand in hand as the full moon sat high in the sky and flooded the darkness with its pale blue light.

"I never imagined when we walked through here that first day everything that would happen," he said.

"What were your initial impressions of the entire affair?" she asked.

"You mean my *First Impressions?*"

That earned him a groan.

"I didn't have as much of a feeling of disbelief as I should," he continued. "It's weird that I wasn't really pinching myself, wondering if it was all some crazy dream. But for some reason, deep down, I just knew it was all real. It didn't add up, and I had no clue how to explain it, but I was certain. And honestly, I think you're the one to thank for that."

"Me?" She laughed in earnest. "How did I manage such a feat?"

"Just by being you, I guess." He lifted her hand to his mouth, kissing the inside of her wrist. "You are one of the realest people I've ever met in my life. If you were here, then that made this place and everything that happened to me seem believable, or at least plausible."

"I don't know what I did to warrant such a compliment, but for now I'll thank you."

"What about you? What did you imagine was going to happen?" he asked.

"I—I recall feeling quite anxious, fearing someone would stumble upon us and notice your shoes. They're far too unconventional, too out of place for this era. I couldn't shake the thought . . . if someone catches sight of those shoes, there will be quite the uproar."

"What happened to my shoes anyway? They disappeared after we got to the house. Along with my clothing."

"That was my doing," she said matter-of-factly. "I couldn't risk anyone finding anything."

He groaned. "Don't tell me you buried them?"

"Of course not, don't be ridiculous." She sniffed. "I stuffed everything into the privy by the barn."

He pulled up short. "You put my Regals jersey into a toilet?"

"What's a jersey?"

"My hockey shirt. It had our logo—my lucky number . . . and my name."

"Oh, that. I do remember it. The material was too strange. If anyone stumbled on it, there would be questions for months, if not years. I couldn't risk it. It would draw too much attention."

He understood the logic but still gave her a look of mock horror. "How can you be a Regals wife if my jersey is stuck in shit? You're supposed to want to borrow it because I *am* the shit."

"I won't apologize for not fully understanding what you are saying," she said crisply. "I stand by what I did to protect you and I'd do it all over again."

"I just wish I could've seen you wear my jersey one time. Nothing else." He squeezed her hand as they resumed walking. "Just the jersey."

"This seems like a very primitive sensibility, like wanting me to wear the fur of an animal you've hunted."

"Maybe it is, in a roundabout way."

A light fog drifted between the trunks of the trees. It wasn't dense enough to obscure the moonlight, but its presence lent the forest an eerie, ethereal quality. The rustling of nocturnal creatures fleeing added to the atmosphere of secrecy and danger.

Their conversation dwindled to a hush, and they clung to each other's hand with increasing intensity. As they ventured further, the trees began to thin, eventually yielding to the expanse of the meadow.

Tuck's heart quickened as he noticed Lizzy's sharp intake of breath at the sight of the pond. Her hand trembled in his.

"You okay?"

"No. You?"

"Not at all." He stopped and faced her. "We don't have to do this."

She shook her head. "We do. You cannot remain here. It is not prudent. Should your illness resurface and there be no means to procure the assistance you require, the burden of guilt would destroy me. Moreover, there is your sister to consider. As you've mentioned, you are essentially her sole family. And then there is your hockey, a pursuit I must confess I still do not comprehend, but I am aware of its significance to you."

His throat was so tight it felt like he was choking. "I'm not going to ask you to come."

"Please . . ." Her voice hitched. "Don't."

"I know this is your home. You have your friends. Your life. Your dreams. I'm not going to ask you to leave everything and everyone you've ever known."

"This feels like a test." Her eyes shone with tears. "It's as if I've received this gift that I've always wanted, and here I am ready to open it. I still want it—I do—I want it with all my heart. Except I want another gift too. Us. And so now I'm just greedy."

"No." He pulled her to him, hugging her tight. "Don't talk like that about yourself."

"I want to live so many versions of my life. But I can only have one. And I need to choose me. This is my world. And you have given me a true gift. My freedom."

"You've given it to yourself," he murmured into the top of her head. "I'm just the guy who has to disappear."

"You are . . ." Her voice trembled as she trailed off, wiping her eyes. "You are the first person who has ever seen me, all of my parts, the good and bad, and didn't turn away or ask me to be someone else. You have taught me what it truly means to open one's heart to another. It's a lesson I never fully grasped until now. Even though you are bound for a place so distant, where I will cease to exist, I know there will always be a part of you within me. And I dearly hope that I will remain with you as well."

"Lizzy."

"Go now." She folded her arms as if holding herself together. "Please. Let us not prolong farewells. It's time."

"Fuck time." He stepped forward and lifted her chin, searching her face. "I'm never going to forget you." He kissed her softly, trying to commit her taste to memory.

"Please." She put her hands on his chest and gave a small push. "Please."

He knew she was asking him to go. But also, there was so much else. So many things that they hadn't said. So many things that they hadn't done.

"My time with you has been unforgettable," he said.

"And now it's over." She forced a laugh. "But we did have fun."

He glanced at the pond. "Are you going to watch me go?"

"I hadn't been sure, but yes. I need to. I was here when you arrived. I will be here to see you out."

"Promise me something?"

She cocked her head. "It depends on the request."

"Please finish your book, I mean it, really prove it to yourself. I know Jane Austen is going to be hot shit someday, and good for her, but why not you too? I want to go to some bookstore and find your words there, printed on a page."

"I will try my best."

"Try?"

"Oh, fine." She stamped a foot. "I'll bloody well do it, and you shall be able to buy that bloody book, put it on your pillow, and I'll haunt your dreams for the rest of your life. Happy? Is that the promise you want?"

"That, Pocket Rocket, is exactly the promise I wanted. I want you haunting my dreams every night—becoming my own personal sleep paralysis demon."

"I don't know what you are talking about."

"But you know you are going to write a book. And I'll read every word."

"Very well." She pushed back her shoulders. "Goodbye, Tucker Taylor. I'm very glad we have met and married. Also, my middle name? It's Hortense."

His brows lifted. "You're joking. Is that even a real name?"

She wrinkled her nose. "I told you it was horrid."

"On you? It's lovely. Goodbye, Elizabeth Hortense Wooddash. I'm very glad to have met you, married you, and I hope you have the best widowhood in all of England."

He took a step into the water. The frogs stopped croaking. The temperature was cool, but not as cold as he had imagined. He took a step and another and another. Nothing happened. Nothing looked different. His heart pounded. Maybe it was all a fluke. Maybe he'd be walking home with Lizzy tonight. Did he want that?

There, just beyond his position, a light emerged from the water. It took him a moment to grasp that it wasn't a figment of his imagination; it was real. He turned back and saw Lizzy on the hill, her hand covering her mouth. She looked smaller, fragile somehow. He hadn't even told her the most important truth of all. He'd been afraid it would hurt her. That it would hurt him.

But that was cowardly. He knew he had to do it. They'd begun with honesty. They needed to end there too.

"Lizzy. I—"

But he was gone. The night sky vanished. He fought to keep his eyes open, but the pressure was too great. A sickening sensation bore down, his internal compass gone. There was no left or right or up or down. East turned west. North became south.

And then silence. The scent of antiseptic assaulted his nostrils. A rhythmic beeping was in the background.

He tried to open his eyes but they were so heavy. He gritted his teeth and put everything he had into it, and . . . there. Fluorescent light. He wasn't in a pond. But he wasn't in some medieval plague village either. He was in a hospital bed, and that beeping? It was a heart monitor. He glanced over and there was Nora, in a chair, reading by the window.

"Nor?" His voice was so weak. Why was his mouth so dry?

But it was enough. She heard him. The book tipped from her hands as she stumbled to her feet. "Tucker? Tuck! Oh my God, you're awake."

"Hey, sis." He forced a grin. "I'm back."

CHAPTER THIRTY

All the very best love stories end tragically.

Lizzy repeated this refrain to herself in the days and weeks after Tuck disappeared from her life.

The pain she felt upon waking, lingering until it was time to retire in the evening, the sense that she was missing a part of her body . . . this was how it was supposed to be. For who could have a love affair and walk away unscathed?

The fact she hurt meant it was a good thing. She should be grateful for the pain, glad that it happened, happy it was over. Now she could get on with her business of widowhood.

Should. Such a useless word. It lingered in the realm of missed opportunities, dwelling on what could have been but wasn't. It should be relegated to the same trash heap as the word *try.*

Lizzy doodled two intersecting rings on the corner of the blank page of her vellum notebook, her thin gold band on her ring finger teasing her. She could take it off anytime she wanted. No one would have such bad manners as to comment on it. But she couldn't bring herself to twist it off. Every time she went to do it, her fingers found some other way to occupy themselves.

She set aside her lap desk and strolled to the window. Beyond, the oaks encircling the yard had taken on hues of flame, their leaves a vivid reminder that the August day Tuck departed had long passed, and autumn was encroaching.

In the end, she couldn't muster the resolve to execute Jane's scheme. No staged fishing trip to Southampton Water or a contrived accident. The notion of becoming a widow no longer held any appeal. She glanced down at her green walking dress, its hue reminiscent of fresh grass, a far cry from the somber black of mourning. The thought of Tuck meeting his demise—even a fictitious one—was too agonizing. Instead, she penned a letter to her family, explaining that Tuck had been summoned back to Baltimore for urgent and pressing business.

This new deception certainly complicated matters. When was he expected to return? Would it eventually cast her in the light of an abandoned woman, subject to society's pity and scorn?

She exhaled slowly, her breath clouding the glass before she traced a heart in the condensation, then wiped it away.

That could be an issue for future Lizzy to deal with. For now, she needed to shake off the stupor that had gripped her for the past weeks. She used to drift off to sleep effortlessly, but now she tossed and turned until dawn, her reflection in the mirror revealing dark circles under her eyes, signs of exhaustion and what appeared to be a broken heart.

Her hand drifted to the concealed pocket nestled within the folds of her skirts, brushing against the folded parchment within. Surely she couldn't bring herself to read it for the fourth time today. She ought to return to her desk and resume her attempts to try to complete the story she had pledged to him.

Should. Try. The words grated on her nerves like sandpaper.

With a low groan of frustration bubbling in her throat, she retrieved the letter. Who was she attempting to deceive? Herself?

Of course she was going to read the words Tuck left her. The letter she'd found beneath her pillow when she returned from the pond trembling and tearful.

Dear Lizzy,

It feels weird to write those words. It feels weird to write words, period. I should be leaving that work to better people, like Jane or you. But I couldn't leave without telling you a few things. First off, I never pushed you to come with me for a simple reason—and it had nothing to do with me not wanting you. It's that I want you to always get to choose your path. Your future. Your destiny. I saw how your family used you like a piece on a chessboard—and I'm never going to do that.

But let's say that at some point you wake up one day and think that you'd like to come. And you decide to enter the pond on one of those Druid holy days, and you appear in my time. I realized, how are you going to find me? I don't live in Hallow's Gate. Hell, I don't even live in England, so what am I going to do to help you?

Well, I came up with a plan. If you ever do come, I want you to go to Ye Olde King's Head. It still exists in my time. So, make your way there and approach the barkeep. You're going to want to give them the numbers written at the bottom of this note. This will let them contact my sister Nora. I'll have told her all about you. She will come. Bath isn't far, especially in my time. And then she'll figure out how to get you to me. Again, this isn't to pressure you. If you want to hear me say I want to see you again? Please know I'll always

want you, Lizzy. That's never going to stop. You're it for
me. And if the time we had together is all I ever get? Then
I'll count myself luckier than most. But our marriage? It's
as real as anything to me. And I'm always going to be yours.

Tuck

Lizzy folded the letter back up and returned it to her pocket. She was well on her way to having every word memorized.

Footsteps echoed down the hall—Jane's unmistakable pace. Lizzy recognized it by the swift, purposeful rhythm; her friend was never one to dawdle. Her movements resembled those of a songbird—nimble and precise.

"Hello," Lizzy greeted as Jane entered.

Jane responded with a small yelp. "Goodness. I didn't realize anyone was in here. The servants said Georgie would be out for a few hours. You're haunting the room like a ghost."

"I feel rather like one," Lizzy admitted with a forced smile that felt more like a grimace. "How are you?"

"Tired. But happy. I have finished my novel."

"Oh, congratulations." Lizzy was relieved no envy cropped up despite all her empty pages impatiently waiting for her. Her own success wouldn't come at the expense of her friendship. "How shall we celebrate?"

"The book is at a stage where it doesn't feel real, so celebrations aren't quite in order. All I can do is ponder the three to four plot points that are still very much amiss and endeavor to find a solution."

"I can leave you to your thoughts." Lizzy made to move toward the door.

"Darling. Stop." Jane blocked the exit, a frown tugging at the corners of her mouth. "You are behaving so small and skittish. What's gotten into you?"

Lizzy parted her lips, yet for once, words eluded her. There were so many to say that it rendered the next sentence perplexing. Where to start? Everything seemed congested, akin to a river blocked after a storm.

Jane's mouth spread into a slow smile. "It's love, isn't it?"

Lizzy looked away. "I've never used that word directly."

"Does that make it any less real?"

"I had rather hoped that avoiding speaking it would mean everything might hurt less."

"That's a sweet, but ultimately flawed, idea. Come sit with me a moment, dear, I want to tell you a story. A real one this time."

Lizzy joined Jane on the camelback settee. "Real?"

"I don't believe I've ever shared the tale of my past love with you, have I?"

"Love?" Lizzy huffed a little in surprise. "You?"

Jane laughed, genuinely amused. "Do not appear so astonished, or you shall wound my sensibilities. Yes, indeed, I had a suitor once, Tom Lefroy, an Irishman."

"An Irishman!" she blurted out, her mind racing so she was left to just repeat words dumbly. She thought she knew her friend inside out, but now she felt like she might as well be talking to a stranger.

"Our initial connection was forged through books. He took pleasure in *Tom Jones*, a sentiment I didn't quite share. Yet, his striking appearance was hard to ignore—fine eyes, admirable ears, and a manly physique, all wrapped in gentlemanly charm. He was quite the flirt, leaving me feeling rather bashful and tongue-tied whenever we were together. Interestingly, I've since imbued this similar reticence into my latest literary hero. Some may read my work and assume the heroine is a reflection of myself, but how lacking in imagination they are! In truth, I've woven aspects of myself into my Mr. Darcy."

"And while I do want to know more of this book, I desire to hear more of this man! What happened?"

"When we first crossed paths, he hadn't a sixpence to his name, and you're well aware of my own modest circumstances—no dowry to speak of. Despite this, he did propose to me, and in a moment of impulsiveness, I accepted. However, his parents, acting with wisdom and prudence, quickly intervened."

"Oh no! How dreadful of them."

"Sometimes, the most difficult decisions are the right ones. Love doesn't always conquer all, as I came to realize. Reality must take precedence, and life isn't always adorned with happily-ever-afters and picturesque sunsets. It can quickly become little more than a succession of busy nothings."

"I understand."

"No." Jane's gaze sharpened. "You don't understand. Disregard everything I've said. I opted for the practical route, yielding to others out of mere logic. And every day since, I've regretted my decision. I will continue to do so until my last breath, for I loved Tom deeply, and I'll never love another in the same way. Nor would I wish to. Once is sufficient for such intense emotion. Yet, I'll spend the rest of my days endeavoring to capture those feelings on paper—to compose a happiness denied to me. And that's not what I desire for you, Lizzy. If there's still a chance for you to find love, pursue it."

"What if I want too much?" There. She was finally asking the question that had been nagging at her.

"Elaborate, please."

"First, writing. I'm afraid that I've left it too late. The comic sketches I've done in the past, or the amusing stories to be read during Christmas, all the pieces that I've ever finished are childish and amateur. I should have been more diligent since girlhood and now I'm afraid my ambitions are all a bit of a joke."

"You poor dear." Jane scootched over and gave her a hip bump. "I don't think it's a bad thing to have waited as long as you have to take up the pen in earnest. You have spent much time reading, and therefore absorbing how a story is meant to feel to the audience. What counts the most is to know you'll take what you've learned and trust yourself. The most intimidating moment is prior to initiating. As for me, I'm often not at all in a humor for writing, so I persist until I am. It will be the same for you, and yet different. I want you to find your happiness, but it will be in your own way."

"Thank you." Lizzy seized her friend's hand and squeezed. "I'm sorry if I'm a bother with my problems."

"Don't be silly. There's nothing I wouldn't do for those who are my true friends. I don't love my people in halves. It's not in my character. What else is on your mind?"

"What if I want Tuck, to be with him, to . . . to . . . love him, to know him and see if it gets better, and deeper and richer with time. But . . ." She tossed her hair over her shoulder, grimacing in frustration. "But what if I don't want to leave my whole life? What if I want to have love, but also have me?"

"I see." Jane stared thoughtfully into space for a few moments, nibbling the corner of her lower lip. "And you believe that it's a choice? That you're unable to have both?"

"Yes. If I go to him in his time, I leave you, Georgie, this place that I love and feels like home. But if I remain—I'm afraid my heart might really break."

Jane's brows pushed toward each other. "Who says you have to choose?"

Lizzy rolled her eyes. "The laws of the universe seem to be quite clear on this point."

"Perhaps." Jane was monitoring her carefully. "Perhaps not."

"I'm getting the sense you're dancing around some truth you want me to grasp. It would be much kinder and more useful if you'd speak plainly."

"Lizzy. Do you know what's the most powerful thing a woman can be? Happy. Why can't you go to see him and then return? Live some of your life there, some here. You explained how time travel works. The lodestone theory. Goodness, he could return for a season as well. You've gone and complicated what appears to me to be very simple. It isn't our words or thoughts that define us, but what we do."

"So continue my marriage but with the idea that Tuck and I don't need to be with each other all the time?"

"Or even more to the point, in the same time." Jane sat back against the sofa and kicked out her legs, crossing them at the ankles. "Why are you making such a face?"

"I feel a little bewildered. But what you say makes sense. It felt as if since he was too far for me to hold, I'd have to resign myself to letting him go. However, I've been studying the Druid's Wheel of the Year. Tomorrow marks Alban Elfed—the time of equal balance between day and night. It's possible that I could make the journey then."

"And I say you should. I know yours is not an easy path. It's unconventional. There are those who think to love a person is to need to be with them at all times, but in my limited experience, love often doesn't come easy. It's approaching obstacles and figuring out a way around them. You may hold each other's hands only sometimes, but who says you can't hold each other's hearts forever?"

CHAPTER THIRTY-ONE

I love you.

Lizzy, I love you.

As long as I live . . . I'm going to love you and only you.

I love you so much that I've tried to invent new ways to say it, but always circle back to those three perfect words.

Tuck opened his eyes to find his teammate Knight staring at him. Seven weeks had passed since Tuck had regained consciousness in that English hospital bed, and tonight marked his second game with the Regals since receiving medical clearance.

Tuck thrust out the thermos he'd been cradling. "Want some oolong? It's not souchong, unfortunately, that's hard to find these days. Go on, I put some lemon in it, and lots of sugar. No milk, of course, never milk with lemon. It's good, try some."

Knight blinked. "Uh, thanks, but I'm good, man."

"What are you and Wilson getting up to later?" Tuck asked, taking a sip of the tea.

Knight frowned. "Who?"

Tuck gestured at Knight's thick scruff. "You look like Tom Hanks in *Castaway* with that lucky beard. I gotta get you a volleyball to be your BFF."

"Oh. Ha. Wilson. Yeah." Knight chuckled, turning away with

a half-relieved expression, as if thinking, *Everything's fine, Taylor's a weirdo as per usual.*

Tuck took another swig of tea, swishing the hot, sweet water around in his mouth. How long had he been zoned out in his stall inside the Regals' locker room, not focusing on the upcoming game against the Maple Leafs? His thoughts all circled back to Lizzy. Her presence loomed in his mind, a persistent echo of the words he wished he'd found the guts to say before leaving—words that now haunted him with regret.

Regret was a new feeling. He had always charged ahead to achieve his goals, and perhaps it had made him cocky. Now he found himself carrying his wedding ring on a gold chain around his neck. The team locker room was no place for distraction. It was so steeped in superstition that the Regals logo adorned the Jumbotron on the ceiling, ensuring no one would ever make the mistake of stepping on it. That crown symbolized the team, the fans, and their collective pride. Painted on the wall opposite were the words "I see no virtue where I smell no sweat." Tuck grimaced. If that were true, his teammates would be candidates for sainthood, because even with state-of-the-art ventilation, the place got fragrant.

He cranked up the volume on the audiobook playing through his AirPods. The female narrator's voice grew louder: "There is a stubbornness about me that never can bear to be frightened at the will of others. My courage always rises at every attempt to intimidate me."

He'd been immersing himself in Jane's books since returning. It turned out, not only was she funny as hell, but she'd taken his suggestion to heart and really named her book *Pride and Prejudice.*

Pretty cool.

The press had caught wind of Tuck and his newfound Regency obsession, and in an interview yesterday he'd been told, "Didn't know hockey players even read."

To which he'd shot back, "I don't. I listen." Audiobooks were his favorite.

When Tuck first woke up in the hospital, Nora informed him that it was the end of January. This made sense to Tuck, as he recalled that when he had first gone through the cow pond in December, he had ended up in Lizzy's time during the summer month of June. Therefore, it was logical that leaving in Lizzy's time in August would have thrust him forward another six months. However, Tuck was less interested in the confusing-ass intricacies of time travel. His thoughts were fixed on Lizzy and how much he missed her.

And if his sister thought he was crazy, she didn't let on.

"Your story is too detailed," she had kept repeating. "And then there's the ring. I can't quite wrap my head around it, but strangely, I believe you. It all seems too real." And with that, she'd launched into a barrage of questions . . . most of them about Jane Austen.

The night before he flew back to the States, she burst into his room, waving her phone. "Oh my God. Oh my God. Tuck. Look. You gotta see this." He had taken the phone, and his insides froze as he read the headline: "Search Given Up for Missing Scholar." The online news article, dated a few years back, detailed the disappearance of UC Berkeley professor of Celtic history, Ezekiel Fairweather, who had vanished during a walk in Oxfordshire. He hadn't been seen since. Foul play seemed unlikely, and there were no clues in the case.

"Is that him?" Nora had pointed at the photo. "The time traveler you met?"

"He didn't have that goatee and his hair was shorter, but yeah. That's the same guy. No doubt."

"Ready for tonight?" Someone squeezed his shoulder, snapping him back to the now. It was Coach. "Feeling good, T?"

Tuck popped out his AirPods and paused the book. "I'm great. Fired up. My little sister is here tonight. She flew in today, and hasn't seen me play since before Covid."

Coach gave him a thumbs-up. "I don't know how you do it. Cancer. Car accident. Coma. But I saw you in practice this morning and you have no quit."

"Never have." Tuck's shrug was one-shouldered. "Stop pucks and ask questions later."

This was true. Technically. He just wasn't going to share what kind of questions kept him tossing and turning all night—big ones about life, the universe, and love.

Tonight was a home game. As he skated out, he couldn't help but grin—pumping his arms to increase the crowd's roar. Damn, it felt good to be back in the arena, gazing up at a sea of white-and-navy fans. He nodded to the mascot, hyping up the crowd in the stands—officially called Highness, but everyone in Austin knew him as the Puck King, with the rowdiest fans often adding a lewd gesture. Tuck turned around, scanning for where Nora should be—he'd given her two ringside tickets behind the net, one for her and the other for the friend she was bringing along.

After about thirty seconds, he spotted her—and it was as if the ice melted beneath his skates. Lizzy stood next to Nora, wearing his jersey and shaking a giant foam hand giving a number one sign. For once in his life, he didn't trust his eyes. He closed them tight and counted to five. She was still there. His heart thundered so loudly he couldn't hear the crowd's roar or the pulsing music.

How? What?

Lizzy threw her arms over her head, waving first wildly and then frantically.

He glanced over his shoulder. Fuck. Face-off. The game had started.

He'd never played for anyone else before. Winning for himself always seemed to make everyone else happy enough. But today? He wanted to impress a girl. He was going to put up a brick wall in front of the net. And he did.

When they finished the game 3–0, Toronto going home empty-handed, he threw himself at the boards, tearing off his helmet. Lizzy stood on the other side of the tempered glass, so close he could drown in her baby blues, yet he couldn't get his hands on her. He wasn't with her. He wasn't holding her. He sure as hell wasn't kissing her until he'd ripped off his uniform and changed at light speed, avoiding the reporters circling after his performance and charging out to meet her.

"I found you," she managed to say before he crushed his mouth on hers, and for the first time since he left her, he felt like himself. Her soft lips tasted like fruit ChapStick, new, but he didn't mind. It was still Lizzy. His Lizzy.

He braced her face between his hands. "I love you."

Her big eyes widened even further. Maybe he was rushing the moment, but the missed opportunity had weighed on his chest. "I love you, and I should have told you that before I left. I was an idiot, and I'm never going to miss a chance to tell you the truth again."

"I . . . I love you too."

He had to have his mouth on hers again. He kept his arms wrapped around her lower back, though his hands ached to touch her all over, to reassure himself that this was real. She was really here. They were getting this second chance.

"Toss me your keys, big brother," Nora chimed in. "I'll be designated driver as long as you don't traumatize me while you're in the back seat. Any funny business and I'm dropping you on the nearest curb and calling you an Uber."

As they walked to his parking spot, he knew everyone was watching him holding Lizzy's hand, wondering who the hell she was. His team would have questions, and so would the media. But everyone could wait because this was his time, and right now, he got to ask the questions.

"How? When? What?" he asked as they slid into the back of his Jeep.

"I decided you were worth risking plagues and the other perils of time," she said in a teasing voice. "If I can give credit, it was Jane who made me see reason. You are my lodestone. I trusted and dove in."

"That's Jane *Austen*," Nora piped up from the front, turning out of the underground parking garage and onto the street. "Just so everyone is clear."

"Yes, Nor," Tuck said. "You can have your fan time, but right now I'm gonna have mine."

"I must admit, I was previously at a loss to fully grasp the nature of your endeavors." Lizzy was watching him raptly, eyes bright. "The grandeur, the brilliance, the roar of the crowd, and the speed of movement—all were quite beyond my comprehension. Yet, having now witnessed it firsthand, I find it exhilarating. It is now apparent to me what you meant in saying that your occupation involves impeding a puck."

"Yeah? Good." He was pleased she liked to see him play and had watched him doing the thing that he was second best at. "It's pretty cool seeing you in my jersey. And the hat looks all kinds of cute." He tugged the side of her Regals beanie.

"And these jeans?" Lizzy ran her hands over her thighs. "Your sister let me borrow hers, and they are so practical. They make moving around so much easier, although they are a bit tight on my waist. I do prefer the other kind better. What are they called again, Nora? The stretchy ones?"

"Leggings." Nora glanced in the rearview mirror, her expression amused but fond.

"And no corsets! And I learned about deodorant. And I have been trying ever so many toothbrushes. Your sister taught me how to use a curling iron and mascara. Oh, and I have gotten to try on the panties you told me about. I can show you if—"

"I'm sure my brother would love to have a close inspection," Nora broke in. "But that can be for your special alone time, hmmm? Not for a special little-sister-in-the-front-of-the-car time. Hard pass, people. Hard pass."

Tuck threw his arm around Lizzy, drawing her close, unable to fully believe she was beside him. "Tell me about your crossing."

"The lodestone theory worked. I came directly to your time, but precisely six months later. Quite useful to confirm this lag, really, because I can't risk overstaying and finding the pond frozen come winter!"

"Wait." His chest tightened. "You aren't staying?"

"Yes. And no." She reached out and touched his cheek, roughing her hands over the beard he'd been growing for luck. "I would not have thought I'd like all this hair, but I very much do. It suits you. Very Viking."

"Thanks, but let's keep focused on the you-not-staying part of the conversation."

"Yes." She sat back in the seat, fiddling with her seat belt strap. "I came to the slow realization that I desire everything life has to offer. I wish to be your wife and share my life with you." Her words tumbled out in a rush. "However, I cannot forsake my identity or my desire to live among friends or in my own time. Therefore, throughout the year, I shall come to you, and we shall seize those opportunities to be together. And as your schedule permits, you may visit me as well? Let us discuss such plans in due time. All that matters now is that we have this moment, and know that we shall have more ahead of us."

"Lizzy asked the bartender to call me from Ye Olde King's Head like you instructed," Nora smoothly cut in. "And look, I know it sounds crazy, but I have to say I wasn't that surprised to hear from her. I've never seen you so rattled over a woman, Tuck. Or anything, for that matter. I figured what you both have must be something pretty special. And you're just really lucky that I know a girl who knows a guy who knows another guy in London who might have mad skills in passport forgery and the less we all know about that, the better."

Later that night, after Nora discreetly turned in early and they had fallen into his king-size bed to make up for lost time, Lizzy crawled into his plaid bathrobe and they padded around his condo, Lizzy turning on lamps, exploring the designer kitchen he never used, the dining room with a wine fridge, the master bathroom's floor-to-ceiling mirror and large porcelain soaking tub, before stepping out onto the terrace off his bedroom. "We are up so high. It's as if I could reach out and touch the moon."

"Fiftieth story. Penthouse, baby." He stepped behind and hugged her close. The wraparound deck offered panoramic views of the vibrant cityscape and Lady Bird Lake. It was a sight he'd seen often, but tonight? It felt as though they stood together on the edge of a new world, one where anything was possible, where time itself couldn't get in their way.

"Will this be enough for you?" he asked, entwining his fingers with hers. They were looking to take the concept of long-distance relationships to the next level. "Will you be able to remember that my heart will always hold on tight, even during moments when I can't physically do the same?"

"I know this will be a challenge, one that requires commitment and perseverance. But I'm determined for us to triumph. I want nothing more than to be yours as long as time allows. It's you and I, together, now and for all eternity. Even if not always in body, surely in soul."

"Eternity, huh? Is that all?" He touched his lips to hers, a sweet, soft kiss, one of many more that would come tonight. "Doesn't seem long enough, but I guess it's as good a place to start as any."

EPILOGUE

Two Years Later

The floor of Ye Olde King's Head was still sticky, but Tuck was used to it by now. He moved easily through the crowded pub, dodging elbows and jovial back slaps, carrying a tray with two porters, a lager, and a glass of barley wine.

"No, no, no!" Nora was barely containing her excitement for the impending punchline. "What do you call an English major at a restaurant?"

Lizzy grinned at Tuck as she plucked her glass off his tray, taking a quick sip of the barley wine before the foam spilled down the side of the glass. "I can't begin to guess," she said.

"Garçon!" Siobhan, Nora's newest partner, chimed in with the answer.

Tuck groaned, handing them both their dark beers before sliding into the seat next to Lizzy.

"That hurts, right?" Nora grinned, in high spirits after recently receiving a lecturer position, which they had been celebrating.

Reaching under the small table, Tuck took Lizzy's hand, his thumb toying with her wedding ring, one of his favorite habits.

"Do you really have to leave tonight?" Siobhan turned to Lizzy, disappointment in their voice. "It's been so much fun hanging out the last few weeks."

While it was disappointing that the Regals hadn't secured a spot in the playoffs this year, there was a silver lining. The early end to the season meant that he and Lizzy had gotten to spend a little time with Nora in England.

"This guy has to get back to Texas." Lizzy nodded toward Tuck. "And I have my own plane to catch."

Crossing through time was on a strictly need-to-know basis. Only three people at the table knew the truth: Tuck, Nora, and Lizzy. If Siobhan stuck around, eventually they could be brought into the circle. Tuck knew Lizzy liked Siobhan, especially as they had recently discovered a new Regency-era author—E. H. Wooddash.

"You have to try Wooddash," Siobhan had said earlier that day. "I found the book in London last spring and I'm fan-geeking so hard. I swear, once you read her, you'll find yourself more acquainted with the intricacies of Regency life than by reading some scholarly research specializing in the era's culture and customs. She's still lesser known, but I'm on a mission to make her just as famous as Austen, the Brontës, Hardy, or Gaskell."

He loved the way Lizzy had beamed. He was so damn proud that she'd finished writing her book at last. It was about an unconventional heroine who disrupts her relatives' conservative household and draws the begrudging attention of a visiting soldier. Soon the pair are forced to confront their feelings amidst a whirlwind of failed matchmaking attempts and different social classes.

"I just finished my last Jane Austen. *Persuasion.* It was enjoyable, but I'll tell you a secret"—Tuck leaned in, dropping his voice to an exaggerated hush—"*I* prefer Wooddash."

Siobhan shook their head in evident disbelief. "Who knew? Hockey players *can* read."

"It's a newer passion," Nora said smugly. "How long have you been into this reading-as-a-hobby thing, brother? Two years?"

He mock-glared at her feigned ignorance. "That's right."

It was Beltane—or May Day—and that meant it was a time when Lizzy could cross. The official story was that she worked in New Zealand, and no one seemed to question that beyond expressing sympathy for her flights and the couple's long-distance relationship. The media's attention was focused on the contract negotiations with Regals' center Gale Knight, leaving little interest in the personal life of a dedicated goalie who rarely saw his wife.

As night descended outside the window, Lizzy glanced over at Tuck. "I'll have to head out to catch my flight," she said gently.

After a quick exchange of goodbyes with Siobhan and Nora, they stepped out onto the quiet street of Hallow's Gate, in stark contrast to the lively atmosphere inside the pub. Hand in hand, they walked in contented silence toward the bridge that led them over the field.

"Send my love to Georgie and Jane?" he asked.

"I always do," she assured him.

"And tell Jane not to overdo it. She was looking far too pale last time I saw her."

Lizzy's smile faded. "I will."

Suddenly, Tuck pulled up short. "Hold up," he said. Ahead, beneath the last streetlight, a pair of teens approached. He recognized the shock of blond hair—it was the kid from the farmhouse down the road, grown up a bit, leaning in to give the girl a hug.

Tuck's mind wandered to that fateful night when his quick

decision-making had allowed the boy to remain here, alive, and able to experience his first love. And now Tuck stood beside the most remarkable woman to ever exist, also deeply in love.

"What's rattling around inside that pretty head?" Lizzy teased, her voice pulling him back.

He drew her close, silencing her with a kiss, then glanced up at the stars. "Just thinking about fate."

"Now you must tell me more," she urged.

"Fate may bring people into our lives, but we're the ones who choose who we refuse to part with."

"I'm afraid you're stuck with me, then," Lizzy said, a playful smile on her lips.

"All in," he murmured, his commitment unwavering. The intensity of his love sent a wave of vertigo through him, and he found grounding in the connection with her lips. "Forever." And another kiss. With them, there would always be another kiss. "I have all the time in the world for you."

ACKNOWLEDGMENTS

Big thank-yous:

First and foremost to my agent, Emily Sylvan Kim, who didn't blink at the initial idea for this book—and encouraged me to go big or go home, but nicely. Also, to my editor, Alessandra Roche, whom I genuinely believe the universe conspired me to meet—my gratitude is vast. And to the wonderful Ellen Brescia at Prospect Agency and the team at Avon (including Samantha Larrabee, DJ DeSmyter, Linda Sawicki, Jeanie Lee, and more).

To Megan Erickson and Amy Pine, who are my sisters from another mother, and our entire *AfterNoona Delight* Patreon community, who feel like extended family—I love you all.

To my ARMY GC crew: Tonya, Alison, Megan, Cyn, Becky, and Erin—Borahae, obviously.

To Bangtan Sonyeondan, because hey, you nice—keep going!

To Korean drama writers for bringing me back to my love of tropes.

To Lexi: I already thanked you in the dedication, so I won't make it weirder.

To Chanel Cleeton, Jennifer Blackwood, and Jennifer Ryan: You're all the best people.

To Jarah, Bronte, and Poppy, because their mom is a cringey

romance writer, except romance isn't cringey, it's awesome, and life isn't that serious, and that's a FANTASTIC LESSON TO LEARN YOUNG AND GO FIND JOY WHERE YOU CAN.

To Nick—I have a lot of time for you.

And to Mom, Dad, Kevin, Megan, Bridget, Kristi, Owen, Maya, Jabran, Malcolm, Oliver, and Arden for being fam.

ABOUT THE AUTHOR

LIA RILEY is a contemporary romance author. She loves redwood forests, beach fog, procrastinating, and a perfect pour-over coffee. She is 25 percent sarcastic, 54 percent optimistic, and 122 percent bad at math (good thing she writes happy endings for a living). She and her family live mostly in Northern California. You can also find Lia cohosting the weekly *AfterNoona Delight* podcast, exploring the wonderful (and trope-filled) world of Korean dramas through a writer's lens.

Discover More by LIA RILEY

REGALS HOCKEY ROMANCE

HELLIONS HOCKEY ROMANCE

TWO-IN-ONE BOOK!

BRIGHTWATER